"BEST OF THE YEAR!"

COSMOPOLITAN

John "Duke" Anderson was a man with a dream. He wanted to invade a Manhattan luxury apartment building, take it over, and systematically loot it. To do this, he first had to seduce one of the occupants, then enlist the aid of a prostitute, a homosexual art expert and thief, a black stud, a pair of hoods, an electronics expert, and a Mafia chieftain to help him complete his perfect plan.

But Anderson's brilliant mind had not calculated one factor. Every man and woman he dealt with was being secretly tape-recorded by a federal, state, city, or private agency. But in spite of that, there was no one to stop Anderson and his followers when they moved into the building. . . .

Sound incredible? Then examine the evidence in—

(Please turn page)

NATIONWIDE

"With this first novel, Lawrence Sanders establishes himself as the writer to watch in the 1970s"

CHICAGO SUN TIMES

"A new kind of book:
An electronic novel!"

PLAYBOY

"Authentic and dramatic . . . The author has given us a hero with charisma, an intriguing sex life and an audacious plan"

THE NEW YORK TIMES

"Grips the reader from first page and never lets him go . . . guaranteed to keep you fascinated from first page to last"

AUBURN CITIZEN ADVERTISER

SENSATION ! ! !

"Meet a new master"

CLEVELAND PLAIN DEALER

"Astonishingly entertaining"

LOOK

"Exciting, tense entertainment"

LOS ANGELES TIMES

"A spectacular thriller"

SAN FRANCISCO CHRONICLE

"A winner . . . Get comfortable in your favorite chair and dare anyone to interrupt you. Once you've begun *The Anderson Tapes,* you'll never forgive anyone who does"

ATLANTA JOURNAL AND CONSTITUTION

A Novel by
LAWRENCE SANDERS

A DELL BOOK

Published by
DELL PUBLISHING CO., INC.
750 Third Avenue
New York, New York 10017

Reprinted by arrangement with
G. P. Putnam's Sons
New York, New York

Printed in the U.S.A.
First Dell printing—January 1971

Author's Note

The following account of a crime committed in the City of New York on the night of 31 August and the early morning hours of 1 September, 1968, has been assembled from a variety of sources, including:

—Eyewitness reports dictated to the author, and eyewitness reports available from official sources, on tape recordings and in transcriptions.

—Records of courts, penal institutions, and investigative agencies.

—Tape recordings and transcriptions made by "bugging" and other electronic surveillance devices, by crime prevention and detection agencies of the City of New York, the State of New York, the U.S. government, and by private investigative agencies.

—Personal correspondence, speeches, and private documents of the individuals involved, made available to the author.

—Newspaper reports.

—Official reports and testimony which are a matter of public record, including deathbed statements.

—The author's personal experiences.

It would be impractical to name all the individuals, official and civilian, who provided valuable assistance to the author. However, I am especially grateful to Louis J. Girardi, Managing Editor of the Newark (N.J.) *Post-Ledger,* who granted me a leave of absence from my crime reporting duties with that newspaper in order that I might research and write the full story of this crime, as part of a continuing investigation into the uses and abuses of electronic surveillance equipment by public and private agencies.

LAWRENCE SANDERS

The
Anderson
Tapes

[1]

The building at 535 East Seventy-third Street, New York City, was erected in 1912 as a city residence for Erwin K. Barthold, a Manhattan merchant who owned Barthold, Inc., a firm that dealt in rope, tar, ships' supplies, and marine gear of all types. On the death of Mr. Barthold in 1931, his widow, Edwina, and his son, Erwin, Jr., lived in the house until 1943. Erwin Barthold, Jr., was killed on 14 July, 1943, while engaged on a bombing mission over Bremen, Germany. This was, incidentally, the city in which his father had been born. Mrs. Barthold died six months after the death of her son, from cancer of the uterus.

The house on Seventy-third Street then passed to a brother of the original owner and builder. He was Emil Barthold, a resident of Palm Beach, Florida, and shortly after the will was probated, Emil Barthold sold the house (16 February, 1946) to Baxter & Bailey, 7456 Park Avenue, New York City.

This investment company then converted the town house into eight separate apartments and two professional suites on the ground floor. A self-service elevator and central air conditioning were installed. The apartments and suites were sold as cooperatives, at prices ranging from $26,768 to $72,359.

The building itself is a handsome structure of gray stone, the architecture generally in the French chateau style. The building has been certified and listed by the New York City Landmark Society. Outside decoration is minimal and chaste; the roof is tarnished copper. The lobby is lined with veined gray marble slabs interspersed with antiqued mirrors. In addition to the main entrance, there is a service entrance reached by a narrow alleyway which stretches from the street to a back door that leads to a wide flight of concrete stairs. The two apartments on the top floor have small terraces. There is a small apartment in the basement occupied by the superintendent. The building is managed by Shovey & White, 1324 Madison Avenue, New York.

Prior to 1 September, 1967, for a period of several years, Apartment 3B at 535 East Seventy-third Street had been occupied by a married couple (childless), Agnes and David Everleigh. On or about that date, they separated, and Mrs. Agnes Everleigh remained in possession of Apartment 3B, while David Everleigh took up residence at the Simeon Club, Twenty-third Street and Madison Avenue.

On approximately 1 March, 1968 (this is an assumption), David Everleigh engaged the services of Peace of Mind, Inc., a private investigation agency located at 983 West Forty-second Street, New York. With David Everleigh's assistance—

this is presumed, since he still possessed a key to Apartment 3B and was its legal owner—an electronic device was installed in the base of the telephone in Apartment 3B.

It was a microphone transmitter—an Intel Model MT-146B—capable of picking up and transmitting telephone calls as well as conversations taking place in the apartment. A sum of $25 per month was paid to the superintendent of 534 East Seventy-third Street—the building across the street—to allow Peace of Mind, Inc., to emplace a voice-actuated tape recorder in a broom closet on the third floor of that building.

Thus, it was not necessary for an investigator to be present. The voice-actuated tape recorder recorded all telephone calls and interior conversations taking place in Apartment 3B, 535 East Seventy-third Street. The tape was retrieved each morning by an operative from Peace of Mind, Inc., and a fresh tape installed.

The resulting recordings became the basis of David Everleigh's suit for divorce (Supreme Court, New York County) on the grounds of adultery (*Everleigh v. Everleigh,* NYSC-148532), and transcriptions of the tapes have become a matter of public record, which allows them to be reproduced here. It is of some interest to note that the verdict of the trial judge, in favor of David Everleigh, has been appealed by Mrs. Everleigh's attorneys on the grounds that David Everleigh did not obtain a court order, and had no legal right, to implant an electronic surveillance device in Apartment 3B, despite the fact that he was legal owner of the premises in question.

It is expected this litigation will eventually reach the Supreme Court of the United States and will result in a landmark decision.

The following is an excerpt from the transcription made from the Peace of Mind, Inc., tape recording made at approximately 1:15 A.M. on the morning of 24 March, 1968.

This is tape POM-24MAR68-EVERLEIGH. Those present, Mrs. Agnes Everleigh and John Anderson, have been identified by voice prints and interior evidence.

[Sound of door opening and closing.]

MRS. EVERLEIGH: Here we are . . . make yourself at home. Throw your coat anywhere.

ANDERSON: How come a classy place like this don't have a doorman?

MRS. EVERLEIGH: Oh, we have one, but he's probably down in the basement with the super, sucking on a jug of muscatel. They're both a couple of winos.

ANDERSON: Oh?

[Lapse of seven seconds.]

ANDERSON: Nice place you got here.

MRS. EVERLEIGH: *So* glad you like it. Mix us a drink. The stuff's over there. Ice in the kitchen.

ANDERSON: What'll you have?

MRS. EVERLEIGH: Jameson's. On the rocks. With a little soda. What do you drink?

ANDERSON: Got any cognac? Or brandy?

MRS. EVERLEIGH: I have some Martell.

ANDERSON: That'll do fine.

[Lapse of forty-two seconds.]

ANDERSON: Here you are.

MRS. EVERLEIGH: Cheers.

ANDERSON: Yeah.

[Lapse of six seconds.]

MRS. EVERLEIGH: Sit down and relax. I'm going to take off my girdle.

ANDERSON: Sure.

[Lapse of two minutes sixteen seconds.]

MRS. EVERLEIGH: That's better. Thank God.

ANDERSON: Are all the apartments in the building like this?

MRS. EVERLEIGH: Most of them are larger. Why?

ANDERSON: I like it. Class.

MRS. EVERLEIGH: Class? Jesus, you're too much. What do you do for a living?

ANDERSON: I work on a folding machine in a printing plant. For a supermarket newspaper. A daily. Their specials and things like that.

MRS. EVERLEIGH: Aren't you going to ask me what I do?

ANDERSON: Do you do anything?

MRS. EVERLEIGH: That's a laugh. My husband owns this apartment. We're separated. He doesn't give me a cent. But I do all right. I'm the buyer for a chain of women's lingerie shops.

ANDERSON: That sounds interesting.

MRS. EVERLEIGH: Go to hell.

ANDERSON: Are you lushed?

MRS. EVERLEIGH: Some. Not enough.

[Lapse of seventeen seconds.]

MRS. EVERLEIGH: I hope you don't think I make a habit of picking men up off the street?

ANDERSON: Why me?

MRS. EVERLEIGH: You looked clean and reasonably well dressed. Except for that tie. God, I hate that tie. Are you married?

ANDERSON: No.

MRS. EVERLEIGH: Ever been?

ANDERSON: No.

MRS. EVERLEIGH: Jesus Christ, I don't even know your name. What the hell's your name?

ANDERSON: Another drink?

MRS. EVERLEIGH: Sure.

[Lapse of thirty-four seconds.]

MRS. EVERLEIGH: I thank you. What the hell's your name?

ANDERSON: John Anderson.

MRS. EVERLEIGH: That's a nice, clean, neat name. My name's Agnes Everleigh—Mrs. David Everleigh that was. What do I call you—Jack?

ANDERSON: Mostly I'm called Duke.

MRS. EVERLEIGH: Duke? Royalty, for God's sake. Jesus, I'm sleepy. . . .

[Lapse of four minutes thirteen seconds. At this point there is evidence (not admissible) that Mrs. Everleigh dozed off. Anderson wandered about the apartment (supposition). He inspected the intercom system connected to the bells and the microphone in the lobby.

He inspected the locks on the windows. He inspected the lock on the front door.]

MRS. EVERLEIGH: What are you doing?

ANDERSON: Just stretching my legs.

MRS. EVERLEIGH: Would you like to stay the night?

ANDERSON: No. But I don't want to go home yet.

MRS. EVERLEIGH: Thanks a lot, bum.

[Sound of loud slap.]

MRS. EVERLEIGH [gasping]: What did you do that for?

ANDERSON: That's what you wanted, isn't it?

MRS. EVERLEIGH: How did you know?

ANDERSON: A big, beefy lady executive like you . . . it had to be.

MRS. EVERLEIGH: Does it show that plainly?

ANDERSON: No. Unless you're looking for it. Should I use my belt?

MRS. EVERLEIGH: All right.

The following is supposition, supported in part by eyewitness testimony.

When he left Apartment 3B at 3:04 A.M., John Anderson spent a few moments examining the lock on Apartment 3A, across the foyer. He then took the self-service elevator up to the fifth floor, examined the locks, and made his way slowly downward, examining doors and locks. There were no peepholes in apartment doors above the ground floor.

When he exited from the lobby—still unattended by a doorman—he was able to examine the security arrangements of the outside doors and the bell system. He then waited on the corner of East

Seventy-third Street and York Avenue for a cab, and rode home to his Brooklyn apartment, arriving there at 4:26 A.M. The lights in his apartment were extinguished at 4:43 (testimony of eyewitness).

[2]

At 2:35 P.M., on the afternoon of Wednesday, 17 April, 1968, a black sedan was parked on the north side of Fifty-ninth Street, New York City, between Fifth Avenue and Avenue of the Americas. The vehicle was a 1966 Cadillac Eldorado (with air conditioning), license HGR-45-9159. It was registered as a company car by the Benefix Realty Co., Inc., 6501 Fifth Avenue, New York, New York.

The chauffeur of the car—later identified as Leonard Goldberg, forty-two, a resident of 19778 Grant Parkway, the Bronx, New York—was observed lounging nearby.

The sole occupant of the parked car, seated in the back, was Frederick Simons, vice-president of the Benefix Realty Co., Inc. He was fifty-three years old; approximately 5 feet 7 inches; 190 pounds. He wore a black bowler and a double-breasted tweed topcoat. His hair and mustache were white. He was a graduate of Rawlins Law College, Erskine, Virginia, and was also licensed as a certified public accountant in the State of New York (#41-5G-1943). He had no criminal record, although he had twice been questioned—by the New York Federal District Attorney (Southern District) and by a grand jury convened by Manhattan Supreme Court—regarding the control of the Benefix Realty Co., Inc., by an organized criminal syndicate, and the role Benefix had played in the procurement of liquor licenses for several taverns and restaurants in New York City and Buffalo, New York.

Approximately five months prior to this date, on 14 November, 1967, a court order (MCC-B-189M16) had been obtained for the emplacement of an electronic transmitting device in the vehicle described. Application was made by the Frauds Division, New York State Income Tax Bureau. A Gregory MT-146-GB microphone transmitter was concealed under the dashboard of the aforesaid vehicle. It was implanted in the garage where cars registered to the Benefix Realty Co., Inc., were serviced.

At 2:38 P.M., on the afternoon of Wednesday, 17 April, 1968, a man was seen approaching this car. He was later identified by an eyewitness at the scene and by voice prints.

John "Duke" Anderson, thirty-seven, was a resident of 314 Harrar Street, Brooklyn, New York. He was 5 feet 11 inches; 178 pounds; brown hair and brown eyes; no physical scars; dressed neatly and spoke with a slight Southern accent. Anderson was a professional thief, and four months previously had been paroled after serving twenty-three months at Sing Sing (#562-8491) after his conviction on 21 January, 1966, in Manhattan Criminal Court on a charge of breaking and entering. Although it was the first conviction on his record, he had been arrested twice before in New York State, once for burglary, once for simple assault. Both charges had been dropped with no record of trial.

Tape NYSITB-FD-17APR68-106-1A begins:

SIMONS: Duke! My Lord, it's good to see you! Come in, come in! Sit here next to me.

ANDERSON: Mr. Simons. Mighty fine to see you. How you been?

SIMONS: Fine, Duke, just fine. You're looking well. A little thinner, maybe.

ANDERSON: I expect so.

SIMONS: Of course, of course! We've got this little refreshment stand here. As you can see, I'm already partaking. Can I offer you something?

ANDERSON: Cognac? Or brandy?

SIMONS: How will Rémy Martin suit you?

ANDERSON: Just right.

SIMONS: Pardon the paper cups, Duke. We find it's easier that way.

ANDERSON: Sure, Mr. Simons.

[Lapse of five seconds.]

SIMONS: Well . . . here's to crime.

[Lapse of four seconds.]

ANDERSON: God . . . that's good.

SIMONS: Tell me, Duke—how have things been going for you?

ANDERSON: I got no complaints, Mr. Simons. I appreciate everything you all did for me.

SIMONS: You did a lot for us, too, Duke.

ANDERSON: Yes. But it wasn't much. I got the letters through when I could. Sometimes I couldn't.

SIMONS: We understood, I assure you. We don't expect perfection when you're inside.

ANDERSON: I'll never forget that night I got back to Manhattan. The hotel room. The money. The booze. And that cow you sent over. And the clothes! How did you know my sizes?

SIMONS: We have ways, Duke. You know that. I hope you liked the woman. I picked her out myself.

ANDERSON: Just what the doctor ordered.

SIMONS [laughing]: Exactly right.

[Lapse of nine seconds.]

ANDERSON: Mr. Simons, since I got out I been walking the arrow. I work nights on a folding machine in a printing plant. We do a daily sheet a chain of supermarkets gets out. You know—special buys for the day, things like that. And I report regular. I don't see any of the old gang.

SIMONS: We know, Duke, we know.

ANDERSON: But something came up I wanted to ask you about. A wild idea. I can't handle it myself. That's why I called.

SIMONS: What is it, Duke?

ANDERSON: You'll probably think I'm nuts, that

those twenty-three months scrambled my brains.

SIMONS: We don't think you're nuts, Duke. What is it . . . a campaign?

ANDERSON: Yes. Something I came across about three weeks ago. It's been chewing at me ever since. It might be good.

SIMONS: You say you can't handle it yourself? How many will you need?

ANDERSON: More than five. No more than ten.

SIMONS: I don't like it. It isn't simple.

ANDERSON: It is simple, Mr. Simons. Maybe I could do with five.

SIMONS: Let's have another.

ANDERSON: Sure . . . thanks.

[Lapse of eleven seconds.]

SIMONS: What income do you anticipate?

ANDERSON: You want me to guess? That's all I can do—guess. I guess a minimum of a hundred thou.

[Lapse of six seconds.]

SIMONS: And you want to talk to the Doctor?

ANDERSON: Yes. If you can set it up.

SIMONS: You better tell me a little more about it.

ANDERSON: You'll laugh at me.

SIMONS: I won't laugh at you, Duke. I promise.

ANDERSON: There's a house on the East Side. Way over near the river. Used to be a privately owned town house. Now it's apartments. Doctors' offices on the ground floor. Eight apartments on the four floors above. Rich people. Doorman. Self-service elevator.

SIMONS: You want to hit one of the apartments?

ANDERSON: No, Mr. Simons. I want to hit the whole building. I want to take over the entire fucking building and clean it out.

[3]

Anthony "Doctor" D'Medico, fifty-four, legal residence at 14325 Mulberry Lane, Great Neck, Long Island, was identified before the U.S. Senate Special Subcommittee to Investigate Organized Crime, Eighty-seventh Congress first session), on 15 March, 1965 (Report of Hearings, pp. 413-19), as being the third-ranking *capo* (captain) of the Angelo family. The Angelos were one of six families controlling the distribution of illicit drugs, extortion, prostitution, loan-sharking, and other illegal activities in the New York, New Jersey, Connecticut, and eastern Pennsylvania area.

D'Medico was president of the Benefix Realty Co., Inc., 6501 Fifth Avenue, New York City. His other holdings included half-partnership in the Great Frontier Steak House, 106-372 Flatbush Avenue, Brooklyn, New York; full ownership of the New Finnish Sauna and Health Club, 746 West Forty-eighth Street, Manhattan; one-third ownership of Lafferty, Riley, Riley & D'Amato, brokers (twice fined by the Securities and Exchange Commission), of 1441 Wall Street, Manhattan; and suspected but unproved ownership or interest in several small taverns, restaurants, and private clubs on the East Side of Manhattan catering to male homosexuals and lesbians.

D'Medico was a tall man, 6 feet 5 inches, portly, and he dressed conservatively (his suits were made by Quint Riddle, tailor, 1486 Saville Row, London; shirts by Trioni, 142-F Via Veneto, Rome; shoes by B. Halley, Geneva). For many years he had been the victim of a chronic and apparently incurable *tic douloureux,* an extremely painful neuralgia of the facial muscles that resulted in a spasmodic twitching of his right eye and cheek.

His criminal record was minimal. At the age of seventeen he was arrested on a charge of assault with a knife upon a uniformed officer. No injury resulted. The case was dropped by Bronx Juvenile Court on the plea of D'Medico's parents. There is no other record of charges, arrests, or convictions.

On 22 April, 1968, the premises of the Benefix Realty Co., Inc., 6501 Fifth Avenue, New York, were under electronic surveillance by three agencies: the Federal Bureau of Investigation, the Frauds Division of the New York State Income Tax Bureau, and the New York Police Department. Apparently none of these agencies was aware of the others' activities.

The following tape, dated 22 April, 1968, is NYPD-SIS-564-03.

ANDERSON: Mr. D'Medico, please. My name is John Anderson.

RECEPTIONIST: Is Mr. D'Medico expecting you?

ANDERSON: Yes. Mr. Simons set up the appointment.

RECEPTIONIST: Just a moment, please, sir.

[Lapse of fourteen seconds.]

RECEPTIONIST: You may go right in, sir. Through that door and down the hall. First door on your right.

ANDERSON: Thanks.

RECEPTIONIST: You're quite welcome, sir.

[Lapse of twenty-three seconds.]

D'MEDICO: Come in.

ANDERSON: Afternoon, Mr. D'Medico.

D'MEDICO: Duke! Good to see you.

ANDERSON: Doc . . . it's fine seeing you again. You're looking well.

D'MEDICO: Too much weight. Look at this. Too much. It's the pasta that does it. But I can't resist it. How have you been, Duke?

ANDERSON: Can't complain. I want to thank you. . . .

D'MEDICO: Of course, of course. Duke, have you ever seen the view from our roof? Suppose we go up and take a look around? Get a breath of fresh air.

ANDERSON: Fine.

[Lapse of five seconds.]

D'MEDICO: Miss Riley? I'll be out of my office for a few moments. Will you ask Sam to switch on the air conditioner? It's very stuffy in here. Thank you.

[Lapse of three minutes forty-two seconds.

Remainder of recording is garbled and indistinct due to mechanical difficulties.]

D'MEDICO: . . . do we know? A guy comes in every morning . . . the place . . . but. . . . You wouldn't believe . . . phones . . . gadgets that. . . . The building over there, across the street . . . windows . . . long-range. . . . We try to keep . . . murder. Don't trust. . . . Over here by the air conditioner. The noise. . . . Cold for you?

ANDERSON: No. It's. . . .

D'MEDICO: Fred told me . . . campaign. . . . Interesting. About five men you figured or . . . me more.

ANDERSON: I know . . . idea . . . still. . . . Of course, I haven't even gone . . . it. So I . . . you a package, Mr. D'Medico.

D'MEDICO: [Completely garbled.]

ANDERSON: No. No, I. . . . Two months, I'd say . . . be careful. . . . first investigation. Good men . . . be in . . . if we went ahead. So all I got . . . right . . . is a hustle. I hoped . . . might stake . . . piece of the action.

D'MEDICO: I see. . . . much do you . . . for this initial. . . .

ANDERSON: Three grand tops I . . . most . . . good men. But no use cutting . . . like this. . . .

D'MEDICO: You've got . . . –stand, is personal. My own funds. If it . . . good, I'll have . . . bring in others. You understand? It will . . . more . . . and also we'll want . . . man in. Ours.

ANDERSON: I understand. And thanks . . . help. I really . . . can bring it. . . .

D'MEDICO: Duke . . . anyone . . . you can. You . . .

think . . . Fred Simons will . . . funds . . . from him. Let's . . . downstairs. Cold . . . hell. My face . . . act up. Jesus.

End of recording. It is assumed the two men returned to the Benefix offices, but that Anderson did not reenter D'Medico's private office. He departed from the building at 2:34 P.M.

[4]

Patsy's Delicious Meat Market, 11901 Ninth Avenue, New York. Four months previously these premises had been placed under electronic surveillance by the Investigative Division, Food and Drug Administration. The following tape recording, labeled FDA-PMM-#198-08, is dated 24 April, 1968. Time: approximately 11:15 A.M.

ANDERSON: Are you Patsy?

PATSY: Yes.

ANDERSON: My name is Simons. I called for three of your best steaks. You said you'd have them ready when I came in.

PATSY: Sure. Here they are, all wrapped.

ANDERSON: Thanks. Add that to my bill, will you?

PATSY: A pleasure.

[5]

Thomas Haskins (alias Timothy Hawkins, Terence Hall, etc.); thirty-two; 5 feet 4 inches; 128 pounds; faint white scar on left temple; slight figure; blond hair bleached whiter; a confessed male homosexual. This man's record included two arrests on charges of molesting male juveniles. Charges dropped when parents refused to prosecute. Arrested on 18 March, 1964, during raid on bucket shop operation at 1432 Wall Street, Manhattan. Charge dropped. Arrested on 23 October, 1964, on conspiracy to defraud, complaint of Mrs. Eloise MacLevy, 41105 Central Park West, Manhattan, claiming subject had mulcted her of $10,131.56 while promising her high return on investment in pork-belly futures. Charge dropped. Last known address: 713 West Seventy-sixth Street, New York City. Subject lived with sister (see below).

Cynthia "Snapper" Haskins; thirty-six; 5 feet 8 inches; 148 pounds; red hair (dyed; frequently wore wigs); no physical scars. Four convictions for shoplifting, three for prostitution, and one for fraud, in that she charged $1,061.78 worth of merchandise against a stolen credit card of the

Buy-Everything Credit Co., Inc., 4501 Marvella Street, Los Angeles, California. Subject had served a total of four years, seven months, thirteen days in the Women's House of Detention, Manhattan; Barnaby House for Women, Losset, New York; and the McAllister Home for Women, Carburn, New York. Subject was author of *I Was a B-Girl* (Smith & Townsend, published 10 March, 1963) and *Women's Prison: A Story of Lust and Frustration* (Nu-World Publishing Corp., published 26 July, 1964).

The premises at 713 West Seventy-sixth Street, New York, were under surveillance by the Bureau of Narcotics, Department of the Treasury. The following is transcription BN-DT-TH-0018-95GT, from a tape recording of the same number (except that the final digits are 95G). Those present have been identified by voice prints and by internal and external evidence. The date and time have not been determined exactly.

HASKINS: . . . so we're on the old uppers, darling. The sad story of our lives. Would you like a stick?

ANDERSON: No. You go ahead. What about you, Snap?

CYNTHIA: We live. I boost a little, and Tommy hustles his ass. We get by.

ANDERSON: I got something for you.

CYNTHIA: Both of us?

ANDERSON: Yes.

CYNTHIA: How much?

ANDERSON: Five bills. Shouldn't take over a week.

No sweat.

HASKINS: Sounds divine.

CYNTHIA: Let's hear it.

ANDERSON: I'll tell you what you need to know. After that . . . no questions.

HASKINS: Wouldn't dream, darling.

ANDERSON: There's this house on the East Side. I'll leave you the address and everything I know about the schedules of the doormen and the super. Tommy, I want a complete list of everyone who lives in the place or who works there. That includes day-only servants, doormen, and super. Anything and everything. Names, ages, businesses they're in, daily schedules—the whole schmear.

HASKINS: A lark, darling.

ANDERSON: Snap, there are two professional offices on the ground floor, one a doctor, one a psychiatrist. I want you to look around. Furnishings? Safes? Maybe paintings on the walls? Shoe boxes in the back closet? These fucking doctors collect a lot in cash and never declare. Look it over and decide how you'll handle it. Then let me know before you move.

CYNTHIA: Like you said—no sweat. How do we contact you, Duke?

ANDERSON: I'll call at noon every Friday until you're set. Is your phone clean?

CYNTHIA: Here . . . I'll write it down. It's a phone booth in a candy store on West End Avenue. I'll be there at twelve o'clock every Friday.

ANDERSON: All right.

CYNTHIA: A little something down?

ANDERSON: Two bills.

CYNTHIA: You're a darling.

HASKINS: He's a sweetheart, a messenger from heaven. How's your love life, Duke?

ANDERSON: All right.

HASKINS: I saw Ingrid the other night. She heard you were out. She asked about you. Do you want to see her?

ANDERSON: I don't know.

HASKINS: She wants to see you.

ANDERSON: Yes? All right. Is she still at the old place?

HASKINS: She is indeed, darling. You don't blame her . . . do you?

ANDERSON: No. It wasn't her fault. I got busted from my own stupidity. How did she look?

HASKINS: The same. The pale, white little mouse made of wire and steel. The essence of bitchery.

ANDERSON: Yes.

[6]

Fun City Electronic Supply & Repair Co., Inc., 1975 Avenue D, New York City.

The following tape recording was made by the Federal Trade Commission through a rather unusual set of circumstances. The FTC established electronic surveillance of the aforementioned premises (court order MCC-#198-67BC) following complaints from several large recording companies that the proprietor of the Fun City Electronic Supply & Repair Co., Inc., Ernest Heinrich Mann, was engaged in a criminal activity, in that he purchased expensive commercial LP's and tape recordings of classical music—operas and symphonies—rerecorded them onto his own tapes, and sold the tapes at a greatly reduced (but profitable) price to a large list of clients.

Tape FTC-30APR68-EHM-14.

CLERK: Yes?

ANDERSON: The owner around?

CLERK: Mr. Mann?

ANDERSON: Yes. Could I see him for a minute? I want to complain about an air conditioner you people sold me.

CLERK: I'll get him.

[Lapse of nine seconds.]

ANDERSON: You installed an air conditioner in my place and it conked out after I turned it on. I tested it and it ran a few minutes, then it stopped.

MANN: Would you step into the back office for a few minutes, sir, and we'll try to solve your problem. Al, handle things.

CLERK: Yes, Mr. Mann.

[Lapse of thirteen seconds.]

ANDERSON: Professor . . . you're looking good.

MANN: All goes well. With you, Duke?

ANDERSON: Can't complain. Took me a while to track you down. Nice setup you've got here.

MANN: What I've wanted always. Radio, television, hi-fi equipment, tape recorders, air conditioners. I do good.

ANDERSON: In other words, you're making money?

MANN: Yes, that is true.

ANDERSON: In other words, it will cost me more?

MANN [laughing]: Duke, Duke, you have always been a—how do you say it?—you have always been a very sharp man. Yes, it will now cost you more. What is it?

ANDERSON: There's this house on the East Side. Not too far from here. Five floors. Service entrance to basement. I want the basement washed—telephone system, trunk lines, alarms, whatever is down there. The works.

[Lapse of nine seconds.]

MANN: Difficult. With all these terrible robberies on the East Side recently, everyone is most alert. Doorman?

ANDERSON: Yes.

MANN: Back entrance?

ANDERSON: Yes.

MANN: I would guess closed-circuit TV from the back service entrance to the doorman's cubbyhole in the lobby. He doesn't press the button that releases the service door until he sees who is ringing. Am I correct?

ANDERSON: One hundred percent.

MANN: So. Let me think. . . .

ANDERSON: Do that, Professor.

MANN: "Professor." You are the only man I know who calls me Professor.

ANDERSON: Aren't you a professor?

MANN: I *was* a professor. But please . . . let me think. Now. . . . Yes. . . . We are telephone repairmen. The authentic truck is parked in front where the doorman can see it. Uniforms, equipment, identity cards . . . everything. We are bringing a new trunk line down the block. We must inspect the telephone connections in the basement. Duke? All right so far?

ANDERSON: Yes.

MANN: The doorman insists we pull over to the service entrance. . . .

ANDERSON: It's an alleyway leading to the back of the building.

MANN: Excellent. We pull in after he has inspected my identity card. All is well. The driver stays with the truck. I go in. The doorman sees me on his TV monitor. He releases the lock. Yes, I think so.

ANDERSON: I do, too.

MANN: So? What do you want?

ANDERSON: Everything down there. How the telephone lines come in. Can we break them? How? Is it a one-trunk line? Can it be cut or bypassed? How many phones in the whole building? Extensions? Alarm systems? To the local precinct house or private agencies? I want a blueprint of the whole wiring system. And look around down there. Probably nothing, but you never can tell. Can you operate a Polaroid with flash?

MANN: Of course. Clear, complete views. Every angle. Details. Instructions on what to bridge and what to cut. Satisfaction guaranteed.

ANDERSON: That's why I looked you up.

MANN: The cost will be one thousand dollars with half down in advance.

ANDERSON: The cost will be seven hundred dollars with three in advance.

MANN: The cost will be eight with four ahead.

ANDERSON: All right.

MANN: The cost will not include telephone truck and driver. I have no one I can trust. You must provide. Telephone truck, driver, uniform, and paper. You will pay for this?

[Lapse of four seconds.]

ANDERSON: All right. You'll get your own?

MANN: Yes.

ANDERSON: I'll let you know when. Thank you, Professor.

MANN: Any time.

[7]

From tape recording POM-14MAY68-EVERLEIGH, Segment I, approximately 9:45 A.M.

MRS. EVERLEIGH: Jesus, you're too much. I've never

met anyone like you. How did you learn to do these things?

ANDERSON: Practice.

MRS. EVERLEIGH: You turn me upside down and inside out. You know all the buttons—just what turns me on. About a half hour ago I was down to one little nerve end, red and raw. You get me out.

ANDERSON: Yes.

MRS. EVERLEIGH: For a moment there I wanted to scream.

ANDERSON: Why didn't you?

MRS. EVERLEIGH: That bitch next door—she'd probably tell the doorman to call the cops.

ANDERSON: What bitch?

MRS. EVERLEIGH: Old Mrs. Horowitz. She and her husband have Apartment Three A, across the foyer.

ANDERSON: She's home during the day?

MRS. EVERLEIGH: Of course. He is, too—most days, when he's not at his broker's. He's retired and plays the market for kicks. Why—I don't know. He's got the first buck he ever earned.

ANDERSON: Loaded?

MRS. EVERLEIGH: Loaded *and* cheap. I've seen her put dog-food cans in the incinerator, and they don't even have a dog. I was in their place once. I don't socialize with them, but he called me in one night when she fainted. He panicked and rang my bell. It was just a faint—nothing to it. But while I was in their bedroom I saw a safe that must date from Year One. I'll bet that thing is bulging. He used to be a wholesale jeweler. Do it again, baby.

ANDERSON: Do what?

MRS. EVERLEIGH: You know. . . . with your finger . . . here . . .

ANDERSON: I know something better than that. Open up a little. More. Yes. Keep your knees up, you stupid cow.

MRS. EVERLEIGH: No. Don't do that. Please.

ANDERSON: I'm just starting. It gets better.

MRS. EVERLEIGH: Please, don't. Please, Duke. You're hurting me.

ANDERSON: That's the name of the game.

MRS. EVERLEIGH: I can't . . . oh Jesus, don't . . . please . . . God . . . Duke, I beg . . . oh, oh, oh . . .

ANDERSON: What a fat slob you are. For Chrissakes, you're crying . . .

[8]

Helmas Job Printing, 8901 Amsterdam Avenue, New York; 14 May, 1968; 10:46 A.M. Electronic surveillance by the Internal Revenue Service, using a Teletek Model MT-18-48B, transmitting to a voice-actuated tape recorder in the basement of the delicatessen next door. This is tape IRS-HJB-14MAY68-106.

CLERK: Yeah?

HASKINS: Is your employer about?

CLERK: Smitty? He's in back. Hey, Smitty! Someone to see you!

[Lapse of six seconds.]

HASKINS: Hello, Smitty.

SMITTY: Where's my twenty?

HASKINS: Right here, Smitty. Sorry it took so long to pay you. I do apologize. But I assure you, I didn't forget it.

SMITTY: Yeah. Thanks, Tommy.

HASKINS: Could I speak to you for a moment, Smitty?

SMITTY: Well . . . yeah . . . all right. Come on in back.

[Lapse of eleven seconds.]

HASKINS: I need some paper, Smitty. I've got the cash. See? Plenty of bread. Cash on delivery.

SMITTY: What do you need?

HASKINS: I typed it all out for you on Snapper's typewriter. One identification card in the name of Sidney Brevoort. I've always loved the name Sidney. The company is the New Urban Reorganization Committee, a nonprofit outfit. Any clean address. Make sure you use this phone number. Here's a snapshot of me to staple on the card. Here is what it should say: "This will identify . . ." and so forth and so forth. Then I'll want about twenty Sidney Brevoort business cards. While you're at it, better make up about ten letterheads and envelopes for the New Urban Reorganization Committee. You never know. Okay so far?

SMITTY: Sure. What else?

HASKINS: Snapper wants twenty cards. Very ladylike and elegant. Script. Here's the name and address: Mrs. Doreen Margolies, five-eight-five East Seventy-third Street. Something with taste. You know?

SMITTY: Sure. I got taste. That's it?

HASKINS: Yes, that's everything.

SMITTY: Three o'clock this afternoon. Twenty-five bucks.

HASKINS: Thanks so much, Smitty. You're a sweet. I'll see you at three.

SMITTY: With the loot.

HASKINS: Of course. Have. . . .

[The recording was halted by mechanical failure.]

[9]

Tape recording POM-14MAY68-EVERLEIGH, Segment II; approximately 11:45 A.M.

MRS. EVERLEIGH: I've got to get to the office. I've been away too long. God, I feel drained.

ANDERSON: Have another shot; you'll feel better.

MRS. EVERLEIGH: I suppose so. Do you think we should leave together?

ANDERSON: Why not? He knows I'm up here, don't he?

MRS. EVERLEIGH: Yes. He called first. Christ, I hope he doesn't shoot his mouth off to the other owners.

ANDERSON: Give him a tip. He won't talk.

MRS. EVERLEIGH: How much should I give him?

ANDERSON: Have him call you a cab and slip him two bucks.

MRS. EVERLEIGH: Two dollars? Is that enough?

ANDERSON: Plenty.

MRS. EVERLEIGH: Where are you going when you leave?

ANDERSON: It's a nice day—maybe I'll walk over to Ninth and get a downtown bus to work.

MRS. EVERLEIGH: I won't be able to see you for a while. For about two weeks.

ANDERSON: How's that?

MRS. EVERLEIGH: I've got to go to Paris on a buying trip. If you'd give me your address, I'll send you a dirty French postcard.

ANDERSON: I'll wait till you get back. You go on these trips often?

MRS. EVERLEIGH: Almost every month. Either to Europe or some other place to shoot ads. I'm gone at least a week out of every month.

ANDERSON: Nice. I'd like to travel.

MRS. EVERLEIGH: It's just working in a different place. Will you miss me?

ANDERSON: Sure.

MRS. EVERLEIGH: Oh, my God. . . . Well . . . all ready?

ANDERSON: Yes. Let's go.

MRS. EVERLEIGH: Oh, by the way . . . here's something I bought for you. It's a gold cigarette lighter from Dunhill's. I hope you like it.

ANDERSON: Thanks.

MRS. EVERLEIGH: Oh my God . . .

[10]

Approximately three weeks after the parole of John Anderson from Sing Sing Penitentiary, intermittent electronic surveillance was established on his newly rented furnished rooms at 314 Harrar Street, Brooklyn, New York. The device used has not been verified. The following tape is coded NYPD-JDA-146-09. It is not dated. Speakers have been identified by voice prints and internal evidence.

ANDERSON: Ed Brodsky?

BILLY: He ain't here.

ANDERSON: Is that you, Billy?

BILLY: Who's this?

ANDERSON: I'm the guy you went to the Peters-McCoy fight with, at the old Garden.

BILLY: Gee, this is great! Duke, how. . . .

ANDERSON: Shut up and listen to me. Got a pencil?

BILLY: Wait a sec . . . yeah . . . okay, Duke, I got a pencil.

ANDERSON: How long will it take you to get to a

pay phone?

BILLY: Five minutes maybe.

ANDERSON: Call me at this number, Billy. Now write it down.

BILLY: Okay, go ahead, I'm ready.

ANDERSON: Five-five-five-six-six-seven-one. Got that?

BILLY: Yeah. Sure.

ANDERSON: Read it back.

BILLY: Five-five-five-six-six-one-seven.

ANDERSON: Seven-one. The last two numbers are seven-one.

BILLY: Seven-one. Yeah, I got it now. Five-five-five, six-six-seven-one. How you been, Duke? I sure been. . . .

ANDERSON: Just hang up and go call, Billy. I'll be here.

BILLY: Oh . . . yeah. Okay, Duke, I'll hang up now.

[Lapse of three minutes forty-two seconds.]

BILLY: Duke?

ANDERSON: How are you, Billy?

BILLY: Gee, it's good to hear from you, Duke. We heard you was out. Ed was saying just the other. . . .

ANDERSON: Where is Ed?

BILLY: He took a fall, Duke.

ANDERSON: A fall? What the hell for?

BILLY: He was a . . . he was a . . . Duke, what's that word—you know—you got a lot of traffic tickets and you throw them away?

ANDERSON: A scofflaw?

BILLY: Yeah! That's it! Ed was a scofflaw. The judge said Ed was the biggest scofflaw in Brooklyn.

How about that! So he got thirty days.

ANDERSON: Beautiful. When's he springing?

BILLY: What's today?

ANDERSON: It's Friday, Billy. The seventeenth of May.

BILLY: Yeah. Let's see . . . eighteen, nineteen, twenty, twenty-one. Yeah. The twenty-oneth. That's Tuesday . . . right?

ANDERSON: That's right, Billy.

BILLY: Ed will be out on Tuesday.

ANDERSON: I'll call late Tuesday or Wednesday morning. Tell him, will you, kid?

BILLY: I sure will. Duke, you got a job for us?

ANDERSON: Something like that.

BILLY: We sure could use a job, Duke. Things ain't been so great for me since Ed's been in the can. Listen, Duke, is it something maybe I could handle? I mean, if it's something right away, I could handle it. No use waiting for Ed to spring.

ANDERSON: Well, it's really a two-man job, Billy. If it was a one-man job, I'd tell you right away because I know you could handle anything I'd give you.

BILLY: I sure could, Duke. You know me.

ANDERSON: But this is really a two-man job so I think maybe we should wait for Ed. Okay?

BILLY: Oh, yeah, sure, Duke . . . if you say so.

ANDERSON: Listen, kid, is it really bad? I mean, if you need a couple of plasters until Ed gets out, tell me right now.

BILLY: Oh, no, Duke, thanks. Gee, no. It's not that bad. I mean I can get by till Ed gets sprung. Gee, thanks, Duke, I really do appreciate it. Hey, when you mentioned about that night at the Garden it really took me back. Hey, what a night that was . . . hey? Remember that guy I decked in the restaurant? Gee, what a night that was . . . hey, Duke?

ANDERSON: A great night, Billy. I remember it. Well, listen, keep out of trouble, will you, kid?

BILLY: Oh, sure, Duke. I'll be careful.

ANDERSON: And tell Ed I'll call on Tuesday night or early Wednesday.

BILLY: I won't forget, Duke. Honest I won't. Tuesday night or early Wednesday. Duke will call. When I get back to the room I'll write it down.

ANDERSON: That's a good boy, Billy. Keep your nose clean. I'll be seeing you soon.

BILLY: Sure, Duke, sure. It was real good talking to you. Thank you very much.

[11]

Ingrid Macht, thirty-four, a resident of 627 West Twenty-fourth Street, New York City, was of German or Polish birth (not determined); 5 feet 5 inches; 112 pounds; black hair usually worn very short. Brown eyes. Healed lash marks on left buttock. Healed knife scar in X pattern on inside of left thigh. Scar of second-degree burns on right forearm. Spoke German, English, French, Spanish, and Italian fluently. (See Interpol file #35S-

M49876.) Believed to be Jewish. There is evidence (unsubstantiated) that this woman entered the United States illegally from Cuba in 1964 in a group of authentic refugees. Interpol file (see above) lists arrests in Hamburg for solicitation, prostitution, robbery, and blackmail. Served eighteen months in corrective institution in Munich. Arrested on 16 November, 1964, in Miami, Florida, charged with complicity in a scheme to extort money from Cuban refugees on the promise of getting their relatives to the United States. Charges dropped for lack of evidence. Employed as dance instructor at Fandango Dance Ballroom, 11563, Broadway, New York.

Electronic surveillance of Miss Macht's apartment had been established on 15 January, 1968, by the Investigative Branch, Securities and Exchange Commission, on application in Federal Court, claiming that Miss Macht was involved in the theft and sale of securities, including stock shares, corporate bonds, and U.S. government bonds. On the granting of court order FDC-1719M-89C, a Bottomley 956-MT microphone transmitter was installed, tapping both telephone calls and interior conversations.

By coincidence, an employee of the SEC lived in the apartment directly below Miss Macht's. With his kind permission, a voice-actuated tape recorder was installed in his linen closet.

The following transcription was made from tape SEC-21MAY68-IM-12:18PM-130C.

ANDERSON: Is your apartment clean?

INGRID: Why not? I have been living a clean life. Duke, I heard you were out. How was it?

ANDERSON: Inside? A lot of faggots. You know how it was. You've been there.

INGRID: Yes. I have been there. A brandy—as usual?

ANDERSON: Yes. I like this place now. It looks different.

[Lapse of twenty-nine seconds.]

INGRID: Thank you. I have spent much money on it. *Prosit.*

[Lapse of five seconds.]

INGRID: Frankly, it is a surprise to see you. I did not think you would wish to see me again.

ANDERSON: Why not?

INGRID: I thought you would blame me.

ANDERSON: No. I don't blame you. What could you have done—confessed and taken a fall? What for? How would that have helped?

INGRID: That is what I thought.

ANDERSON: I was stupid and got caught. It happens. You have to pay for stupidity in this world. You did exactly what I would have done.

INGRID: I thank you, Duke. Now . . . that makes me feel better.

ANDERSON: You've put on weight?

INGRID: Perhaps. A little. Here and there.

ANDERSON: You look good, real good. Here, I brought you something. A gold cigarette lighter from Dunhill's. You still smoke as much as ever?

INGRID: Oh, yes—more than ever. Thank you. Very handsome. Expensive—no? Are things going so good for you . . . or did a woman give it to you?

ANDERSON: You guess.

INGRID [laughing]: I don't care how you got it. It was very nice, and you were very sweet to think of me. So . . . what happens now? What do you want?

ANDERSON: I don't know. I really don't know. What do *you* want?

INGRID: Oh, *Schatzie,* I stopped wanting many years ago. Now I just accept. It is easier that way.

ANDERSON: It made no difference to you whether I looked you up or not?

INGRID: No difference . . . no. I was curious, naturally. But it makes no difference either way.

[Lapse of fourteen seconds.]

ANDERSON: You're a cold woman.

INGRID: Yes. I have learned to be cold.

ANDERSON: Tommy Haskins said you wanted to see me.

INGRID: Did he? That's Tommy.

ANDERSON: You didn't want to see me?

INGRID: Did—didn't. What difference does it make?

ANDERSON: What time do you go to work?

INGRID: I leave here at seven. I must be at the hall by eight.

ANDERSON: I'm working. Not too far from here. I've got to be there by four.

INGRID: So?

ANDERSON: So we have three hours. I want you to make love to me.

INGRID: If you wish.

ANDERSON: That's what I like—a hot woman.

INGRID: Oh, Duke. . . . If I was a hot woman you would not bother with me.

ANDERSON: Take off your robe. You know what I like.

INGRID: All right.

ANDERSON: You have gained weight. But it looks good.

INGRID: Thank you. Do you wish to undress?

ANDERSON: Not now. Later.

INGRID: Yes.

[Lapse of seventeen seconds.]

ANDERSON: Oh, God. A week ago a woman asked me where I learned these things. I should have told her.

INGRID: Yes. But you don't know everything, Duke. A few things I have held back. Like this. . . .

ANDERSON: I . . . oh, Jesus, don't . . . I can't. . . .

INGRID: But of course you can. You will not die from this, *Schatzie,* I assure you. It can be endured. I think now you will undress.

ANDERSON: Yes. Can we go in the bedroom?

INGRID: Please, no. I have just changed the bedding. I will get the soiled sheet from the hamper and we will spread it here, on the rug.

ANDERSON: All right.

[Lapse of twenty-three seconds.]

ANDERSON: What is that?

INGRID: A girl at the dance hall told me about it, so I went out and bought one. Less than five dollars at a discount drugstore. It is intended for massage. Would you like to try it?

ANDERSON: All right.

INGRID: Look at this shape. So obvious. It makes a buzzing noise when I switch it on. Do not be startled. You will like it. I use it on myself.

[Buzzing sound. Lapse of eighteen seconds.]

ANDERSON: No . . . stop. I can't take that.

INGRID: From me? But Duke, you once said you could take anything from me.

ANDERSON: God . . .

INGRID: Let me get closer to you. Look at me.

ANDERSON: What? I . . . what?

INGRID: In my eyes. At me, Duke. In my eyes . . .

ANDERSON: Oh . . . oh . . .

INGRID: "Oh, oh!" What kind of love talk is that? I must punish you for that. There is a nerve near . . . ah, yes, here. Am I not clever, *Schatzie?*

ANDERSON: Uhh . . .

INGRID: Please do not become unconscious so soon. I have several new things I would like to show you. Some are old things that will be new to you. And some are truly new things I have learned since . . . since you have been away. Open your eyes; you are no longer looking at me. You must look at me, *Schatzie*. You must look into my eyes. That is very important . . .

ANDERSON: Why . . .

INGRID: It is very important to me.

ANDERSON: Ah, ah, ah, ah . . .

INGRID: Just spread yourself a little wider and I will get you out. Watch carefully, Duke, and learn. . . . And who knows? Perhaps she will give you another cigarette lighter. . . .

[12]

Residence of Thomas and Cynthia Haskins, 713 West Seventy-sixth Street, New York; 24 May, 1968. Excerpt from tape recording BN-DT-TH-0018-96G.

THOMAS: . . . and then the nasty turd stiffed me. He said he only had ten dollars with him. He opened his wallet to show me.

CYNTHIA: Bastard.

THOMAS: And then he laughed and asked if I took credit cards. I swear if I had a razor with me, he'd have been a member of the castrati right then. I was just furious. I thought he was good for at least fifty. Midwesterner, of course. Pillar of the church. PTA. Rotarians. Elks. And all that shit.

CYNTHIA: And Odd Fellows.

THOMAS: You wouldn't *believe!* He said he was in New York on a business trip—but I know better, luv. He probably comes in twice a year to get his ashes hauled. I hope the next time he meets some rough trade from uptown. They'll shove his credit cards right up his hairy ass.

CYNTHIA: Duke called today.

THOMAS: What did you say?

CYNTHIA: I said we were working on it. I said we had the paper and were working it out. He was satisfied.

THOMAS: That's good. I don't think we should appear too anxious . . . do you, luv?

CYNTHIA: No I guess not. But I really want to do a good job for him, Tommy. Maybe then he'll let us in on it. I got the feeling it's something big.

THOMAS: Why do you think that?

CYNTHIA: He's being so very, very careful. And five bills is a lot of bread for what he wants us to do. Someone is behind him on this. He just got out of poke a few months ago. He wouldn't have that kind of loot.

THOMAS: We'll do a good job for him. He scares me sometimes. His eyes are so pale and they look right through you.

CYNTHIA: I know. And that Ingrid is no Mother Goose, either.

[Lapse of seven seconds.]

THOMAS: Tell me something, Snap. Did you ever swing with her?

[Lapse of five seconds.]

CYNTHIA: Twice. No more.

THOMAS: Bent–isn't she?

CYNTHIA: You have no idea. I couldn't describe it.

THOMAS: I thought so, luv. She's got the look. And I bet I can guess her hang-up. . . .

CYNTHIA: What?

THOMAS: Whips, chains, feathers . . . the whole bit.

CYNTHIA: You're warm.

THOMAS [laughing]: I bet I am. That's what I don't understand–Duke going that route. It's not like him.

CYNTHIA: Every man's got to get out sooner or later. I told him we'd be ready by next Friday. Okay?

THOMAS: Why not? I'm ready now.

[Lapse of six seconds.]

CYNTHIA: I walked past that house on Seventy-third Street this morning.

THOMAS: My God, you didn't go in, did you?

CYNTHIA: Do you think I've got shit for brains? He told us not to . . . didn't he? Until we get his go-ahead. . . . I walked by across the street.

THOMAS: How did it look? Want a stick, luv?

CYNTHIA: Yes, all right, light me one. Good-looking town house. Gray stone. Black canopy from the doorway to the curb. I saw two brass plates–the doctors' names. There was a doorman talking to the beat fuzz out in front. Rich-looking building. Smells like money. I wonder what's on Duke's mind?

THOMAS: One of the apartments, I expect. How are you going to work it?

CYNTHIA: I'm going to call the doctor-doctor for an appointment, giving the name on those cards you got me. No one recommended me; I just moved into the neighborhood and need a doctor and saw his sign. Before I go to see him, I'll bite all my nails off down to the quick. I'll ask him for something to keep me from biting my nails. If he suggests something, I'll tell him I tried all kinds of liquids and paints and they didn't work. I'll ask if he thinks it might be a mental or emotional problem. I'll get him to recommend me to the shrink next door.

THOMAS: Sounds good.

CYNTHIA: I'll stop by the shrink's office and see him or make an appointment. I'll leave another card and tell him the doctor-doctor sent me. If I don't get enough on the first visits, I'll make some excuse for going back. How does it sound? Anything wrong?

THOMAS: Well . . . one thing. You got the cards and a good address. They'll never in a billion years check to see if you actually live there—until their bills are returned. And then it'll probably be too late. But you better check with Duke to make sure. Find out how you should handle the bills. My God, if the doctor-doctor sent out a bill after the day you visited him, and it was returned, it might fuck the whole thing. You better ask Duke.

CYNTHIA: Yes, that makes sense, Tommy. Doctors usually send bills out a few weeks or a month later—but no use taking chances. I didn't think about how I was going to pay them. You know, you've got some brains in that tiny, pointed head of yours.

THOMAS: And I worship you, too, luv!

CYNTHIA: This is lousy grass . . . you know? Where did you get it?

THOMAS: I just got it. No like?

CYNTHIA: All twigs and seeds. Didn't you strain it?

THOMAS: He told me it had been strained.

CYNTHIA: Who?

THOMAS: Paul.

CYNTHIA: That little scut? No wonder it's lousy. I'd rather have a Chesterfield. Tommy, how are you going to handle your end?

THOMAS: All front. I waltz in, flash my paper, and get a complete list of everyone in the building. After all, I'm making an informal neighborhood census on behalf of the New Urban Reorganization Committee. And by the way, the day I hit you'll have to sit in that booth in the candy store most of the morning. That's the number on my ID card. In case anyone decides to check.

CYNTHIA: All right.

THOMAS: Shouldn't be more than an hour or so, at the most. I'll call as soon as I leave. After I get the list from him, I'll ask him to call individual tenants and see if they'd be willing to be interviewed. Purely voluntary. No pressure. No hard line. Easy does it. If they don't want to, they don't have to. I might get into two or three apartments. Those rich bitches get lonely in the afternoon. They want to talk to someone.

CYNTHIA: Just one visit?

THOMAS: Yes. Let's not push our luck, luv. I'll get what I can on one visit. If Duke isn't satisfied, screw him.

CYNTHIA: You'd like that, wouldn't you? Or vice versa.

THOMAS: How do you like your vice–versa? I

guess I would. Maybe. I'm not sure. I told you he frightens me sometimes. He's so cold and aloof and withdrawn. Someday he's going to kill.

CYNTHIA: Do you really think so?

THOMAS: Oh, yes.

CYNTHIA: He never carries a piece.

THOMAS: I know. But he'll do it someday. Maybe he'll kick someone to death. Or with his hands or whatever is handy. That would be like him—standing there coldly kicking someone in their balls and stomping on them. Until they're dead.

CYNTHIA: Jesus, Tommy!

THOMAS: It's true. You know, I'm very psychic about people. Those are the emanations I get from him.

CYNTHIA: Then I won't even suggest it.

THOMAS: Suggest what?

CYNTHIA: Well . . . the whole deal is so interesting—I mean Duke giving us all that loot for what we're doing. I'm sure it's something big. So I thought. . . .

THOMAS: Yes?

CYNTHIA: Well, I thought that if we . . . if you and me . . . we could discover what it was, maybe we could . . . somehow, you know . . . move first and take. . . .

THOMAS [yelling]: You bloody scut! Forget it! Forget it . . . do you hear? If I ever hear you mention such a thing again I'm going right to Duke and tell him. We're getting paid for what we do. That's it! You understand? That's all we know and all we do unless Duke gives us something more. Do you have that straight?

CYNTHIA: Jesus Christ, Tommy, you don't have to scream at me.

THOMAS: Frigging cunt. You get ideas like that and we're dead. You understand what I'm saying? We're dead.

CYNTHIA: All right, Tommy, *all right.* I won't say any more about it.

THOMAS: Don't even think about it. Don't even let the idea get into your stupid little brain again. I know men better than you and. . . .

CYNTHIA: I'm sure you do, Tommy.

THOMAS: . . . and Duke isn't like you and me. If he found out what you said, he'd do things to us you wouldn't believe. And it wouldn't mean a thing to him. Not a thing. Ignorant slut!

CYNTHIA: All right, Tommy, *all right.*

[Lapse of sixteen seconds.]

CYNTHIA: When Duke calls next Friday, you want me to give him what we've got and get the go-ahead?

THOMAS: Yes. Outline it for him. Ask him how you should handle paying the doctors. He'll come up with something.

CYNTHIA: All right.

[Lapse of six seconds.]

THOMAS: Snap, I'm sorry I yelled at you. But I was frightened at what you said. Please, please, forgive me.

CYNTHIA: Sure.

THOMAS: Would you like a nice hot bath, luv? I'll get it all ready for you. With bath oil.

CYNTHIA: That would. . . .

[End of recording due to tape runout.]

[13]

Edward J. Brodsky; thirty-six; 5 feet 9½ inches; 178 pounds; black, oily hair, center part, worn long. Middle finger of right hand amputated. Faint knife scar on right forearm. Brown eyes. This man had a record of four arrests, one conviction. Arrested on charge of assault, 2 March, 1963. Case dismissed. Arrested for breaking and entering, 31 May, 1964. Case dismissed for lack of evidence. Arrested for conspiracy to defraud, 27 September, 1964. Charges withdrawn. Arrested as scofflaw, 14 April, 1968. Sentenced to thirty days in the Brooklyn jail. Completed sentence and released 21 May, 1968. Member of Brooklyn Longshoremen's Union, Local 418 (Steward, 5 May, 1965, to 6 May, 1966). Questioned in connection with fatal stabbing of union official, BLU, Local 526, 28 December, 1965. No charge. Residence: 124-159 Flatbush Avenue, Brooklyn, New York. Older brother of William K. Brodsky (see below).

William "Billy" K. Brodsky; twenty-seven; 6 feet 5 inches; 215 pounds; fair, wavy hair; blue eyes; no physical scars. Extremely muscular build.

Elected "Mr. Young Brooklyn" 1963, 1964, and 1965. Arrested 14 May, 1964, on a charge of molesting a minor (female). Charge dropped. Arrested on 30 October, 1966, for assault with a deadly weapon—namely, his fists. Convicted; suspended sentence. Questioned on 16 July, 1967, in case involving attack and rape of two juveniles (female), Brooklyn, New York. Released for lack of evidence. This man dropped out of school after the seventh grade. The investigator's report leading to the suspended sentence in the assault case of 1966 states he had the mentality of a ten-year-old. Lived with his older brother at address given above.

The following meeting took place at the You-Know-It Bar & Grill, 136-943 Flatbush Avenue, Brooklyn, New York, on the afternoon of 25 May, 1968. At the time, these premises were under electronic surveillance by the New York State Liquor Authority, on the suspicion that the owners of record were selling liquor to minors and that the premises were a gathering place for undesirables, including prostitutes and homosexuals.

This tape is coded SLA-25MAY68-146-JB.

ANDERSON: Wait'll we get our drinks, then we'll talk.

EDWARD: Sure.

BILLY: Duke, gee, it's. . . .

WAITER: Here we are, gents . . . three beers. Call me when you're ready for a refill.

EDWARD: Yeah.

ANDERSON: The old ex-con.

EDWARD: Ah, come on, Duke, don't put me on. Isn't that a pile of crap? After what I've done and I get jugged for parking in the wrong places? Honest to God, I'd laugh . . . if it happened to someone else.

BILLY: The judge said Ed was the biggest scofflaw in Brooklyn. Ain't that right, Ed?

EDWARD: *Isn't* that right. . . . You're absolutely correct, kid. That's what the judge said.

ANDERSON: Beautiful. Got anything on?

EDWARD: Not right now. I got a promise of something in October, but that's a long way away.

BILLY: Duke said he had a job for us . . . didn't you, Duke?

ANDERSON: That's right, Billy.

BILLY: Duke said it was a two-man job or I could have handled it. Ain't that right, Duke? I told him I could handle something while you were away, Edward, but Duke said he'd wait until you got out because it was a two-man job.

ANDERSON: You're right, Billy.

EDWARD: Listen, kid, why don't you drink your beer and keep quiet for a while . . . huh? Duke and I want to talk business. Don't interrupt. Just drink your beer and listen. Okay?

BILLY: Oh, yeah, sure, Edward. Can I have another beer?

EDWARD: Sure you can, kid . . . as soon as you finish that one. You got something, Duke?

ANDERSON: There's this house on the East Side in Manhattan. I need the basement swept. I got a guy to do it—a tech named Ernie Mann. You know him?

EDWARD: No.

ANDERSON: Good, solid guy. Knows his stuff. He'll be the only one to go in. But he needs a driver. He wants a telephone company truck. A Manhattan truck. Clothes and ID cards. All the equipment. I can tell you where to get the paper; you'll have to take care of the rest. It's only for a few hours. Three hours at the most.

EDWARD: Where will I be?

ANDERSON: Outside. In the truck. It's like a small van. You've seen them.

BILLY: It's a two-man job . . . right, Duke?

ANDERSON: That's up to Ed. How about it?

EDWARD: Tell me more.

ANDERSON: Converted town house on a quiet block. Doorman. Alley that leads to the service entrance. You can't get in the back door until the doorman sees you on closed-circuit TV and presses the button. You pull up in front. Ernie goes in the lobby and flashes his potsy. Real good odds that the doorman won't ask to see yours. You're sitting outside in the regulation van where he can see it. Ernie tells the doorman the telephone company is bringing a new trunk line down the block and he's got to examine the connections. All right so far?

EDWARD: So far.

ANDERSON: What could go wrong? The tech just wants to get into the basement; he doesn't want to case the apartments. The doorman says okay, that you should pull into the alley and drive to the back entrance. Like I said, only Ernie goes in. You stay with the truck.

BILLY: Me, too, Duke. Don't forget me.

ANDERSON: Yeah. How does it sound, Ed?

EDWARD: Where do we get the ID cards?

ANDERSON: There's a paper man on Amsterdam Avenue. Helmas. Ever use him?

EDWARD: No.

ANDERSON: The best. He's got the blank cards. Not copies. The real thing. You'll need snapshots to staple on—you know, the kind of four-for-a-quarter shots you get on Forty-second Street.

EDWARD: What about the truck, uniforms, equipment, and all that shit?

ANDERSON: That's your problem.

EDWARD: How much?

ANDERSON: Four bills.

EDWARD: When?

ANDERSON: As soon as you're ready. Then I'll call Ernie, and we'll set it up. This is not a hit, Ed. It's just a wash.

EDWARD: I understand, but still. . . . Can't go to five, can you, Duke?

ANDERSON: I can't, Ed. I'm on a budget. But if it works out, it might be something more for you . . . for all of us. You understand?

EDWARD: Sure.

BILLY: What are you talking about? I don't understand what you're talking about.

EDWARD: Shut up a minute, kid. Let's go over it once more, Duke; I want to be sure I got it right.

It's just a wash, not a hit. I don't go inside the building. I pick up a Manhattan telephone company van with all the gear. I have the uniform and crap hanging from my belt. What about the tech?

ANDERSON: He'll bring his own.

EDWARD: Good. I lift the truck. I pick up this Ernie guy somewhere. Right?

ANDERSON: Right.

EDWARD: We drive up in front of the house. He gets out, braces the doorman, and shows his ID. We drive up the alley to the back entrance. This Ernie gets out, shows on the TV, and gets let in. I stick in the truck. Have I got it?

ANDERSON: That's it.

EDWARD: How long do I stick around?

ANDERSON: Three hours tops.

EDWARD: And then . . . ?

ANDERSON: If he's not out by then, take off.

EDWARD: Good. That's what I wanted to hear. So he's out in under three hours. Then what?

ANDERSON: Drop him where he wants to go. Ditch the truck. Change back to your regular clothes. Walk away.

BILLY: Gee, that sounds easy . . . doesn't it, Edward? Doesn't that sound easy?

EDWARD: They all sound easy, kid. How do I contact you, Duke?

ANDERSON: It's on?

EDWARD: Yeah. It's on.

ANDERSON: I'll call you every day at one o'clock in

the afternoon. If you miss it, don't worry; I'll call the next day. After you get it set, I'll call the tech and we'll set up a meet. Want two bills?

EDWARD: Jesus, do I? Waiter . . . another round!

[14]

The premises at 4678 West End Avenue, New York City, a candy and cigar store, were placed under surveillance on 16 November, 1967, by the New York Police Department, on suspicion that the store was being used as a policy (numbers racket) drop. Taps were installed on the two pay phones in booths in the rear of the store.

The following transcription was made from a tape identified as NYPD-SIS-182-BL. It is not dated definitely but is believed to have been recorded on 31 May, 1968.

CYNTHIA: . . . so that's how it shapes up, Duke. How does it sound?

ANDERSON: All right. It sounds all right.

CYNTHIA: The only hang-up we can see is that business of paying the doctors. You know doctors usually wait a few weeks or a month before they bill. But if the doctor-doctor or the shrink happens to bill within a few days, and the letter comes back from my freak address, it means I couldn't make a second visit.

ANDERSON: What does Tommy say?

CYNTHIA: He says to tell you we could handle it a couple of ways. I can tell them I'm going on a cruise or vacation or something and not to bill for a month at least because I don't want mail piling up in the mailbox because that's a tip-off to crooks that no one is home. Or, Tommy says, we can get me a book of personalized checks from Helmas. I can give them a freak check right then and there. That'll guarantee me at least three or four days before it bounces, and during that time I might be able to arrange another visit.

ANDERSON: Why not just pay cash before you leave?

CYNTHIA: Tommy says it would be out of character.

ANDERSON: Shit. That brother of yours should have been a play actor. Look, let's not get so fucking tricky. This is just a dry run. Don't take chances. Get what you can on your first visit. Pay them in cash. Then you can go back a second time whenever you like.

CYNTHIA: Okay, Duke, if you say so. How does Tommy's campaign sound?

ANDERSON: I can't see any holes, Snap. Both of you go ahead. If anything comes up, play it smart and lay off. Don't push. I'll call you next Friday, same time, and set up a meet.

[15]

Transcription from tape recording FTC-1JUN68-EHM-29L. Premises of Fun City Electronic Supply & Repair Co., Inc., 1975 Avenue D, New York.

ANDERSON: Professor?

MANN: Yes.

ANDERSON: Duke. Your phone clean?

MANN: Of course.

ANDERSON: I have your drivers.

MANN: Drivers? More than one?

ANDERSON: Two brothers.

MANN: This is necessary?

ANDERSON: They're a team. Professionals. No sweat. They'll sit there for three hours tops.

MANN: Plenty. More than plenty. I'll be out in one.

ANDERSON: Good. When?

MANN: Precisely nine forty-five A.M., on the morning of June fourth.

ANDERSON: That's next Tuesday morning? Correct?

MANN: Correct.

ANDERSON: Where?

MANN: On the northwest corner of Seventy-ninth Street and Lexington Avenue. I shall be wearing a light tan raincoat and carrying a small black suitcase. I shall be wearing no hat. You have that?

ANDERSON: Yes, I have it.

MANN: Duke, the two men . . . is it necessary?

ANDERSON: I told you, they're a team. The old one drives. The young one is strictly muscle.

MANN: Why should muscle be necessary?

ANDERSON: It won't be, Professor. The kid's a little light in the head. His brother takes care of him. The kid needs to be with him. You understand?

MANN: No.

ANDERSON: Professor, the two will sit in the truck and wait for you. There will be no trouble. There will be no need for muscle. Everything will go well.

[Lapse of six seconds.]

MANN: Very well.

ANDERSON: I'll call you on Wednesday, June fifth, and we'll set up a meet.

MANN: As you wish.

[16]

The following is a transcription of a personal tape recording made by the author on 19 November, 1968. To my knowledge, the testimony it contains is not duplicated in any official recording, transcription, or document now in existence.

AUTHOR: This will be a recording GO-1A. Will you identify yourself, please, and state your place of residence.

RYAN: My name is Kenneth Ryan. I live at one-one-nine-eight West Nineteenth Street, New York.

AUTHOR: And will you please state your occupation and where you work.

RYAN: I'm a doorman. I'm on the door at five-three-five East Seventy-third Street in Manhattan. I'm usually on eight in the morning until four in the afternoon. Sometimes we switch around, you understand. There's three of us, and sometimes we switch around, like when a guy wants to go somewhere, like he's got a family thing to go to. Then we switch around. But generally I'm on eight to four during the day.

AUTHOR: Thank you. Mr. Ryan, as I explained to you previously, this recording will be solely for my own use in preparing a record of a crime that occurred in New York City on the night and morning of August thirty-first and September first, 1968. I am not an officer of any branch of the government—city, state, or federal. I shall not ask you to swear to the testimony you are about to give, nor will it be used in a court of law or in any legal proceeding. The statement you make will be for my personal use only and will not be published without your permission, which can only be granted by a signed statement from you, giving approval of such use. In return, I have paid you the sum of one hundred dollars, this sum paid whether or not you agree to the publication of your statement. In addition, I will furnish you—at my expense—a duplicate recording of this interrogation. Is all that understood?

RYAN: Sure.

AUTHOR: Now then . . . this photograph I showed you. . . . Do you recognize him?

RYAN: Sure. That's the fly who told me his name was Sidney Brevoort.

AUTHOR: Well . . . actually this man's name is Thomas Haskins. But he told you he was Sidney Brevoort?

RYAN: That's right.

AUTHOR: When did this happen?

RYAN: It was early in June. This year. Maybe the third, maybe the fourth, maybe the fifth. Around then. This little guy comes up to me in the lobby where I work. That's five-three-five East Seventy-third Street, like I told you.

AUTHOR: About what time was this?

RYAN: Oh, I don't remember exactly. Maybe nine forty-five in the morning. Maybe ten. Around then. "Good morning," he says, and I say, "Good morning." And he says, "My name is Sidney Brevoort, and I am a field representative of the New Urban Reorganization Committee. Here is my identification card." And then he shows me his card, and it's just like he says.

AUTHOR: Did the card have his photo on it?

RYAN: Oh, sure. All printed and regular like. Official—know what I mean? So he says, "Sir . . ." —he always called me sir—he says, "Sir, my organization is making an informal census of the dwellings and population of the East Side of Manhattan from Fifth Avenue to the river, and from Twenty-third Street on the south to Eighty-sixth Street on the north. We are trying to get legislation passed by New York State allowing for a bond issue to finance the cost of a Second Avenue subway." That's as near as I can remember to what he says. He's talking very official, you know. Very impressive, it was. So I says, "You're damned right. They had the bonds for that years ago, and then they went and pissed the money away on other things. Right into the politicians' pocket," I tells him. And he says, "I can see you keep up on civic affairs." And I says to him, "I know what's going on." And he says, "I am certain you do, sir. Well, to help convince New York State legislators that this bill should be passed, the New Urban Reorganization Committee is making an actual count of everyone on the East Side of Manhattan in the area I mentioned who might conceivably benefit by a Second Avenue subway. What I'd like from you are the names of people living in this building and the numbers of the apartments they occupy."

AUTHOR: And what did you say to that?

RYAN: I told him to go to hell. Well, I didn't put it

in those exact words, you understand. But I told him I couldn't do it.

AUTHOR: What did he say then?

RYAN: He said it would be voluntary. He said that any tenant who wanted to volunteer information—why, that would be confidential, and their names wouldn't be given to anyone. They'd just be—you know, like statistics. What he wanted to know was who lived in what apartment, did they have servants, and how they traveled to work, and what time did they go to work and what time did they come home. Stuff like that. So I said, "Sorry, no can do." I told him Shovey and White at one-three-two-four Madison Avenue managed the house, and all us doors got strict orders not to talk to anyone about the tenants, not to give out no information, and not to let anyone into tenants' apartments unless we get the okay from Shovey and White.

AUTHOR: What was his reaction to that?

RYAN: That little shit. He said he could understand it because of all the robberies on the East Side recently, and would it be all right if he called Shovey and White and asked for permission to talk to me and interview the tenants who would volunteer to talk to him. So I said sure, call Shovey and White, and if they say it's okay, then it's okay with me. He said he'd call them and if it was okay, he'd have them call me to give me the go-ahead. He asks me who he should talk to at Shovey and White, and I told him to talk to Mr. Walsh who handles our building. I even gave him the phone number . . . oh, the filth of him! Then he asks me if I had ever seen Mr. Walsh, and I had to tell him no, I had never set eyes on the guy. I only talked to him twice on the phone. You gotta understand, these managers don't take no personal interest. They just sit on their ass behind a phone.

AUTHOR: What did the man you know as Sidney Brevoort do then?

RYAN: He said he'd call Shovey and White and explain what he wanted and have Mr. Walsh contact me. So I said if it was okay with them, it was okay with me. So he thanked me for my trouble—very polite, you understand—and walked away. The dirty little crud.

AUTHOR: Thank you, Mr. Ryan.

[17]

Tape NYPD-SIS-196-BL. Premises of candy store at 4678 West End Avenue. Approximately 10:28 A.M., 3 June, 1968.

CYNTHIA HASKINS: The New Urban Reorganization Committee. May I help you?

THOMAS: It's me, Snap.

CYNTHIA: What's wrong?

THOMAS: I bombed out. The fucking Irishman on the door won't talk unless he gets a go-ahead from the management agents, Shovey and White, on Madison Avenue.

CYNTHIA: Oh, my God. Duke will kill us.

THOMAS: Don't get your balls in an uproar, luv. I thought of something on the way here. I'm calling from a pay phone on the corner of Seventy-third Street and York Avenue.

CYNTHIA: Jesus' sake, Tommy, take it easy. Duke said not to take any chances. Duke said if anything came up to lay off. Now you say you thought of something. Tommy, don't. . . .

THOMAS: You think he's paying us five bills to lay off? He wants us to use our brains, doesn't he? That's why he looked us up, isn't it? If he wanted a couple of dumdums he could have bought them for a bill. Duke wants results. If we don't blow the whole goddamned thing—whatever it is—he won't care how we did it.

CYNTHIA: Tommy, I. . . .

THOMAS: Shut up and listen. Here's how we'll work it. . . .

[18]

Approximately 10:37 A.M., 3 June, 1968.

RYAN: Five thirty-five East Seventy-third Street.

CYNTHIA: Is this the doorman?

RYAN: Yeah. Who's this?

CYNTHIA: This is Ruth David at Shovey and White. Did you just talk to a man named Sidney Brevoort who said he was from the New Urban Reorganization Committee?

RYAN: Yeah. He was here a few minutes ago. He wanted a list of people in the building and wanted to talk to them. I told him to call Mr. Walsh.

CYNTHIA: You did exactly right. But Mr. Walsh is out sick. The flu or something. He was out yesterday and he's out today. I'm handling his buildings while he's gone. How did this Brevoort guy look to you?

RYAN: A mousy little swish. I could chew him up and spit him over the left-field fence.

CYNTHIA: He didn't look like a thief, I mean?

RYAN: No, but that don't mean nothing. What do you want me to do if he comes back?

CYNTHIA: Well, I called the New Urban Reorganization Committee, and it's a legitimate outfit. They said yes, Sidney Brevoort was one of their field representatives. Did he have an identification card?

RYAN: Yeah. He showed it to me.

CYNTHIA: Well, I don't want to take the responsibility of giving him the names of tenants or letting him talk to them.

RYAN: You're right. I don't neither.

CYNTHIA: Tell you what . . . Mr. Walsh told me to call him at home in case something came up I couldn't handle. I've got his home phone number. If he says it's okay, you can talk to Brevoort. If Walsh says no, then to hell with Brevoort and the New Urban Reorganization Committee. Either way, you and I are out of it; we'll leave it up to Walsh.

RYAN: Yeah. That's smart.

CYNTHIA: All right. I'll hang up now and call Walsh. I'll call you back in a few minutes and tell you what he said.

RYAN: I'll be here.

[19]

Approximately 10:48 A.M., 3 June, 1968.

CYNTHIA: Doorman? This is Ruth David again.

RYAN: Yeah. You talk to Mr. Walsh?

CYNTHIA: Yes. He said it was perfectly all right. He knows this New Urban Reorganization Committee. He says it's okay to give Brevoort the names of tenants. Also, he can talk to any tenants who voluntarily agree. But you ask them first on the intercom. Don't let Brevoort wander around the house. And make sure he comes down to the lobby after every interview.

RYAN: Don't worry, Miss David. I know how to handle it.

CYNTHIA: Good. Well, that's a load off my mind. I didn't want to take the responsibility.

RYAN: I didn't neither.

CYNTHIA: Mr. Walsh said to tell you that you did exactly right, making Brevoort call us. He said to tell you he won't forget how you handled this.

RYAN: Yeah. Fine. Okay, then I'll talk to Brevoort. Thanks for calling, Miss David.

CYNTHIA: Thank you, sir.

[20]

Transcription from tape SEC-3JUN68-IM-01:48-PM-142C. Premises of Ingrid Macht, 627 West Twenty-fourth Street, New York.

INGRID: Come in, *Schatzie*.

ANDERSON: Glasses? You're wearing glasses now?

INGRID: For perhaps a year. Only for reading. You like them?

ANDERSON: Yes. You're doing something?

INGRID: I am just finishing my breakfast. I slept late today. Coffee?

ANDERSON: All right. Black.

[Lapse of one minute thirteen seconds.]

INGRID: A little brandy perhaps?

ANDERSON: Fine. You join me?

INGRID: Thank you, no. I will take a sip of yours.

ANDERSON: Then you'll tell me I drink too much, and meanwhile you're sipping half my booze.

INGRID: Oh, *Schatzie,* when did I ever tell you that you drank too much? When did I ever criticize anything you do?

ANDERSON: Never . . . that I can remember. I was just kidding you. Don't be so serious. You have no sense of humor.

INGRID: That is true. Is something bothering you?

ANDERSON: No. Why?

INGRID: You have a look I recognize. Something in your eyes—faraway. You are thinking very hard about something. Do I guess right?

ANDERSON: Maybe.

INGRID: Please do not tell me. I want to know absolutely nothing. I do not wish to go through all that again. You understand?

ANDERSON: Sure. Sit on my lap. No . . . leave your glasses on.

INGRID: You do like them?

ANDERSON: Yes. When I was down South I had an idea of what a big-city woman was like. I could see her. Very thin. Not too tall. Hard. Bony. Open eyes. Pale lips. And heavy, black-rimmed glasses.

INGRID: A strange dream for a man to have. Usually it is a sweet, plump little blonde with big tits.

ANDERSON: Well, that was my dream. And long, straight black hair that hung to her waist.

INGRID: I have a wig like that.
ANDERSON: I know. I gave it to you.
INGRID: So you did, *Schatzie*. I had forgotten. Shall I put it on?
ANDERSON: Yes.

[Lapse of four minutes fourteen seconds.]

INGRID: So. Am I now your dream?
ANDERSON: Close. Very close. Sit here again.
INGRID: And what have you brought me today, Duke . . . another cigarette lighter?
ANDERSON: No. I brought you a hundred dollars.
INGRID: That is nice. I like money.
ANDERSON: I know. More stocks?
INGRID: Of course. I have been doing very well. My broker tells me I have an instinct for trading.
ANDERSON: I could have told him that. Am I hurting you?
INGRID: No. Perhaps we should go into the bedroom.

[Lapse of two minutes thirty-four seconds.]

INGRID: You are thinner . . . and harder. This scar . . . you told me once but I have forgotten.
ANDERSON: Knife fight.
INGRID: Did you kill him?
ANDERSON: Yes.
INGRID: Why did you fight?
ANDERSON: I forget. At the time it seemed important. Do you want me to give you the money now?
INGRID: Do not be nasty, Duke. It is not like you.
ANDERSON: Then start. Jesus, I need it. I've got to get out.

INGRID: Getting out—that is so important to you?

ANDERSON: I need it. I'm hooked. Slowly. . . .

INGRID: Of course. No . . . I told you, don't close your eyes. Look at me.

ANDERSON: Yes. All right.

INGRID: You know, I think I shall write a book. Relax your muscles, *Schatzie;* you are too tense.

ANDERSON: All right . . . yes. Is that better?

INGRID: Much. See . . . isn't that better?

ANDERSON: Oh, God, yes. Yes. A book about what?

INGRID: About pain and about crime. You know, I think criminals—most criminals—do what they do so that they may cause pain to someone. Also, so that they may be caught and be punished. To cause pain and to feel pain. That is why they lie, cheat, steal, and kill.

ANDERSON: Yes. . . .

INGRID: Look . . . I will tie my long, black hair about you. I will pull it tight and knot it . . . like so. There. How funny you look . . . like a strange Christmas package, a gift. . . .

ANDERSON: It's starting. I can feel it. . . .

INGRID: You are getting out?

ANDERSON: Slowly. You may be right. I don't know about those things. But it makes sense. When I was inside I met a guy who drew a minimum of thirty. He would have gotten eight to ten, but he hurt the people he robbed. He didn't have to. They gave him everything he wanted. They didn't yell. But he hurt them bad. And then he left his prints all over the place.

INGRID: Yes, that is understandable. You are tensing

up again, *Schatzie*. Relax. Yes, that is better. And now. . . .

ANDERSON: Oh, God, Ingrid, please . . . please don't. . . .

INGRID: First you beg me to start, and then you beg me to stop. But I must help you to get out. Is that not so, Duke?

ANDERSON: You are the only one who can do it . . . the only one. . . .

INGRID: So . . . Now, bite down hard and try not to scream. There . . . and there . . .

ANDERSON: Your teeth . . . I can't . . . please, I . . . oh God . . .

INGRID: Just a little more. You are getting out . . . I can see it in your eyes. Just a little more. And now . . . so . . . so. . . . Oh, you are getting out now, Duke . . . are you not? Yes, now you have escaped. But not me, Duke . . . not me. . . .

[21]

Starting on 12 April, 1968, a number of letters—obviously written by a mentally deranged person—were received threatening the personal safety of the President of the United States, Justices of the Supreme Court of the United States, and certain U.S. Senators. Incredibly, the unsigned letters were typed on stationery of the Excalibur Arms Hotel, 14896 Broadway, New York, New York.

On 19 April, 1968, with the cooperation of the owners of record, the U.S. Secret Service established electronic surveillance of the premises. A master tap was placed on the main telephone line coming into the building. In addition, several rooms and suites were equipped with bugs to record interior conversations. All these devices fed into an Emplex 47-83B voice-actuated tape recorder connected to a backup Emplex 47-82B-1 in case two conversations came in simultaneously. These machines were emplaced in the basement of the Excalibur Arms.

The following tape, coded USSS-VS-901KD-432, is dated 5 June, 1968. It was recorded from Room 432. The two men present, John Anderson and Thomas Haskins, have been identified by voice prints and interior evidence.

[Knock on door.]

ANDERSON: Who is it?

HASKINS: Me . . . Tommy.

ANDERSON: Come on in. Everything look all right downstairs?

HASKINS: Clear. What a filthy fleabag, darling.

ANDERSON: I just took the room for our meet. I'm not going to sleep here. Sit down over here. I have some brandy.

HASKINS: Thanks, no. But I do believe I'll have a joint. Join me?

ANDERSON: I'll stick to brandy. How did you make out?

HASKINS: Very well, I think. I hit two days ago. Snapper will hit tomorrow.

ANDERSON: Any beef?

HASKINS: A little difficulty. Nothing important. We handled it.

ANDERSON: Get much?

HASKINS: As much as I could. Not as complete as you'd wish, I'm sure, but interesting.

ANDERSON: Tommy, I won't shit you. You've got brains. You know I can't pay out five bills for a wash if I wasn't planning a hustle. Before you give me your report, give it to me straight—would it be worth it?

HASKINS: Which apartment, darling?

ANDERSON: All of them.

HASKINS: Jesus Christ Almighty.

ANDERSON: Would it be worth it?

HASKINS: My God, yes!

ANDERSON: Guess at the income?

HASKINS: Guess? I'd guess a minimum of a hundred G's. But maybe twice that.

ANDERSON: You and I think alike. That's what I guessed. All right, let's have it.

HASKINS: I typed out a report and one carbon on Snapper's machine, so we could go over it together. Naturally you get both copies.

ANDERSON: Naturally.

HASKINS: All right . . . let's start with the doormen. Three of them: Timothy O'Leary, Kenneth Ryan, Ed Bakely. In order, they're on midnight to eight A.M., eight A.M. to four P.M., four P.M. to midnight. O'Leary, the guy on midnight to eight A.M., is the lush. An ex-cop. When one of them takes his day off, the other two work twelve-hour shifts and get paid double. Occasionally, like around Christmas, two of them are off at once, and the union sends over a temporary. Okay?

ANDERSON: Go ahead.

HASKINS: I have all this in the report in more detail, darling, but I just want to go over the highlights with you in case you have any questions.

ANDERSON: Go ahead.

HASKINS: The super. Ivan Block. A Hungarian, I think, or maybe a Pole. A wino. He lives in the basement. He's there twenty-four hours a day, six days a week. On Mondays he goes to visit his married sister in New Jersey. In case of emergency, the super next door at five-three-seven East Seventy-third Street fills in for him. He also fills in when Block takes his two-week vacation every May. Block is sixty-four years old and blind in one eye. His basement apartment is one room and bath. Ryan hinted that he's a cheap son of a bitch. He may have something under the mattress.

ANDERSON: Maybe. These Old World farts don't believe in banks. Let's get on with it. I don't want to spend too much time here. This place bugs me.

HASKINS: Literally, I'm sure. I just saw one. Suite One A, first floor, off the lobby. Dr. Erwin

Leister, MD, an internist.

ANDERSON: What's that?

HASKINS: A doctor who specializes in internal medicine. One nurse, one combination secretary-receptionist. Office hours from about nine A.M. to six P.M. Occasionally he's there later. Usually the nurse and secretary are gone by five thirty. The headshrinker is Dr. Dmitri Rubicoff, Suite One B. He's got one secretary-nurse. Office hours usually from nine to nine. Occasionally later. Snapper will give you a more complete rundown on these doctors after Thursday.

ANDERSON: You're doing fine.

HASKINS: Two apartments on each floor. By the way, the lobby floor is called one. Up one flight and you're on floor two. The top floor is the fifth, where the terraces are.

ANDERSON: I know.

HASKINS: Second floor. Apartment Two A. Eric Sabine. A male interior decorator who sounds divine. His apartment got a big write-up in the *Times* last year. I looked it up. Original Picassos and Klees. A nice collection of pre-Columbian art. A gorgeous nine-by-twelve Oriental carpet that's valued at twenty G's. In the photo in the *Times* he was wearing three rings that looked legit. Not really my type, darling, but obviously loaded. I shouldn't have any trouble finding out more about him if you're interested.

ANDERSON: We'll see.

HASKINS: Apartment Two B. Mr. and Mrs. Aron Rabinowitz. Rich, young Jews. He's in a Wall

Street law firm. Junior partner. They're active in opera and ballet and theater groups. Shit like that. Very liberal. This is one of the three apartments I actually cased. She was home, delighted to talk about the proposed Second Avenue subway and the plight of the poor. Modern furnishings. I didn't spot anything except her wedding ring, which looked like it had been hacked out of Mount Rushmore. Seeing he's a lawyer, I'd guess a wall safe somewhere. Good paintings, but too big to fool with. All huge, abstract stuff.

ANDERSON: Silver?

HASKINS: You don't miss a trick, do you, darling? Yes, silver . . . on display and very nice. Antique, I think. Probably a wedding gift. It's on a sideboard in their dining room. Any questions?

ANDERSON: Maid?

HASKINS: Not sleep-in. She comes at noon and leaves after she serves their evening meal and cleans up. She's German. A middle-aged woman. Now then . . . up to the third floor. Apartment Three A. Mr. and Mrs. Max Horowitz. He's retired. Used to be a wholesale jeweler. She's got bad arthritis of the knees and uses a cane to walk with. She's also got three fur coats, including one mink and one sable, and drips with ice. At least, that's what the doorman says. He also says they're cheap bastards—a total of five bucks to all employees at Christmastime. But he thinks they're loaded. Apartment Three B. Mrs. Agnes Everleigh. Separated from her hubby. He owns the apartment, but she's living there. Nothing much interesting. A mink coat, maybe. She's a buyer for a chain of woman's lingerie shops. Travels a lot. Incidentally, I've been mentioning the fur coats—but of course you realize, darling, most of them will be in storage this time of year.

ANDERSON: Sure.

HASKINS: Fourth floor. Apartment Four A. Mr. and Mrs. James T. Sheldon, with three-year-old twin girls. A sleep-in maid who goes out shopping in the neighborhood every day at noon. I got into this apartment, too. I was there when the maid left. West Indian. A dish . . . if I was hungry that way. Lovely accent. Big boobs. Flashing smile. Mrs. James T. Sheldon is a perfect fright: horse face, buck teeth, skin like burlap. She must have the money. And Mr. Sheldon must be pronging the maid. He's a partner in a brokerage house, in charge of their Park Avenue branch. Lots of goodies. I caught a quick look at a wood-paneled study with glass display cases lining the walls. Then Mrs. Sheldon closed the door. A coin collection, I think. It would fit. Easy to check.

ANDERSON: Yes. You say the maid goes shopping every day at noon?

HASKINS: That's right. Like clockwork. I verified it with the doorman later. Her name's Andronica.

ANDERSON: Andronica?

HASKINS: That's right. It's in the report. Crazy. Apartment Four B. Mrs. Martha Hathway—not Hathaway but Hathway. A ninety-two-year-old widow, with an eighty-two-year-old companion-housekeeper. Somewhat nutty. Kind of a recluse.

ANDERSON: A what?

HASKINS: Recluse. Like a hermit. She rarely goes out. Watches TV all day. Has no visitors. The housekeeper shops by phone. Ryan, the doorman, said her husband was a politician, a big shit in Tammany Hall about a thousand years ago. The apartment is furnished with stuff from the original Hathway town house on East Sixty-second Street. She sold off a lot of stuff after her husband died, but kept the best. It was a big auction, so you could check it out easy enough or I could do it for you.

ANDERSON: What do you figure she's got?

HASKINS: Silver, jewelry, paintings . . . the works. It's just a feeling I have, but I think Apartment Four B might prove to be a treasure house.

ANDERSON: Could be.

HASKINS: Top floor—the fifth. Both apartments have small terraces. Apartment Five A. Mr. and Mrs. Gerald Bingham and their fifteen-year-old son, Gerald junior. The kid uses a wheelchair; he's dead from the hips down. He has a private tutor who comes in every day. Bingham has his own management consultant firm with offices on Madison Avenue. Also, he has his own limousine, chauffeur-driven, which is garaged over on Lex. He's driven to work every morning, driven home every night. Sweet. He's listed all over the place, so he won't be hard to check out. His wife has money, too. I have nothing specific on this apartment—nothing good.

ANDERSON: Go on.

HASKINS: The other is Five B. Ernest Longene and April Clifford. They're married, they say, but use their own names. He's a theatrical producer and she was a famous actress. Hasn't appeared in ten years—but she remembers. God, does she remember! Sleep-in maid. A big, fat mammy type. This was the third apartment I got into. April was on her way to a luncheon at the Plaza and was wearing her daytime diamonds. Very nice. Some good, small paintings on the walls. A very nice collection of rough gemstones in glass display cases.

ANDERSON: There's money there?

HASKINS: He's got two hits on Broadway right now. That's got to mean loose cash around the place, probably in a wall safe. Well, darling, those are just the highlights. I'm sorry I couldn't be more specific.

ANDERSON: You did better than I hoped. Give me your carbon of the report.

HASKINS: Of course. I assure you no other copy was made.

ANDERSON: I believe you. I'll pay you the balance of the five bills when I get Snapper's report.

HASKINS: No rush, no rush. Do you have any questions, or is there anything you want me to dig into further?

ANDERSON: Not right now. This is like a preliminary report. There may be some more work for you later.

HASKINS: Anytime. You know you can trust me.

ANDERSON: Sure.

[Lapse of six seconds.]

HASKINS: Tell me, darling . . . are you seeing Ingrid again?

ANDERSON: Yes.

HASKINS: And how is the dear girl?

ANDERSON: All right. I think you better leave now. I'll wait about half an hour, and then I'll take off. Tell Snapper I'll call on Friday, as usual.

HASKINS: Are you angry with me, Duke?

ANDERSON: Why should I be angry with you? I think you did a good job on this.

HASKINS: I mean because I mentioned Ingrid. . . .

[Lapse of four seconds.]

ANDERSON: Are you jealous, Tommy?

HASKINS: Well . . . maybe. A little. . . .

ANDERSON: Forget it. I don't like the way you smell.

HASKINS: Well, I guess I. . . .

ANDERSON: Yes. Better go. And don't get any ideas.

HASKINS: Ideas, darling? What kind of ideas would I get?

ANDERSON: About what I'm doing.

HASKINS: Don't be silly, darling. I know better than that.

ANDERSON: That's good.

[22]

Tape NYSITB-FD-6JUN68-106-9H. Location of car: Sixty-fifth Street near Park Avenue.

ANDERSON: Goddammit, I told the Doctor I'd contact him when I was ready. Well, I'm not ready.

SIMONS: Take it easy, Duke. Good heavens, you have the shortest fuse of any man I've ever known.

ANDERSON: I just don't like to get leaned on, that's all.

SIMONS: No one's leaning on you, Duke. The Doctor has invested three thousand dollars of his personal funds in this campaign, and quite naturally and normally he's interested in your progress.

ANDERSON: What if I told him it was a bust . . . a nothing?

SIMONS: Is that what you want me to tell him?

[Lapse of eleven seconds.]

ANDERSON: No. I'm sorry I blew, Mr. Simons, but I like to move at my own speed. This thing is big, probably the biggest thing I've ever been in. Bigger than that Bensonhurst bank job. I want everything to go right. I want to be sure. Another week or two. Three weeks at the most. I'm keeping a very careful account of those three G's. I'm not making a cent out of this. I can tell the Doctor where every cent went. I'm not trying to con him.

SIMONS: Duke, Duke, it's not the money. I assure you the money has very little to do with it. He can drop that in one day at the dogs and never notice it. But Duke, you must recognize that the Doctor is a very proud man, very jealous of his position. He is where he is today because he picked winners. You understand? He would not like the word to get around that he flushed three G's on a free-lancer and got nothing to show for it. It would hurt his reputation, and it would hurt his self-esteem. Perhaps the younger men might say he is slipping, his judgment is going, he should be replaced. The Doctor must consider these things. So, quite naturally, he is concerned. You understand?

ANDERSON: Ah . . . sure. I understand. It's just that I want to make a big score, a *big* score . . . enough to go somewhere for a long, long time. That's why I'm wound up so tight. This one has got to be just right.

SIMONS: Are you trying to tell me it looks good . . . as of this moment?

ANDERSON: Mr. Simons, as of this moment it looks great, just great.

SIMONS: The Doctor will be pleased.

[23]

Ernest Heinrich "Professor" Mann; fifty-three; resident of 529 East Fifty-first Street, New York City. Place of business: Fun City Electronic Supply & Repair Co., 1975 Avenue D, New York City. Five feet six inches tall; 147 pounds; almost completely bald, with gray fringe around scalp; gray eyebrows; small Van Dyke beard, also gray. Walked with slight limp, favoring left leg. Deep scar in calf of left leg (believed to be a knife wound; see Interpol file #96B-J43196). He was a technician, skilled in mechanical, electrical, and electronic engineering. Graduated from Stuttgarter Technische Hochschule, 1938, with highest honors. Assistant professor, mechanical and electrical engineering, Zurich Académie du Mécanique, 1939–46. Emigrated to the United States (with Swiss passport) in 1948. Arrested Stuttgart, 17 June, 1937, on public nuisance charge (exhibiting himself to an elderly woman). Case dismissed with warning. Arrested Paris, 24 October, 1938, for scandalous conduct (urinating on Tomb of Unknown Soldier). Deported, after case was dismissed. In Zurich, a record of three arrests for possession of a dangerous drug (opium), indecent exposure, and illegal possession of a hypodermic needle. Suspended sentences. Extremely intelligent. Speaks German, French, Italian, English, some Spanish. Not believed to be violent. Single. Record indicates intermittent drug addiction (opium, morphine, hashish). FBI file indicates no illegal activities during residence in the United States. Applied for U.S. citizenship 8 May, 1954. Rejected 16 November, 1954. (As of this date, this man's brother was a high official in the finance ministry of West Germany, and his file contained an alert tag: IN CASE OF ARREST, PLEASE CONTACT U.S. STATE DEPARTMENT BEFORE CHARGE.)

The following is the first part of a dictated, sworn, signed, and witnessed statement by Ernest Heinrich Mann. It was obtained after prolonged questioning (the complete transcription numbers fifty-six typewritten pages) from 8 October, 1968, to 17 October, 1968. The interrogator was an assistant district attorney, County of New York. The entire document is coded NYDA-EHM-101A-108B. The following section is labeled *SEGMENT* 101A.

MANN: My name is Ernest Heinrich Mann. I live at five-two-nine East Fifty-first Street, New York, New York, U.S.A. I also have a business, which I own—the Fun City Electronic Supply and Repair Co., Inc., incorporated under the laws of New York State, at one-nine-seven-five Avenue D, New York City. Am I perhaps speaking too rapidly? Good.

On April thirty, 1968, I was contacted at my place of business by a man I know as John Anderson, also known as Duke Anderson. He stated at this time that he wished to employ me to inspect the basement of a house at five-three-five East Seventy-third Street, New York City. He said he wished me to ascertain the telephone, alarm, and security precautions of this house. At no time did he state the purpose of this.

A price was agreed upon, and it was planned that I would approach the house in the uniform of a New York City telephone repairman, arriving in an authentic truck of the telephone company. Anderson said he would supply truck and driver. I provided my own uniform and identification. May I have a glass of water, please? Thank you.

About a month later Anderson called me and said the arrangements for the telephone truck had been made. There would be two drivers. I objected, but he assured me it would be perfectly safe.

On June fourth, at nine forty-five in the morning, I met the truck at the corner of Seventy-ninth Street and Lexington Avenue. There were two men who introduced themselves to me merely as Ed and Billy. I had never seen them before. They were clad in uniforms of New York Telephone Company repairmen. We spoke very little. The actual driver, the man named Ed, seemed reasonably intelligent and alert. The other one, called Billy, was large and muscular but had a childish mentality. I believe he was mentally retarded.

We drove directly to the house on East Seventy-third Street, pulling up in front. As we had agreed, I alighted, walked into the lobby, and presented my credentials to the doorman. He inspected my identification card, glanced out to the curb where the truck was parked, and told me to pull into the alley that runs alongside the building. Do one of you gentlemen have a cigarette? I would appreciate it. Thank you very much.

[Lapse of four seconds.]

So . . . I was identified on the closed-circuit TV screen in the lobby, and the doorman pressed the button unlocking the service door and allowed me entrance into the basement. Pardon?

No, this was merely to be an inspection. There was no intent to steal or destroy. Anderson merely wanted a complete rundown of the basement plus Polaroid photos of anything interesting. You understand? If I thought there was anything illegal required, I never would have accepted this job.

So. I am now in the basement. I went first to the telephone box. Quite ordinary. I made notes of main phones and extensions. I took instant photos of the entrance of the main trunk line into the basement and where it should be cut to isolate the entire house. This was requested by Anderson, you understand. I also ascertained that there were two separate wiring systems which, by their arrangement, I judged to be alarm systems, one to the local precinct house, perhaps triggered by an ultrasonic or radio-wave alarm, and the other to a private security agency which would be, I guessed, activated by opened doors or windows. Quite unexpectedly, both systems bore small tags with the apartment numbers written on them, so I was able to note that the precinct alarm was attached to Apartment Five B, and the private agency alarm to Apartment Four B. I made notes of this, plus photos. As Anderson had requested.

At this moment a door opened into the basement and a man came in. I learned he was Ivan Block, the superintendent of the building. He asked me what I was doing, and I explained that the telephone company was intending to bring a new line down the street and I was examining the premises to see what new equipment would be required. This was the same explanation I had given to the doorman. Another glass of water, please? I thank you.

[Lapse of six seconds.]

Block appeared satisfied with my explanation. Listening to him speak, I realized he was Hungarian or perhaps a Czech. Since I speak neither of these languages, I spoke to him in German, to which he replied in very bad, heavily accented German. However, he was pleased to speak the language. I believe he was somewhat inebriated. He insisted I come into his apartment for a glass of wine. I followed him, happy at the opportunity of making a further examination.

The super's small apartment was dirty and depressing. However, I took a glass of wine with him while looking around. The only thing of value I saw was an antique triptych on his dresser. I guessed it as being at least three hundred years old, beautifully carved. The value, I estimated, might be as much as two thousand dollars. I made no reference to it.

Block continued to drink wine, and I told him I had to call my office, and I left. I then explored the main basement. The only thing of interest I found was quite odd. . . .

It appeared to be a kind of a box—or rather, a small room—built into one corner of the basement. It was obviously quite old, and I judged it had been built into the basement when the building was constructed. Two walls of the basement formed two sides of the boxlike room; the two walls projecting into the basement at a right angle were constructed of fitted wooden slabs. One wood wall had a flush door, closed by an extremely heavy, old-fashioned brass lever and hasp. The big hinges were also of brass. The door was secured with a large padlock.

Closer inspection revealed that the door was also protected by a rather primitive alarm system obviously added years after the boxlike room had been built. It was a simple contact alarm that might ring a bell or flash a light when the door was opened. I traced the wire and judged it went up into the lobby area where it might alert the doorman.

I took complete Polaroid photos of this strange boxlike affair, and made notes of how the alarm might easily be bridged. Almost as an afterthought, I put my hand to the side of this unusual room and found it quite cold to the touch. It reminded me of a large walk-in refrigerator one might find in a butcher's shop in this country.

I took a final look around and decided I had everything that Anderson, my client, required. I then exited from the basement and got into the truck. The two men, Ed and Billy, had waited quite patiently. We pulled out of the driveway. The doorman was standing on the sidewalk, and I smiled and waved as we pulled away.

They dropped me on the corner of Seventy-ninth Street and Lexington Avenue, and then left. I have no knowledge of what they did after that. The entire operation consumed one hour and twenty-six minutes. John Anderson called me on June fifth. I suggested he come over to my shop on the next day. He did, and I delivered to him the photos I had taken, the diagrams, and a complete report of what I saw—which is exactly what I have reported to you gentlemen. I thank you very much for your courtesy.

[24]

Binky's Bar & Grill, 125th Street and Hannox Avenue, New York City; 12 June, 1968; 1:46 P.M. On this date, these premises were under electronic surveillance by the New York State Liquor Authority, on suspicion that the owners of record were knowingly allowing gambling on the premises. The following is tape SLA-94K-KYM. Anderson's presence was verified by voice print and testimony of an eyewitness.

ANDERSON: Brandy.
BARTENDER: This place for blacks, not for whiteys.
ANDERSON: What you going to do—throw me out?
BARTENDER: You a hardnose?
ANDERSON: Hard as I gotta be. Do I get that brandy?
BARTENDER: You from the South?
ANDERSON: Not deep. Kentucky.
BARTENDER: Lexington?
ANDERSON: Gresham.
BARTENDER: I'm from Lex. Cordon Bleu okay?
ANDERSON: Fine.
[Lapse of eight seconds.]
BARTENDER: You want a wash?
ANDERSON: Water on the side.

[Lapse of eleven seconds.]

ANDERSON: There's a guy I want to meet. Light brown. Sam Johnson. Goes by the name of Skeets.

BARTENDER: Never heard of him.

ANDERSON: I know. He's got a razor scar on his left cheek.

BARTENDER: Never saw such a man.

ANDERSON: I know. My name's Duke Anderson. If such a man should come in, I'm going to finish this drink and go across the street and get me some knuckles and collards. I'll be there for at least an hour.

BARTENDER: Won't do you no good. Never saw such a man. Never heard of him.

ANDERSON: He might come in . . . unexpected like. Here's a fin for you in case he does.

BARTENDER: I'll take your pound and thank you kindly. But it won't do you no good. I don't know the man. Never saw him.

ANDERSON: I know. The name's Duke Anderson. I'll be across the street in Mama's. Keep the faith, baby.

BARTENDER: Up yours, mother.

[25]

Tape recording NYSNB (New York State Narcotics Bureau) 48B-1061 (continuing). Taped at

2:11 P.M., 12 June, 1968, Mama's Soul Food, 125th Street and Hannox Avenue, New York City.

JOHNSON: Here's my man, and gimme your han'.

ANDERSON: Hello, Skeets. Sit down and order up.

JOHNSON: Now that I'm here, I'll have a beer.

ANDERSON: How you been?

JOHNSON: I get some jive so I'm still alive.

ANDERSON: Things going good for you?

JOHNSON: I do this and that, but I don't get fat.

ANDERSON: Cut the shit and talk straight. You got some time to do a job for me?

JOHNSON: If it's a crime, I've got the time.

ANDERSON: Jesus Christ. Skeets, there's a house on the East Side. If you're interested I'll give you the address. There's a live-in spade maid works one of the apartments. Every day at noon she comes out to do shopping.

JOHNSON: When you talk a chick, you gotta click.

ANDERSON: Light tan. West Indian. Big lungs. Pretty. I want you to get close to her.

JOHNSON: How close, oh, Lord, how close?

ANDERSON: Everything. Whatever she can tell you about her apartment. Her name's Andronica. That's right—Andronica. She's from Apartment Four A. There may be a coin collection there. But I want to know about the rest of the house, too—whatever she'll spill.

JOHNSON: If she won't spill, then her sister will.

ANDERSON: There's a funny room in the basement. A cold room. It's locked. Try to find out what the hell it is.

JOHNSON: If the room is cold, then I'll be bold.

ANDERSON: You on?

JOHNSON: If you've got the loot, I've got to suit.

ANDERSON: A bill?

JOHNSON: Make it two and I'll be true.

ANDERSON: All right—two. But do a job for me. Here's a loner to get you started. I'll be back here a week from today, same time. All right?

JOHNSON: As a man you're mean, but I like your green.

[26]

Transcription of tape recording POM-14JUN68-EVERLEIGH. Approximately 2:10 A.M.

MRS. EVERLEIGH: Did the doorman see you come in?

ANDERSON: He wasn't there.

MRS. EVERLEIGH: The bastard. We're supposed to get twenty-four-hour doorman service, and this bastard is always down in the basement drinking wine with that drunken super. Brandy?

ANDERSON: Yes.

MRS. EVERLEIGH: Yes, *please*.

ANDERSON: Go fuck yourself.

MRS. EVERLEIGH: My, we're in a pleasant mood tonight. Tired?

ANDERSON: Just my eyes.

MRS. EVERLEIGH: I think it's more than that. You look like a man who's got a lot on his mind. Money problems?

ANDERSON: No.

MRS. EVERLEIGH: If you need some money, I can let you have some.

ANDERSON: No . . . thanks.

MRS. EVERLEIGH: That's better. Drink up. I bought a case of Rémy Martin. What are you smiling about?

ANDERSON: You figure this will last for a case?

MRS. EVERLEIGH: What's that supposed to mean? You want to cut out? Then cut out.

ANDERSON: I didn't want to cut out. I just figured you might get tired of me slamming you around. Are you tired of it?

[Lapse of seven seconds.]

MRS. EVERLEIGH: No. I'm not tired of it. I think about it all the time. When I was in Paris, I missed you. One night I could have screamed, I wanted you so bad. I got a million things on my mind. Business things. Details. Pressure. I'm only as good as my last season. I work for the worst bastards in the business—the *worst.* I only relax when I'm with you. I think about you during the day, when I'm at the office. I think about what we did and what we'll do. I don't suppose I should be telling you these things.

ANDERSON: Why not?

MRS. EVERLEIGH: A girl's supposed to play hard to get.

ANDERSON: Christ, you're a stupid bitch.

[Lapse of five seconds.]

MRS. EVERLEIGH: Yes. Yes, I am. When it comes to you. You've been in prison, haven't you?

ANDERSON: Reform school. When I was a kid. I stole a car.

MRS. EVERLEIGH: And you haven't been in since?

ANDERSON: No. What makes you think so?

MRS. EVERLEIGH: I don't know. Your eyes, maybe. Those Chinese eyes. The way you talk. Or don't talk. Sometimes you frighten me.

ANDERSON: Do I?

MRS. EVERLEIGH: Here's the bottle. Help yourself. Are you hungry? I can fix you a roast beef sandwich.

ANDERSON: I'm not hungry. You going on another trip?

MRS. EVERLEIGH: Why do you ask?

ANDERSON: Just making conversation.

MRS. EVERLEIGH: I've been invited out to Southhampton for the July Fourth weekend. Then, late in August and over the Labor Day weekend I'll be going to Rome. May I sit on the couch next to you?

ANDERSON: No.

MRS. EVERLEIGH: That's what I like—a romantic man.

ANDERSON: If I was a romantic man you wouldn't bother with me.

MRS. EVERLEIGH: I suppose not. Still, it would be nice to know, occasionally, that you're human.

ANDERSON: I'm human. Sit on the floor.

MRS. EVERLEIGH: Here?

ANDERSON: Closer. In front of me.

MRS. EVERLEIGH: Here, darling?

ANDERSON: Yes. Take off my shoes and socks.

[Lapse of fourteen seconds.]

MRS. EVERLEIGH: I've never seen your feet before. How white they are. Your toes look like white worms.

ANDERSON: Take off that thing.

MRS. EVERLEIGH: What are you going to do?

ANDERSON: I'm going to make you forget the bastards you work for, the business, the details, the pressure. That's what you want . . . isn't it?

MRS. EVERLEIGH: Part of it.

ANDERSON: What's the other part?

MRS. EVERLEIGH: I want to forget who I am and what I am. I want to forget you and what I'm doing with my life.

ANDERSON: You want to get out?

MRS. EVERLEIGH: Get out? Yes. I want to get out.

ANDERSON: You've got a good suntan. Take the robe off.

MRS. EVERLEIGH: Like this?

ANDERSON: Yes. God, you're big. Big tits and big ass.

MRS. EVERLEIGH: Duke . . . be nice to me . . . please.

ANDERSON: Nice to you? Is that what you want?

MRS. EVERLEIGH: Not . . . you know . . . not physically. You can do anything you want. Anything. But be nice to me as a person . . . as a human being.

ANDERSON: I don't know what the hell you're talking about. Spread out.

MRS. EVERLEIGH: Oh God, I think I'm going to be sick.

ANDERSON: Go ahead. Puke all over yourself.

MRS. EVERLEIGH: You're not human. You're not.

ANDERSON: All right. So I'm not. But I'm the only man in the world who can get you out. Spread wider.

MRS. EVERLEIGH: Like this? Is this all right, Duke?

ANDERSON: Yes.

[Lapse of one minute eight seconds.]

MRS. EVERLEIGH: You're hurting me, you're hurting me.

ANDERSON: Sure.

MRS. EVERLEIGH: White worms.

ANDERSON: That's right. Getting out?

MRS. EVERLEIGH: Yes . . . yes. . . .

ANDERSON: You've got a body like mush.

MRS. EVERLEIGH: Please, Duke. . . .

ANDERSON: You're a puddle.

MRS. EVERLEIGH: Please, Duke. . . .

ANDERSON: "Please, Duke. Please Duke." Stupid bitch.

MRS. EVERLEIGH: Please, I. . . .

ANDERSON: There. Isn't that nice? Now I'm being nice to you as a person. As a human being. Right?

[27]

The following is a Xerox copy of a handwritten report, identified by Dr. Seymour P. Ernst, president, The New Graphology Institution, 14426 Erskine Avenue, Chicago, Illinois, as being in the true handwriting of Cynthia "Snapper" Haskins (previously identified). The two sheets of unlined paper, inscribed on both sides, revealed latent fingerprints of Cynthia Haskins, Thomas Haskins, and John Anderson. The paper itself—an inexpensive typing paper without watermark—bore miniature serrations on its upper edge (tipped with a red adhesive), indicating the sheets had been torn from a pad. The paper was identified as being a popular brand of typing paper sold in pads of twenty-five sheets. Such pads as available in many stationery and variety stores.

DUKE:

I swept the two offices, you know where. No strain, no pain. I gave both doctors freak checks instead of cash. I won't go back. No point in it.

Both big layouts. I guess they're doing all right. The doctor's got a nurse and a secretary-receptionist. I saw her opening mail. Mostly checks. No safe in outer office. Probably night bank deposits. Two rooms off the doctor's office: examination room and small supply room. Little room has drug safe in corner. Toilet is to left as you walk down corridor to doctor's private office.

Pictures on walls are cheap prints. Doctor has five silver cups in his office—for rowing a scull. Whatever that is.

Sorry I pulled a blank here—but that's all there was.

Headshrinker's office was small outer room with secretary-nurse, big private office and toilet to right of outer room.

Shrink has three nice small paintings: Picasso, Miro, and someone else. Looked like the real thing. I described them to Tommy. He estimates 20 G's for the three, possibly more.

Bottom left of shrink's desk has dial lock. He was putting reel of recording tape in drawer when I came in. When I started to talk, he pressed button in desk well. Everything I said was recorded, I'm sure. Must be some interesting things in that desk safe. Think about it.

He has small lavatory and clothes closet next to his office, at back near windows that overlook garden. Something in closet?

Nurse-secretary is young, about twenty-eight. Shrink is about fifty-five, speaks with accent. Small, fat, tired. I think he's on something. I'd guess Dexies.

That's all I got. Sorry it wasn't more.

Don't forget about those tape recordings. Hot off the couch. Know what I mean?

Rough sketches of both offices on back of this

sheet. If there's anything else we can do for you, please let us know.

The rest of the $$$, Duke? We had some expenses and we're hung up. Thanks.

SNAP

[28]

Recording NYSNB-1157 (continuing). Taped at 2:17 P.M., 19 June, 1968, at Mama's Soul Food, 125th Street and Hannox Avenue, New York City. Participants John Anderson and Samuel Johnson have been identified by a paid informer present at the scene.

Samuel "Skeets" Johnson, thirty-three, was a Negro, light tan, with long black greased hair combed in a high "conk" (pompadour). Approximately 6 feet 2 inches; 178 pounds. Deep razor scar on left cheek. Hearing impairment of 75 percent in left ear. Dressed in expensive clothing of bright hues. Wore light pink polish on fingernails. At last report, drove a 1967 Cadillac convertible (electric blue), New Jersey license plates 4CB-6732A, registered to Jane Martha Goody, 149 Hempy Street, Hackensack, New Jersey. Johnson's criminal record included arrests for loitering, petty larceny, committing a public nuisance, resisting arrest, simple assault, assault with intent to kill, threatening bodily harm, breaking parole, breaking and entering, armed robbery, and expectorating on a public sidewalk. He had served a total of six years, eleven months, fourteen days in Dawson School for Boys, Hillcrest Reformatory, and Dannemora. This man had the unusual ability of being able to add a series of as many as twenty dictated numbers of eight digits each in his head and arriving at the correct sum within seconds. Frequently carried a switchblade knife in a small leather sheath strapped to right ankle. Frequently spoke in rhymed slang.

ANDERSON: How you doing, Skeets?

JOHNSON: Slip me five, I'm still alive. Now that you're here, have a beer. If you're in the mood, make it food.

ANDERSON: Just a beer.

JOHNSON: I thought you dug this soul food crap—knuckles and hocks and greens?

ANDERSON: Yeah, I like it. Don't you?

JOHNSON: Shit no, man. I go for a good Chateaubriand or maybe some of them frogs' legs swimming in butter and garlic. That's eating. This stuff sucks. Just a beer? That all you want?

ANDERSON: That's all. What'd you find out?

JOHNSON: Wait for the beer, and then give ear.

[Lapse of twenty-seven seconds.]

JOHNSON: By the way, I'm picking up the knock.

ANDERSON: Thanks.

JOHNSON: I got to thank you, lad, 'cause you made

me glad.

ANDERSON: How's that?

JOHNSON: That little Andronica you put me onto. Oh, so sweet and juicy. You spend a night with her, all you need is a spoon and a straw. She's a double-dip strawberry sundae with a big whoosh of white whipped cream on top and then a big red cherry sticking up in the air.

ANDERSON: And the first thing you bit off was that cherry.

JOHNSON: Ask me no questions, and I tell you no lies.

ANDERSON: You pushing her?

JOHNSON: Every chance I get—which ain't often. She gets one night off a week. Then we fly. And we had two matinee sessions. Oh, she so cuddly and wiggly and squirming. I could eat her up.

ANDERSON: And I bet you do.

JOHNSON: On occasion, Great White Father, on occasion.

ANDERSON: How did you make the meet?

JOHNSON: What you want to know for?

ANDERSON: How am I going to learn to operate if you don't tell me things?

JOHNSON: Ah, Duke, Duke . . . you got more shit than a Christmas goose. You forgotten more than I could ever teach you. Well, I got this old family friend. A real coon type. But that's just front. This cat is into everything. I mean, he's a black Billy the Kid. Slick. You dig?

ANDERSON: Sure.

JOHNSON: So I slip him a double Z. He meets this

Andronica when she comes out of the supermarket. My pal puts his paws on her. "You dirty sex fiend," I scream at him, "how dare you touch and annoy and defile and molest this dear, sweet, little innocent chick?"

ANDERSON: Beautiful.

JOHNSON: I feed him a knuckle sandwich—which he slips. He takes off down the avenue. Andronica is shook.

ANDERSON: And grateful.

JOHNSON: Yeah—and grateful. So I help her wheel her little wagon of groceries home. One thing leads to another.

ANDERSON: So? What did she spill?

JOHNSON: That coin collection is insured for fifty big ones. There's a wall safe behind a painting of a vase of flowers in the study. That's where Mrs. Sheldon keeps her ice. My baby thinks there's other goodies in there, too. Bonds. Maybe some green. Sound good?

ANDERSON: Not bad. They going to be around all summer?

JOHNSON: I regrets to report, massa, they are not. The family moves out this weekend to Montauk. Old man Sheldon will go out every weekend until after Labor Day. That means no more sweet push for pops for another three months unless we can work something out—like her coming into the city or me going out there.

ANDERSON: You'll work it out.

JOHNSON: I mean to. I really mean to. I must see Andronica so she can blow my harmonica.

ANDERSON: What about the cold room? The room in the basement. Remember?

JOHNSON: I didn't forget, white man who speaks with forked tongue. Guess what it is.

ANDERSON: I been trying to. I can't.

JOHNSON: When the house was built, that's where they kept their fruits and vegetables. Then after they had refrigerators, the old geezer who built the joint kept his wines down there. Those walls are thick.

ANDERSON: And now? What's it used for? Wine?

JOHNSON: No, indeedy. They got a little refrigerator-like in there and a machine that takes the water out of the air. It's cold and it's dry. And everyone who lives in that house—the women, that is—they puts their fur coats in there for storage come warm weather. No extra charge. They got their own fur storage locker right there on the premises. How do you like that?

ANDERSON: I like it. I like it very much.

JOHNSON: Thought you would. Duke, if you planning anything—and notice I say *if*—and you need an extra field hand, you know who's available, don't you?

ANDERSON: I give you your due; it could be you.

JOHNSON: Ah, baby, now you're singing our song!

ANDERSON: Reach under the table; it's your other bill.

JOHNSON: Your gelt I'll take, and that's no fake. But why pay me for just what's due? I should pay you for what I screw.

ANDERSON: See you around.

[29]

Tape SEC-25JUN68-IM-12:48PM-139H. This is a telephone tap.

ANDERSON: Hello? It's me.

INGRID: Yes. Ah. . . .

ANDERSON: Did I wake you up? I'm sorry.

INGRID: What time is it?

ANDERSON: About a quarter to one.

INGRID: You are coming over?

ANDERSON: No. Not today. That's why I called. Is your phone clean?

INGRID: Oh, *Schatzie* . . . why should they bother with me? I am a nobody.

ANDERSON: God, how I'd like to come over. But I can't. Not today. It would put me to sleep. I have a meet tonight.

INGRID: So.

ANDERSON: It's very important. Very big men. I've got to be awake. Sharp. These are the money men.

INGRID: You know what you are doing?

ANDERSON: Yes.

INGRID: I wish you very much good luck.

ANDERSON: I'll probably be through with them by

two or three. It's in Brooklyn. Can I come back?

INGRID: Regretfully, no, *Schatzie*. I am busy tonight.

ANDERSON: Busy?

INGRID: Yes.

ANDERSON: Important?

INGRID: Let us say—profitable. He flies in from Fort Wayne. That is in Indiana. That is something . . . no? To fly to New York from Fort Wayne, Indiana, to see poor old Ingrid Macht.

ANDERSON: I'd fly from Hong Kong.

INGRID: Ah! Now that is romantic! I do thank you. But tomorrow perhaps?

ANDERSON: Yes. All right. I guess that would be best. I'll tell you about it then.

INGRID: As you wish. Duke. . . .

ANDERSON: Yes?

INGRID: Be careful. Be very, very careful.

ANDERSON: I will be.

INGRID: There is something in you that distresses me—a wildness, a strangeness. Think. Duke, promise me you will think . . . very clearly.

ANDERSON: I promise you I will think very clearly.

INGRID: *Das is gut*. And perhaps, tomorrow afternoon, we might get out. Together, Duke. For the first time.

ANDERSON: Together? Yes. I'll get you out. I promise.

INGRID: Good. And now I shall go back to sleep.

[30]

The following manuscript was discovered in a search of the premises of John "Duke" Anderson on 3 September, 1968. It consisted of three sheets of yellow note paper, ruled horizontally with blue lines, and vertically by a thin triple line (red-blue-red) 1¼ inches from the left-hand margin. The sheets themselves measured approximately 8 by 12⅜ inches, with serrations along the top edge indicating they had been torn from a pad or tablet.

Analysis by experts disclosed that this type of paper is commonly sold in pads in stationery and notion stores and is known as legal notepaper. It is frequently used by students, lawyers, professional writers, etc.

The recovered sheets were apparently a part or section of a longer manuscript. The pages were not numbered. Analysts believe they were written approximately ten years before the date of discovery—that is, about 1958. The handwriting was determined to be definitely that of John Anderson. The writing implement used was a ball-point pen with green ink.

The three sheets reproduced below were being used as shelf paper in a small closet in the premises of 314 Harrar Street, Brooklyn, New York, when they were discovered and submitted to analysis.

[First sheet]
it could be everything.

In other words, crime is not just a little thing, a small part of soceity, but is right in there, and it makes up most of what everyone calls normal, right and desent living. Let us list them.

When a woman will not give in to a man unless he marrys her, that could be called extortion or blackmail.

Or a woman who wants a fur coat, and if her husband wont give it to her, and she says no sex if he dont. This also is a kind of a crime, like blackmail.

Maybe a boss lies a secretery because she will loose her job otherwise. Extortion.

A guy says, I know you have been playing around. If you dont give me some, I will tell your husband. Blackmail.

A big grosery store comes in to a neyborhood near a small grosery store. And this big chain cuts there prices and puts the small store out of business. This is mugging. Money mugging but it is mugging all the same.

War. You say to a small country you do what we want or we will blow you up. Extortion or blackmail.

Or a big country like the USA goes into a small country and buys the kind of govt we want. This is criminel bribery.

Or we say we will give you such and so if you do this, and then the country does it, and we say thanks a lot! And dont pay off. That is fraud or conspiracy to defraud.

A busness man or maybe even a professer in a collage thinks the other guy will get the job he wants. So he writes letters he dont sign and sends them to the top man. Poyson pen letters. Nothing he could get busted for but hinting.

There are many other exampels, practicaly endless that I

[Second sheet]

could give here about how much of what we say is common, ordinary human behavier is really crime.

Some of these are personel, like between a man and a woman, or two men or two women, and some are in busness and some are in govt.

A man wants to shiv another guy in his company and he spreds the word hes a queer. Slander.

A guy buys gifts for his wife becase he knows she won't give out if he dont. Bribery.

We teach young kids in the army what is the best way to kill people. Murder.

The local grosery store or department store jacks up the bill if they can get away with it, or maybe shortchanges. Robbery.

A guy wants to go to a cheap restaurant but his woman wants to go to a fancy joint. And she hints if they dont go where she wants, its no push-push for him that night. Extortion.

A guy gives a dame a string of beads and he says

there diamonds but they are really zircons or rinestones and she puts out. Fraud.

A guy in a busness is taking and another guy finds out and lets the first guy know. So the first guy gets something on the second guy. Then they grin and let live. Conspiracy.

Maybe a woman likes to get beat. So her guy slaps her around. He likes it too. But whos to know? Its still assault.

A peter keeps another peter on the string by saying he will nark on him if the first guy doesnt keep playing games. Extortion.

Similer to above, anyone who says I will kill myself if you do no do like I want, that is also extortion. Or maybe blackmail

[Third sheet]

depending on how the lawyers and judges decide on it.

What I am saying is this, that crime is not just breaking laws because everyone does it. I do not know if this is something new or has been going on for many years. But we are all criminels.

We are all criminels. It is just a question of degree, like first, second and third degree. But if the laws against criminel acts are right, then almost everyone should be in the poke. If these laws are right and rigid, then it shouldnt matter what degree. The married woman who wont put out unless her husband buys her a fur coat is just as guilty as a guy whos got a million dollar extortion hustle going for him.

And the poor pop who breaks into his kids piggy bank, yes its funny, and takes out enough change to get to work, well how is he so different from a good bank man like Sonny Brooks, he died yesterday, it was in the papers. Jesus I loved that guy, he taught me all I know, he was so great. He got cut down coming out of a bank in West Va. I cant believe it he was so carefull, a real pro. Worked once a year but he planed for 6 mos. Carefull and good. Layed off for 6 mos. every year. Hit a big one once a year he said and then lay off. I worked two jobs with him and learned so much.

Oh shit, its all crime. Everything. The way we live. Everyone. We are all cons, everyone of us. So what I do is just being smart enough to make it pay.

We lie and we cheat and we steal and we kill, and if it isnt money its other people or there love or just to get some push. Whatever we get hung on. Oh Jesus its so dirty.

When I was inside I thaught those inside were cleaner then those outside. At least we were open and did our crimes in the open. But the rest think they are so normal and clean and desent and they are the biggest and dirtiest criminels of them all because they

[End of third sheet]

[31]

The following is a transcription made from tape recordings of a conversation that took place in Elvira's, an Italian restaurant at 96352 Hammacher Street, Brooklyn, New York, during the early morning hours of 26 June, 1968.

At the time, these premises were under electronic surveillance by at least four, and possibly more, law investigation agencies. Apparently there was no cooperation between these agencies.

A great variety of miniaturized electronic devices was utilized, including telephone taps, bugs implanted beneath certain tables, in the bar, and in both the gents' and the ladies' rooms. In addition, the new Sonex Nailhead 158-JB microphone transmitters had been surreptitiously installed in the baseboards of the kitchen.

Elvira's, a popular and successful restaurant in the Flatbush section of Brooklyn, had for many years been known to law enforcement officers as an eating and meeting place for members of the Angelo family. The restaurant was fire-bombed on 15 October, 1958, during what was apparently a gang war between the Angelo family and a rival organization known as the Snipes Brothers. The bombing resulted in the death of a waiter, Pasquale Gardini.

On 3 February, 1959, Anthony "Wopso" Angelo was shot down in the front phone booth of Elvira's while making a phone call to persons unknown. His killer entered through the glass door, after apparently seeing Angelo go into the phone booth from an outside observation post. Four bullets of .32 caliber were fired into Angelo. He died instantly. His killer has not yet been apprehended.

Present at the meeting in a small, private back room at Elvira's on the morning of 26 June, 1968, were John "Duke" Anderson, Anthony "Doctor" D'Medico, and Patrick "Little Pat" Angelo. These men have been positively identified by voice prints, interior and exterior evidence, and by paid informers present at the scene.

Patrick "Little Pat" Angelo was born in 1932 in Brooklyn, New York. His father, Patsy "The Hook" Angelo, was killed in a waterfront fracas two months before Patrick's birth. Patrick's education was financed by his grandfather, Dominick "Papa" Angelo, don of the Angelo family. Patrick Angelo was 5 feet 8½ inches tall; 193 pounds; blue eyes; thick gray hair worn long, combed straight back, no part. Physical scars: scalp wound above right temple (bullet); depressed wound in left calf (shrapnel); and excised third right rib (grenade). Subject was a graduate of Walsham School of Business Administration, and had attended one year at the Rolley Law Academy. Enlisted in U.S. Army in 1950 and after training was sent to Korea with the 361st Assault Battalion, 498th Regiment, 22d Combat Division. At war's end, he had risen to rank of major (battlefield promotions) and had earned the Purple Heart (3), Silver Star, and Distinguished Service Cross, in addition to decorations from the South Korean and Turkish governments.

Subject resigned from the Army in 1954 with letters of commendation. He then organized and became president of Modern Automanagement, 6501 Fifth Avenue, New York City, a management consultant firm. In addition, he was an officer of record for Sweeteeze Linens, 361 Forbisher Street, Brooklyn, New York; vice-president of Wrenchies Bowling Alleys, 1388 Grand Evarts, the Bronx, New York; and secretary-treasurer of the Fifth National Discount and Service Organization, Palm Credit Co., Inc., and the Thomas Jefferson Trading Corp., all of Wilmington, Delaware.

Subject had no criminal record.

Subject was married (to Maria Angelo, a second cousin) and was the father of two teen-age sons currently students at Harrington Military Academy in Virginia. He also had a four-year-old daughter, Stella.

Supposition: Patrick Angelo will succeed Dominick "Papa" Angelo as don of the Angelo family upon the death of Dominick, who was ninety-four years old.

Due to mechanical difficulties and heavy external noise, no single tape recording contains the entire conversation given below. This is a transcription of parts of four different tapes made by four law enforcement agencies. (At their request, portions of the transcription have been deleted as they concern investigations currently in progress.) This is the author's transcription GO-110T-26JUN68. The time was 1:43 A.M.

D'MEDICO: . . . don't believe you've met Pat Angelo. Pat, this is Duke Anderson, the man I told you about.

ANDERSON: Pleased to make your acquaintance, Mr. Angelo.

ANGELO: Duke, I don't want you to think I'm giving you a fast shuffle, but I've got another meet tonight. Then I've got to drive home to Teaneck. So you'll understand if I make this as short as we can. Okay?

ANDERSON: Sure.

ANGELO: I'll tell you what the Doc told me. See if I got it straight. If not, you correct me. Then I'll start asking questions. You got a campaign. It's a house on the East Side of Manhattan. You want to take the whole place He advanced you three G's. That's out of his own pocket. You been looking it over. Now we're at the point where we decide do we go ahead or do we call the whole thing off. Am I right so far?

ANDERSON: That's right, Mr. Angelo. Mr. D'-Medico, I have a complete list of my expenses with me, and you have three hundred and fifty-nine dollars and sixteen cents coming back on your advance that wasn't spent.

D'MEDICO: I told you, Pat! Didn't I tell you?

ANGELO: Yes. Let's get on with it. So what have we got, Duke?

ANDERSON: I have a report here. It's a handwritten original. No copies. For you and Mr. D'Medico. I think it looks good.

ANGELO: How much?

ANDERSON: Minimum of a hundred thousand. Closer to quarter of a mil, I'd guess.

ANGELO: You'd guess? What the hell are you talking about? What? Retail value? Wholesale value? Resale value? What we can get from fences? What is it? Spell it out.

ANDERSON: It's jewelry, furs, uncut stones, a valuable coin collection, rugs, maybe drugs from two doctors, cash, negotiable securities. These people are loaded.

[Lapse of five seconds.]

ANGELO: So you're talking about original retail value?

ANDERSON: Yes.

ANGELO: So take a third of what you estimate. Maybe thirty G's if we can unload it. Or possibly eighty G's tops. Is that right?

ANDERSON: Yes.

ANGELO: Let's figure the bottom—thirty G's. How many men?

ANDERSON: Five.

ANGELO: Five? And one of ours. Six. So you want six men to put out for five G's each?

ANDERSON: No. I want my men to be paid a flat fee. Whatever I can settle for. But no share. I figure

I can get the five for a total of eight thou tops. I don't know what you'll pay your man. Maybe he's on salary. But figure ten G's tops for employees. That leaves twenty G's for a split. Absolute minimum. I'm no gambler, but I still think it'll run closer to eighty G's. The total, that is.

ANGELO: Forget what you think. We're working on the minimum. So we have twenty G's left for the split. How do you figure that?

ANDERSON: Seventy-thirty.

ANGELO: Seventy to you, of course?

ANDERSON: Yes.

ANGELO: You're a hardnose, aren't you?

D'MEDICO: Pat, take it easy.

ANDERSON: Yes, I'm a hardnose.

ANGELO: Tennessee?

ANDERSON: Kentucky.

ANGELO: I thought so. Duke, put yourself in my place. You want me to okay this thing. You guarantee us about six or seven thousand if we agree to your terms. All right, all right—it may run as high as twenty G's if the take is as big as you guess it might be. I can't figure with guesses. I got to know. So I'm figuring on six G's. Anything over is gravy. All this for six thousand dollars? We can take that legit in one day from our biggest horse parlor. So what's the percentage?

ANDERSON: So what's the risk? One muscle? He's expendable, isn't he?

[Lapse of eight seconds.]

ANGELO: You're no dumdum, are you?

ANDERSON: No, I'm not. And I got to keep repeating that seven G's is the absolute minimum. It'll run more, much more—I swear it.

ANGELO: Put your cock on the line?

ANDERSON: Goddamned right.

D'MEDICO: Jesus, Pat. . . .

ANGELO: He's a hardnose—like I said. I like you, Duke.

ANDERSON: Thanks.

ANGELO: For nothing. Have you started thinking about operations?

ANDERSON: A little. Just a beginning. It should be on a holiday weekend. Half the people will be gone to the beach or on vacation or at their summer places. July Fourth would have been good, but it's too late for that now. If you say okay, we should aim for the Labor Day weekend. We cut all communications. Isolate the house. We pull up a van. We take our time—three hours, four hours, whatever we need.

ANGELO: But you haven't thought it out?

ANDERSON: No, I haven't. I got this report here. It'll give you a rundown on who lives there and where the stuff is and where we should look and how it can be done. But if you say okay, we'll have to dig a lot deeper.

ANGELO: Like what?

ANDERSON: Habits of people in the building. Schedules of the beat fuzz and squad cars in the sector. Private watchmen. People who walk their dogs late at night. Location of call boxes and telephone booths. Bars that are open late at night. A lot of things. . . .

ANGELO: Were you ever in the military?

ANDERSON: Marine Corps. About eighteen months.

ANGELO: What happened?

ANDERSON: I got a dishonorable discharge.

ANGELO: What for?

ANDERSON: I knocked up a captain's wife–amongst other things.

ANGELO: Yes. What did you do? See any action?

ANDERSON: No. I made corporal. I was an instructor on the range at Paris Island.

ANGELO: You're a good shot?

ANDERSON: Yes.

D'MEDICO: But you've never carried a piece on a job–have you, Duke?

ANDERSON: No. I never have.

ANGELO: Christ, I'm thirsty. Doc, get us another bottle of that Volpolicella, will you? But if this campaign goes through, you'll have to pack a piece. You realize that, don't you, Duke?

ANDERSON: Yes.

ANGELO: You're willing?

ANDERSON: Yes.

ANGELO: When you were a corporal of Marines did you ever get any instructions on the technique of a raid? A quick hit-and-run?

ANDERSON: A little.

ANGELO: Did you ever hear about that campaign in Detroit on. . . . We hit the. . . . We used about. . . . What we did was to create a diversion. It pulled off all the precinct buttons to . . . and while they were. . . . And it worked perfectly. Something like that might work here.

ANDERSON: It might.

ANGELO: You don't sound very enthusiastic.

ANDERSON: I got to think about it.

D'MEDICO: Here's the wine, Pat. Chilled just a little . . . the way you like it.

ANGELO: Fine. Thank you, Doctor. So you want to think about it, do you, Duke?

ANDERSON: Yes. It's *my* cock.

ANGELO: It surely is. All right. Supposing Papa gives the go-ahead. What will you need? Have you thought of that?

ANDERSON: Yes, I thought of that. I'll need another two thousand to complete the sweep.

ANGELO: The reconnaissance?

ANDERSON: That's right. To figure how we'll handle it.

ANGELO: Operations and deployment. And then what?

ANDERSON: You'll get a final shakedown on the whole bit. Then if you okay, I'll need the loot to pay off my five men. Half in advance, half when the job's finished.

D'MEDICO: About two thousand for looking, and then another four or five for your staff?

ANDERSON: That's about it.

D'MEDICO: All advances and expenses out of the take before the split?

ANDERSON: Yes.

ANGELO: I've got to get out of here and over to

Manhattan. I'm late as it is. Duke, I want to talk to the Doctor. You understand?

ANDERSON: Sure. I appreciate you giving me this time.

ANGELO: We'll get in touch with you—one way or the other—in a week or so. I've got to talk to Papa and, as you probably know, he's ailing. We should all live to be ninety-four and ailing.

D'MEDICO: Amen.

ANDERSON: Nice to meet you, Mr. Angelo. Thanks, Mr. D'Medico.

D'MEDICO: A pleasure, Duke. We'll be in touch.

[Lapse of seventeen seconds.]

D'MEDICO: How did you know he was from Kentucky, Tennessee—around there?

ANGELO: I recognized him the minute he walked in. Not him, but the type. A mountain man. God knows I saw enough of them in Korea. Kentucky, Tennessee, West Virginia. Rough boys. As rough as the Southerners . . . but they never bugged out. Sometimes you get some freaky Southerners. I never saw a freaky mountain man. They're all born piss-poor. They got nothing but their pride. I had some mountain men who never had a pair of new shoes until they got in the army. This Anderson . . . Jesus Christ, he reminds me so much of a guy I had. He was from Tennessee. Best shot I ever saw. I was a First Looey then. I had this patrol, and we were going down a dry creek bed. This mountain man was point. The target. We went through three points in three days. They fired on the point and that's how we knew where they were.

D'MEDICO: That's nice.

ANGELO: Yes. So this Tennessee mountain man was point, about twenty yards or so ahead of me. A gook comes out of the bushes and charges at him. The gook has a kitchen knife tied to a long pole with string. He was probably hopped up. He comes charging out screaming. My guy could have shot him dead—one, two, three. Like that. But he didn't. He laughed. I swear to God, he laughed. He had his blade on his rifle, and he waited for the gook to come to him. It was classic. Jesus, it was classic. I had been through all the bayonet stuff: advance, parry, thrust. Book stuff. And this was right out of the book. Classic. They could have taken pictures of it for an army manual. My guy took the position, shuffled forward, and when the gook shoved at him, he parried, got his stick in the gook's stomach, withdrew, stuck again into his balls, turned the blade, withdrew, shoved the bayonet into the ground to clean it, and turned and grinned at me. He liked it. There were guys like that. They liked it. They enjoyed it. War, I mean.

D'MEDICO: What happened to him?

ANGELO: Who?

D'MEDICO: Your guy.

ANGELO: Oh. Well, the company went back to Tokyo on leave. This Tennessee guy got caught raping a nine-year-old Japanese girl. He got racked up.

D'MEDICO: Where is he now?

ANGELO: Still in Leavenworth as far as I know. So tell me about this Anderson. What do you know?

D'MEDICO: He came out of the South about ten years ago. A helluva driver. I think he was driving alky for Solly Benedict down there. Anyway, he sliced someone and had to come north. Solly called me about him. About the same time my cousin Gino had a hustle planned. Did you ever meet Gino?

ANGELO: No, I don't believe I ever did.

D'MEDICO: Christ, my face is killing me. Well, it was a warehouse job. Drugs. Pep pills, I think they were. It was cased perfect, but someone tipped the Safe and Loft Squad. We took care of him later. Anyway, I recommended Anderson as the driver, and Gino says okay. The plan was for Gino and two muscles to pull up in this car, Anderson driving. Park a block away. Anderson is told to stay there until Gino returns. The idea is that they'll break the warehouse, the two dumdums will drive the truck out, and Gino will return to where Anderson is waiting in the car.

ANGELO: So?

D'MEDICO: So everything goes wrong. Floodlights, sirens, bullhorns, riot guns, barkers . . . the whole bit. The two muscles get cut down. Gino takes a bad one in the gut and staggers around the corner. He's told Anderson to stay there, and with all this going on, Anderson is still there.

ANGELO: A mountain man.

D'MEDICO: Yes. He didn't cut. Well, he gets Gino into the car and gets him to a sawbones. It saved his life.

ANGELO: What's he doing now?

D'MEDICO: Gino? He's got this little candy store in Newark. He takes some numbers, handles a few loans. Penny-ante stuff. He's not too good . . . but he's alive. I feed him what I can. But I never forgot Duke sitting there while the shit hit the fan. He's some man.

ANGELO: I figured that. Then what happened with him?

D'MEDICO: He didn't want any jobs. He wanted to free-lance. He cleared everything with me first, and I gave him the go-ahead. He did very well. He's a smart boy, Pat. He learned fast. He hit some East Side apartments for a bundle. Ice, mostly. Never carried a stick. Got clever. In and out so fast and so smooth they could never figure how. He was doing all right. Maybe three or four jobs a year. Always made his contribution and never screamed. I kept track and found out he was bent, sex-wise.

ANGELO: How do you mean?

D'MEDICO: Whips . . . you know.

ANGELO: Which way is he? This is important.

D'MEDICO: Both ways, from what I hear. Then he pulled this job and was waiting on a corner for this Jew bitch he had to pass the stuff to—it was only about a block away—when some lucky probationary patrolman decided he didn't like his looks and shook him down. That kid is a Dick

Two now. So Duke went up. The woman wasn't touched; he never mentioned her. I heard she was late for the meet because she was at her stockbroker's.

ANGELO: Beautiful. You been keeping in touch with her?

D'MEDICO: Oh, sure. Since Duke brought up this campaign we been checking her out. She's got a record, and she's hustling right now—shmeck, tail, abortion—the whole bit. She works in a dance hall Sam Bergman owns. We can lean on her any time we want to.

ANGELO: Good. How did Anderson get on to this thing on the East Side?

D'MEDICO: He's pronging a woman who lives there. We don't know how he met her. But he's in and out of the place at least twice a week. A big dame who looks like money.

ANGELO: All right. I guess that's about it. Christ, have we finished another bottle? My God, I've *got* to get to Manhattan.

D'MEDICO: Pat, how do you feel about it?

ANGELO: If it was up to me, I'd say no. Look, Doc, we're in restaurants, hotels, banks, linen supply, insurance, trucking, laundromats, garbage disposal—all nice, clean, legit things. And the profits are good. So why do we need this bang-bang stuff?

D'MEDICO: Still . . . you're interested?

ANGELO: Yes . . . I guess I am. It's a military problem. Look at me . . . I'm a businessman, my gut is swelling, my ass is sinking, I've got a wife and three kids, I belong to four clubs, I play golf every good weekend, I go to the PTA with my wife, I worry about crab grass, I've got a poodle with worms. In other words, I'm a solid citizen. But sometimes I look at myself in the mirror—the belly, the jowls, the fat thighs, the soft cock, and I think I was happier in Korea.

D'MEDICO: Pat, maybe you're one of those guys you were telling me about—the guys who enjoy war.

ANGELO: Maybe. I don't know. All I know is, I hear of something like this and I get all excited. My brain starts working. I'm young again. A campaign. Problems. How to figure it. It's really something. But I wouldn't decide without talking it over with Papa. First of all, I owe it to him. Second of all, he may be bedridden with maybe a fat boy now and then to keep him warm, but his mind is still there—sharp and hard. I'll lay it out for him. He likes to feel he's still needed, still making the decisions. Jesus Christ, we got a thousand lawyers and CPA's making decisions he couldn't even understand—but a problem like this, he can understand. So I'll lay it out for him. If he says no, it's no. If he says yes, it's yes. I'll let you know within a week or so. Is that all right?

D'MEDICO: Of course. Got anyone in mind for the sixth man?

ANGELO: No. Do you?

D'MEDICO: A guy named Sam Heming. A nothing.

All muscle, no brains. But he's one of Paul Washington's boys.

ANGELO: A smoke?

D'MEDICO: He is, but he passes.

ANGELO: Why him?

D'MEDICO: I owe Paul a favor.

ANGELO: Linda Curtis?

D'MEDICO: You don't miss much, do you?

ANGELO: No, Doc, not much. Heming is okay with me if he's solid.

D'MEDICO: He's solid.

ANGELO: Good. Papa will want to know. I'll tell him you go for this guy. Okay?

D'MEDICO: Yes . . . if it's necessary.

ANGELO: It's necessary. Jesus Christ, Doc, you're twitching like a maniac. Can't you do anything about that face of yours?

D'MEDICO: No. Not a thing.

ANGELO: Tough shit. I've got to run. Thanks for the dinner and vino.

D'MEDICO: My pleasure. I'll hear from you on this in a week or so?

ANGELO: Sure. Oh . . . by the way, Doc, keep an eye on Fred Simons.

D'MEDICO: Anything wrong?

ANGELO: Not yet. But he's been hitting the sauce hard lately. Maybe talking a little more than he should. Just a friendly tip.

D'MEDICO: Of course. Thanks. I'll call it to his attention.

ANGELO: You do that.

[32]

Tape recording POM-9JUL68-EVERLEIGH. Time is approximately 2:45 P.M.

MRS. EVERLEIGH: Let me get you a big drink. I want you to sit quietly for a while. I want to show you some pictures—my photo album.

ANDERSON: All right.

[Lapse of sixteen seconds.]

MRS. EVERLEIGH: Here . . . just the way you like it—one ice cube. Here we go. I bought this album at Mark Cross. It's nice, isn't it?

ANDERSON: Yes.

MRS. EVERLEIGH: Here . . . this tintype. This was my great-grandfather on my father's side. He was in the Civil War. That's the uniform of a captain he's wearing. The picture was made when he came home on leave. Then he lost an arm at Antietam. But they let him keep his company. They didn't care so much about things like that in those days.

ANDERSON: I know. My great-grandpappy went through the Second Wilderness with a wooden leg.

MRS. EVERLEIGH: Then, after the war, he came home

and married my great-grandmother. Here's their wedding photo. Wasn't she the tiniest, sweetest, prettiest thing you've ever seen? Raised seven children in Rockford, Illinois. Now this is the only picture I have of my mother's parents. He was an older man, had a general store near Sewickley in Pennsylvania. His wife was a real monster. I remember her vaguely. I guess I got my size from her. She was huge—and ugly. My mother was an only child. Here's my mother's graduating class. She went two years to a teachers' college. The one with the circle is her. This little fellow is my father at the age of ten. Wasn't he cute? Then he went to Yale. Look at that hat he's wearing! Isn't that a scream? He rowed for them. And he was a great swimmer, too. Here he is in a swimsuit. This was taken during his last year at Yale.

ANDERSON: Looks like he was hung.

MRS. EVERLEIGH: Bastard. Well, I can tell you he was all man. Tall and muscular. He met my mother at a prom, and they got married right after he graduated. He started as a junior clerk in Wall Street about three years before World War One. My brother Ernest was born in 1915, but when America got into the war, Daddy enlisted. He went overseas in 1918. I don't think he ever actually saw any action. Here he is in his uniform.

ANDERSON: Those wraparound puttees must have been murder. My mother's first husband got killed with the Marines on the Marne.

MRS. EVERLEIGH: That couldn't have been your father?

ANDERSON: No. My pappy was her third husband.

MRS. EVERLEIGH: Well, here's Mom and Daddy with Ernie and Tom—he was the second-born. He was missing in action in France in World War Two. Then here's Mother holding me in her arms—the first picture ever taken of me. Wasn't I cute?

ANDERSON: Yes.

MRS. EVERLEIGH: Then here are some pictures of me growing up. Bloomers. Gym suit. Bathing suit. We went to a cabin on a lake up in Canada. Here are all the kids—Ernest and Thomas and me and Robert. All of us.

ANDERSON: You were the only girl?

MRS. EVERLEIGH: Yes. But I could keep up with them, and after a while I could outswim them all. Mother got sick and was in bed a lot, and Daddy was busy with his business. So the four of us kids were together a lot. Ernie was the leader because he was oldest, but when he went to Dartmouth, I took over. Tom and Bob never had the authority that Ernie had.

ANDERSON: How old were you when that one was taken?

MRS. EVERLEIGH: About thirteen, I think.

ANDERSON: A great pair of lungs.

MRS. EVERLEIGH: Yes, I matured early. The story of my life. I started bleeding at eleven. Look at the shoulders I had, and those thighs. I could outswim my brothers and all their friends. I think the boys resented it. They liked frail, weak, feminine things. I had this big, strong, muscular body. I thought the boys would like a girl who could swim with them and ride horses with them and wrestle and all that. . . . But when dances came along, I noticed it was the frail, weak, pale feminine things who got invited. Mother insisted I take dancing lessons, but I was never very good at it. I could dive and swim, but on the dance floor I felt like a lump.

ANDERSON: Who copped your cherry?

MRS. EVERLEIGH: My brother Ernie. Does that shock you?

ANDERSON: Why should it? I'm from Kentucky.

MRS. EVERLEIGH: Well, it happened when he was home one Easter vacation from Dartmouth. And he was drunk.

ANDERSON: Sure.

MRS. EVERLEIGH: Here I am at my high school graduation. Don't I look pretty?

ANDERSON: You look like a heifer in a nightgown.

MRS. EVERLEIGH: I guess I do . . . I guess I do. Oh, God, that hat. But then, here, when I started going to Miss Proud's school, I slimmed down. A little. Not much, but a little. I was on the swimming team, captain of the winning intramural field-hockey team, captain of the riding and golf teams, and I played a good game of tennis, too. Not clever, but strong. Here I am with the cup I got for best all-around girl athlete.

ANDERSON: Christ, what a body. I wish I could have stuck you then.

MRS. EVERLEIGH: Plenty of boys did. Maybe I

couldn't dance, but I discovered the secret of how to be popular. A very simple secret. I think they called me Miss Round Heels. All you had to do was ask, and I'd roll over. So I had plenty of dates.

ANDERSON: I'd have figured you for a lez.

MRS. EVERLEIGH: Oh . . . I tried it. I never made the first advance, but I had plenty of those sweet, pale, soft, feminine things touching me up. I tried it, but it didn't take. Maybe it was because of the way they smelled. You didn't shower this morning, did you?

ANDERSON: No.

MRS. EVERLEIGH: That horsey, bitter, acid smell. It really turns me on. Then I met David. He was a friend of my youngest brother, Bob. Here's David.

ANDERSON: Looks like a butterfly.

MRS. EVERLEIGH: He was . . . but I didn't discover that until it was too late. And he drank and drank and drank. . . . But he was funny and kind and considerate. He had money, and he made me laugh and held doors open for me, and if he wasn't so great in the sack, well, I could excuse that because he always had too much to drink. You know?

ANDERSON: Yes.

MRS. EVERLEIGH: Lots of money. Cleveland coal and iron and things like that. Sometimes I wondered if he was a little Jewish.

ANDERSON: A little Jewish?

MRS. EVERLEIGH: You know . . . way back. Anyway,

here we are at the beach, at the prom, at a horse show, at the engagement party, the wedding pictures, reception, and so forth. I wore low heels because I was just a wee bit taller than he was. He had beautiful hair. Didn't he have beautiful hair?

ANDERSON: Beautiful. Much more of this shit?

MRS. EVERLEIGH: No, not much more. Here we are at our summer place in East Hampton. Some good times. Drunken parties. I walked in on him once when he was getting buggered by a Puerto Rican busboy. I don't have a picture of *that!* And that's about all. Some pictures of me on buying trips—Paris, Rome, London, Geneva, Vienna. . . .

ANDERSON: Who's this guy?

MRS. EVERLEIGH: A kid I bought in Stockholm.

ANDERSON: Good lay?

MRS. EVERLEIGH: Not really.

ANDERSON: What the hell are you crying for?

[Lapse of seven seconds.]

MRS. EVERLEIGH: These pictures. A hundred years. My great-grandparents. The Civil War. My parents. The world wars. My brothers. I just think of what all these people went through. To produce me. Me. I'm the result. Ah, Jesus, Duke, what happens to us? How did we get to be what we are? I just can't stand thinking about it—it's so awful. So sad.

ANDERSON: Where's your husband now?

MRS. EVERLEIGH: David? The last time I saw him, he was wearing lipstick. That's what I mean.

And look at me. Am I any better?

ANDERSON: You want me to go?

MRS. EVERLEIGH: And leave me here counting the walls? Duke, for the love of God, get me out. . . .

[33]

Dominick "Papa" Angelo, ninety-four, don of the Angelo family, was a legal resident of 67825 Flint Road, Deal, New Jersey. Born Mario Dominick Nicola Angelo in Mareno, Sicily, 1874. His family was a "left-side" branch of the Angelo family, and for five generations had been tenant farmers in Sicily. There is no record of Dominick's early schooling.

During a New York State investigation in 1934 (see Records of the Murphy Committee, Vol. I, pp. 432-35) evidence was presented that Dominick Angelo entered the United States illegally in 1891 by swimming ashore from a merchant ship on which he was working as cook. In any event, records are confused—or missing—and Dominick Angelo filed for his first citizenship papers in 1896, and became a U.S. citizen in 1903. At that time he listed his occupation as "waiter."

His criminal record includes an arrest for disturbing the peace in 1904 (no disposition) and assault with intent to kill in 1905 (charge withdrawn). In 1907 he was arrested on a charge of assault with a deadly weapon (knife) with the intent to commit grievous bodily harm (he castrated his victim). He was tried, convicted, and served two years, seven months, and fourteen days at Dannemora (#46783).

Upon his release from prison, there is inconclusive evidence that he became a "button" for the Black Hand, as the Italian criminal organization in this country was then called.

(In their treatise *Origins of American Slang*, Hawley and Butanski, Effrim Publishers Co., Inc., 1958, the authors state [pp. 38–39] that in the period 1890–1910, the term "button" was used to describe a gangland executioner, and may have come from a description of a man who could "button the lip" of an informer or enemy. The authors point out that later, in the 1920's and 1930's, the terms "buttons" or "Mr. Buttons" came into use in criminal circles to describe a uniformed policeman.)

In 1910, Dominick Angelo obtained employment with the Alsotto Sand & Gravel Co., of Brooklyn, New York, ostensibly as a loader. In 1917 he volunteered for service with the American Expeditionary Forces, but because of his age, his services were limited to guard duty on the docks at Bayonne, New Jersey.

In 1920 he secured employment as foreman with the Giovanni Shipping Enterprises, Inc. During this period he married Maria Florence Gabriele

Angelo, a distant relative. Their first child, a boy, was born in 1923. He was subsequently killed in action on Guadalcanal Island in 1942.

During World War II, Dominick Angelo volunteered his services to the U.S. government and, according to documents on file, his assistance was "invaluable" in preparing for the invasions of Sicily and Italy. There is in existence a letter from a high official of the OSS attesting to his "magnificent and unique cooperation."

During the period 1948-68, official records reveal his rise to a position of great prominence and power in the Italian-dominated structure controlling organized crime in the United States. From soldier to *capo* to don took him less than ten years, and by 1957 he was recognized as leader of one of the several national "families." His personal fortune was variously estimated as $20,000,000 to $45,000,000.

Students and observers of organized crime in the United States—of what has been described as the Black Hand, the Syndicate, the Mafia, the Cosa Nostra, the Family, etc.—generally agree that Dominick Angelo was the guiding spirit, brain, and power behind the conversion of the violent system to a semilegitimate cartel that increasingly avoided the strong-arm methods of previous years and invested more funds in loan companies, real estate, entertainment enterprises, brokerage houses, garbage collection, banks, linen supply companies, restaurants, laundromats, insurance companies, and advertising agencies.

In 1968,* Dominick Angelo was ninety-four; 124 pounds; 5 feet 6 inches tall; almost totally bald; almost completely bedridden from diabetes, arthritis, and the effects of two severe coronary occlusions. Very dark eyes; extraordinarily long fingers; a habit of stroking his upper lip with one finger (he wore a long mustache until 1946).

His home in Deal, New Jersey, was large, comfortable, and situated in the center of a generous acreage, without being ostentatious. The estate was surrounded by a 12-foot brick wall topped with cement into which pieces of broken glass had been studded. It is believed the staff consisted of several people—housekeeper, two or three groundsmen, a personal valet, butler, a male medical attendant, a female nurse, three maids, and two chauffeurs.

On 16 May, 1966, an explosion occurred at the locked gate leading to the Angelo estate. Officers investigating the incident reported it had been caused by several sticks of dynamite wired to a crude time fuse—a cheap alarm clock. No injuries were reported, and no arrests were made. The investigation is continuing.

Of peripheral interest are two unsubstantiated reports on Dominick Angelo: After his wife's death in 1952, he engaged in homosexual liaisons, preferring the company of very young boys; and he was the inventor of the split-level coffin, although this "credit" has since been given to others. The split-level coffin is a device to get rid of victims of

* Dominick Angelo died on February 19, 1969.

gangland slayings. The coffins are built somewhat deeper than usual, and the victim is buried in a section beneath the legitimate corpse. This scheme, of course, depends upon the cooperation of funeral parlors, in which the family has a substantial financial interest.

The following transcription is from a tape recording made by agents of the New Jersey Special Legislative Subcommittee to Investigate Organized Crime. The transcription is labeled NJSLC-DA-#206-IC, and is dated 10 July, 1968. The time was approximately 11:45 P.M., and the recording was made at Dominick Angelo's home at 67825 Flint Road, Deal, New Jersey. The transmitting device was a Socklet MT-Model K.

From internal evidence, the two persons present were Dominick "Papa" Angelo and Patrick "Little Pat" Angelo. Although the tape recording from which this transcription was made ran for slightly less than three hours, portions have been deleted that repeat evidence already presented. In addition, law enforcement agencies of New Jersey, New York, and Las Vegas, Nevada, have requested that certain portions be withheld, since they concern possible criminal prosecutions presently under investigation. All such deletions have been indicated by "lapse of time" notations.

[Lapse of thirty-two minutes during which Patrick Angelo inquired as to his grandfather's health and was informed that it was "as well as could be expected." Patrick Angelo then reported on the meeting with John Anderson and Anthony D'Medico.]

PATRICK: Well, Papa, what do you think?

PAPA: What do *you* think?

PATRICK: I say no. Too many people involved. Too complex, considering the possible profit.

PAPA: But I see your eyes shining. I see you are interested. You say to yourself, this is action! You are excited. You say to yourself, I am getting old and fat. I need action. This is how it was in Korea. I will plan this like a military raid. To me you say no—but in yourself you want this thing.

PATRICK [laughing]: Papa, you're wonderful! You've got it all exactly right. My brain tells me this is nothing. But my blood wants it. I am sorry.

PAPA: Why be sorry? You think it is a good thing to be all brain and no blood? It is as bad as being all blood and no brain. The right mixture—that is what is important. This man Anderson—what is your feeling on him?

PATRICK: A hardnose. He has never carried a piece, but he is hard. And proud. From Kentucky. A mountain man. Everything the Doctor told me about him was good.

PAPA: Anderson? From the South? About ten years ago Gino Belli—he is the Doctor's cousin—had a thing planned. It seemed good but it went sour. He had a driver named Anderson. Is that the man?

PATRICK: The same one. What a memory you've got, Papa!

PAPA: The body grows old; the mind remains young, praise to God. This Anderson brought Gino to a doctor. I remember it all now. I met him, very briefly. Tall and thin. A long, sunken face. Proud. Yes, you are right—a very proud man. I remember.

PATRICK: So what do you want to do, Papa?

PAPA: Be quiet and let me think.

[Lapse of two minutes thirteen seconds.]

PAPA: This Anderson—you say he has his own staff?

PATRICK: Yes. Five men. One's a smoke. One's a tech. Two are drivers, one of them a dumdum.

[Lapse of nine seconds.]

PAPA: That is four. And the other? The fifth man?

[Lapse of sixteen seconds.]

PAPA: Well? The fifth man?

PATRICK: He's fancy. Knows about paintings, rugs, art collections—things like that.

PAPA: I see. Is his name Bailey?

PATRICK: I don't know what his name is, Papa. I can find out.

PAPA: There was a fancy boy named Bailey out in Vegas. We did a. . . .

[Lapse of four minutes thirty-two seconds.]

PAPA: But that is not important. Besides, I suspect it is not Bailey. I suspect Bailey is dead. And who does the Doctor recommend as our representative?

PATRICK: A man named Sam Heming. One of Paul Washington's boys.

PAPA: Another dinge?

PATRICK: Yes.

PAPA: No. That won't do.
PATRICK: Papa? You mean you approve of this campaign?
PAPA: Yes. I approve. Go ahead with it.
PATRICK: But why? The money is. . . .
PAPA: I know. The money is nothing. There are too many people involved. It will end in disaster.
PATRICK: So . . . ?
[Lapse of seventeen seconds.]
PAPA: Little Pat is thinking why should Papa okay something like this? All these years we work hard to get legit. We deal with Wall Street bankers, Madison Avenue advertising agencies, political parties. We are in all good businesses. The profits are good. Everything is clean. We keep trouble down. And now here is Papa, ninety-four years old, and maybe his mind is getting feeble, too—here is Papa saying all right to this silly plan, this *meshugeneh* raid, where people will be hurt and probably killed. Maybe Papa is no longer to be trusted. Is that what Patrick thinks?
PATRICK: I swear to God, Papa, I never. If you say it's okay, it's okay.
PAPA: Little Pat, you will be don soon enough. Soon enough. A year. Two at the most.
PATRICK: Papa, Papa . . . you'll outlive us all.
PAPA: Two years at the most. Probably one. But if you are to be don you must learn to think . . . *think*. Not only must you think should we do this thing, can we profit from this thing, but also, what are the consequences of this thing? What will result from this thing a year, five years, ten

years from now? Most men—even big executives in the best American companies—gather all the facts and make a decision. But they fail to consider the consequences of their decision. The long-term consequences. Do you understand me?

PATRICK: I think so, Papa.

PAPA: Suppose there is a man we must put down. We consider what he has done and what a danger he represents to us. On the basis of these facts, we say he must be put down. But we must also consider the consequences of his death. Does he have relatives who will be embittered? Will the blues get upset? What will the papers say? Is there a young, smart, ambitious politician who will take this man's death and get elected on it? You understand? It is not enough to consider the immediate facts. You must also project your mind and consider the future. In the long run, will it help us or hurt us?

PATRICK: Now I understand, Papa. But what has that to do with Anderson's hustle?

PAPA: Remember about four years ago in Buffalo, we. . . .

[Lapse of four minutes nine seconds.]

PAPA: So what did that teach us? The advantage of fear. We first create and then maintain an atmosphere of fear. Why do you think we have been so successful in our legitimate dealings? In real estate and garbage collection and banks and linen service? Because our rates are lower? Ah, you know our rates are higher. Higher! But they fear us. And because of their fear, we do good business. The steel fist in the velvet glove. But if this is to continue, if our legitimate enterprises are to flourish, we must maintain our reputation. We must let businessmen know who we are, of what we are capable. Not frequently, but occasionally, choosing incidents that we know will not be lost on them, we must let the public know that beneath that soft velvet glove is bright, shining steel. Only then will they fear us, and our legitimate enterprises will continue to grow.

PATRICK: And you want to use Anderson's campaign as an example? You feel it will end in failure, but you want the newspapers to play it up as ours? You want people hurt and people killed? You want businessmen who read about it in the papers to shiver, and then call us and say yes, they'll take another million yards of our rayons or use our trucking firms or our insurance business?

PAPA: Yes. That is exactly what I want.

PATRICK: Is that why you okayed Al Petty's job two years ago when. . . .

[Lapse of forty-seven seconds.]

PAPA: Of course. I knew he could never succeed. But it made headlines all over the country, and the men arrested were linked to us. Three people, one a child, were killed on that job, and our collections took a five point two percent jump in the following six months. Fear. Let others—the English and the Americans—use persuasion and business pressure. We use fear. Because we know it always works.

PATRICK: But Anderson, he's not. . . .

PAPA: I know he is not linked closely with us. So we must put a man in who is. Toast came to visit me yesterday.

PATRICK: Toast? I didn't know he was in town. Why didn't he call me?

PAPA: He asked me to apologize to you. He was between flights. He just had time for a quick trip out here by car, and then on to Palm Beach.

PATRICK: How old was she this time?

PAPA: About fifteen. A real beauty. Long blond hair. And blind.

PATRICK: Blind? That's good—for her sake.

PAPA: Yes. But Toast has a problem. Perhaps we can solve it for him with this Anderson thing.

PATRICK: What is the problem?

PAPA: Toast has a man—Vincent Parelli. You know him? They call him Socks.

PATRICK: That idiot? I've read about him.

PAPA: Yes. Parelli has gone crazy. He fights people. He runs them down in his car. He shoots them. He just doesn't care. He is a very great embarassment to Toast.

PATRICK: I can imagine.

PAPA: Parelli is very closely linked with us, very closely. Toast wants to get him out. You understand?

PATRICK: Yes.

PAPA: But Parelli is not that easy. He has some muscle of his own. They are all crazy . . . crazy. Al Capones. Throwbacks. They cannot think.

Toast asked if there is anything I can do.

PATRICK: So . . . ?

PAPA: I owe a favor to Toast. You remember last year he got Paolo's nephew into the university after the boy had been turned down all over? So here is what we do. . . . I will tell Toast to send Parelli in from Detroit to be our man on the Anderson campaign. Toast will tell Parelli that we have definite evidence of at least a million dollars' worth of jewelry in the house. Otherwise Parelli would laugh at us. Toast will tell him we want a good, trustworthy man of our own on the scene to make sure there is no chance of a cross. This Parelli is gun-happy. He will probably blast. At the same time, you tell Anderson that we approve his plan providing he carries a piece and, at the end of the action, he puts Parelli down. That is our price for financing his hustle.

[Lapse of eleven seconds.]

PATRICK: Papa, I don't think Anderson will go for it.

PAPA: I think he will. I know these amateurs. Always the big chance, the big hit, and then retirement to South America or the French Riviera for the rest of their lives. They think crime is one big lottery. They don't know what hard work it is . . . hard, grinding work, year after year. No big hits, no big chances. But a job—just like any other. Maybe the profits are larger, but so are the risks. Anderson will stall a while, but then he will go for it. He will put Parelli down. Anderson has the blood and the pride to keep a bargain. I believe the whole thing will be a madness, with innocent people hurt and killed, and Vincent Parelli, who is so closely linked with us, found dead at the scene of the crime.

PATRICK: And you think that will help us, Papa?

PAPA: It will be in headlines all over the country and, eventually, it will help us.

PATRICK: What if the campaign comes off?

PAPA: So much the better. Parelli will no longer be a nuisance to Toast, we will get credit for the grab, and we will also profit. And maybe Anderson will end up in Mexico after all. Patrick, phone me every day and tell me how this is coming. I am very interested. Explain to the Doctor only as much as he needs to know. You understand?

PATRICK: Yes, Papa.

PAPA: I will take care of Toast, and Toast will make certain that Parelli is here when needed. Do you have any questions?

PATRICK: No, Papa. I know what must be done.

PAPA: You are a good boy, Patrick . . . a good boy.

[34]

On 12 July, 1968, at 2:06 P.M., a meeting took place between John Anderson and Patrick Angelo in the dispatcher's office of the Jiffy Trucking & Hauling Co., 11098 Tenth Avenue, New York, New York. This company was a subsidiary of the Thomas Jefferson Trading Corp., of which Patrick Angelo was an officer (secretary-treasurer) of record. The premises were under surveillance by the Bureau of Customs, pursuant to Federal Court Order MFC-#189-605HG, on suspicion that they were being used as a drop for smuggled merchandise. The following is tape USBC-1089756738-B2.

ANDERSON: Well?

ANGELO: It looks good. Papa okayed it.

[Lapse of four seconds.]

ANDERSON [sighing]: Jesus.

ANGELO: But you've got to do something for us.

[Lapse of six seconds.]

ANDERSON: What?

ANGELO: We've got to put our own man in. You know, that's SOP—Standard Operating Procedure.

ANDERSON: I know. I figured that. Who?

ANGELO: A man from Detroit. Vincent Parelli. They call him Socks. You know him?

ANDERSON: No.

ANGELO: You heard about him?

ANDERSON: No.

ANGELO: A good man. Experienced. He's no punk. But you'll be the boss. That's understood. He'll be told he takes orders from you.

ANDERSON: All right. That sounds all right. What else?

ANGELO: You got a brain.

ANDERSON: What else do I got to do?

ANGELO: We want you to cut down on him.

[Lapse of five seconds.]

ANDERSON: What?

ANGELO: Put him down. After it's all over. When you're ready to leave. You put him down.

[Lapse of eleven seconds.]

ANGELO: You understand?

ANDERSON: Yes.

ANGELO: You knew you'd have to carry a barker on this job?

ANDERSON: Yes.

ANGELO: So . . . you cut this Parelli down. Just before you take off.

ANDERSON: You want me to kill him.

[Lapse of seven seconds.]

ANGELO: Yes.

ANDERSON: Why?

ANGELO: You don't have to know that. It's got nothing to do with you, nothing to do with this hustle. We want him out—that's all. You get him out. That's our price.

[Lapse of sixteen seconds.]

ANGELO: Well?

ANDERSON: You want me to answer now?

ANGELO: No. Take a day or two. We'll be in touch. If it's no, then no hard feelings and we'll forget the whole thing. If it's yes, the Doctor will get the scratch to you and we'll start the operations plan. We can get you the schedules of the beat fuzz and the sector cars. But it's up to you. It's your decision.

ANDERSON: Yes.

ANGELO: You know exactly what you must do? There's no misunderstanding? I've made it plain? In things like this, it's best to make absolutely certain everyone knows what's going to happen.

ANDERSON: I know what's going to happen.

ANGELO: Good. You think about it.

ANDERSON: All right. I'll think about it.

[35]

In addition to the microphone transmitter implanted at the home of Dominick Angelo, 67825 Flint Road, Deal, New Jersey, a telephone tap had been installed by the Federal Bureau of Narcotics. This portion of tape FBN-DA-10935 is dated 12 July, 1968. The time: 2:48 P.M.

ANGELO: He was shook, Papa . . . really spooked. I think you were right. I think he'll go for it. Now about this thing with Benefici in Hackensack . . . I think we should. . . .

[36]

Tape SEC-13JUL68-IM-4:24PM-149H. This was a Saturday.

INGRID: So . . . how is it you are here at this hour? You are not working?

ANDERSON: No. I'm off this weekend. I get every other weekend off.

INGRID: You should have called first. I might have been busy.

ANDERSON: Are you busy?

INGRID: No. I have been doing some mending. You would like a drink?

ANDERSON: I brought some Berliner Weisse and raspberry syrup.

INGRID: You darling! How wonderful! You remembered!

ANDERSON: You have big glasses?

INGRID: I will serve it in big brandy snifters I have. How wonderful! You remembered!

[Lapse of two minutes eighteen seconds.]

INGRID: Here you are. Such a beautiful color. *Prosit.*

ANDERSON: *Prosit.*

[Lapse of fourteen seconds.]

INGRID: Ah. So good, so good. Tell me, Duke—how are things with you?

ANDERSON: All right.

INGRID: That meet you had, the last time I spoke to you . . . that turned out well?

ANDERSON: Yes . . . sort of.

INGRID: You are troubled, *Schatzie?* That is why you came? You want to get out?

ANDERSON: No. But I got to talk. I don't mean that the way it sounds. I got to talk to *you.* You're the smartest one I know. I want your opinion. Your advice.

INGRID: This is a job?

ANDERSON: Yes.

INGRID: I don't want to know about it.

ANDERSON: Please. I don't say please very often. I'm saying please to you.

[Lapse of thirteen seconds.]

INGRID: You know, Duke, I have a feeling about you. A very bad feeling.

ANDERSON: What is that?

INGRID: I have this feeling that through you I will meet my death. Just by knowing you and talking to you, I will die before my time.

ANDERSON: Does that scare you?

INGRID: No.

ANDERSON: No. Nothing scares you. Does it make you sad?

INGRID: Perhaps.

ANDERSON: Do you want me to leave?

[Lapse of twenty-two seconds.]

INGRID: What do you want to tell me? Why is this thing so important you need my advice?

ANDERSON: I have this hustle planned. It's a good one. If I hit, it means a lot of money. A lot of money. If it works out, I can go to Mexico, South America, Europe—anywhere. And live for the rest of my life. I mean, *live*. I would ask you to come with me. But don't think about that. Don't let that influence what you tell me.

INGRID: I won't, *Schatzie*. I have heard that before.

ANDERSON: I know, I know. But for this hustle I need money, ready money. To pay people and plan things. You understand?

INGRID: Yes. You want money from me?

ANDERSON: No, I don't want any money from you.

INGRID: Then the people you will get money from, the people whose cooperation you need—they want something . . . *nein?*

ANDERSON: You're so goddamned smart it scares me.

INGRID: Think of what my life has been. What do they want?

ANDERSON: I have a staff. Five men I can get. But these money people must put their own man in. Okay. This is understandable. I'm a free-lance. It happens all the time with free-lancers. You get permission to operate but they must put their own man in to make sure there's no cross, so they know definitely what the take is. You understand?

INGRID: Of course. So?

ANDERSON: They want to bring a man in from Detroit. I've never met him. I've never heard of him. They tell me he's a pro. They tell me he will take orders from me. I will be the boss of this campaign.

INGRID: So?

ANDERSON: They want me to cut down on him. This is their price. After the hit is finished, I am to burn this man. They won't tell me why; it isn't my business. But this is their price.

INGRID: Ah. . . .

[Lapse of one minute twelve seconds.]

INGRID: They know you. They know you so well. They know if you agree to this, you will do it. Not from fear of what they might do if you didn't, but because you are John Anderson, and when you say you will do a thing, you will then do it. Am I right?

ANDERSON: I don't know what they think.

INGRID: You ask me for my advice. I am trying to give it to you. If you say yes, you will then kill this man. Tell me, *Schatzie,* if you say no, are you then in trouble?

ANDERSON: Not in trouble . . . no. They won't kill me. Nothing like that. I'm not worth it. But I couldn't free-lance anymore. I couldn't get clearance from them. I could operate, if I wanted to, but it would never be the same again. It would be very bad—penny-ante stuff. I'd have to go back home. I couldn't operate in this town.

INGRID: Home? Where is home?

ANDERSON: South. Kentucky.

INGRID: And what would you do there?

ANDERSON: Open your robe, will you?

INGRID: Yes. Like this . . . ?

ANDERSON: Yes. Just let me look at you while I'm talking. Christ, I've got to talk.

INGRID: Is this better?

ANDERSON: Yes . . . better. I don't know what I'd do. Run some alky. Gas stations maybe. A bank now and then if I could find the right men.

INGRID: That is all you know?

ANDERSON: Yes, goddammit, that's all I know. Do you think I would become a computer operator in Kentucky, or maybe an insurance salesman?

INGRID: Do not be angry with me, *Schatzie*.

ANDERSON: I'm not angry with you. I told you, I just want your advice. I'm all fucked up.

INGRID: You killed a man before.

ANDERSON: Yes. But that was in blood. I had to. You understand? He said things.

INGRID: So now it is part of a job. How is it different?

ANDERSON: Shit. You foreigners. You don't understand.

INGRID: No, I do not.

ANDERSON: This guy I cut kept pecking at me and pecking at me. We had words. Finally I had to put him down or I couldn't have lived with myself. I *had* to. I was forced into it.

INGRID: You Americans—you are so strange. You "put a man down," or you "cut him," or you "burn him," or you "put him away" or "take him for a ride." But you will never say you killed him. Why is that?

ANDERSON: Yes, you're right. It's funny. I don't know why it is. These people who want me to do this thing I told you about, I finally asked the man, "You want me to kill him?" and he finally admitted that was what they wanted. But I could tell from the way he paused and the way he looked that the word "kill" didn't taste sweet to him. When I was driving for a legger down home we had this old smoke working for us—he could turn out a mighty fine mash—and he said everybody's got to go—everybody. He said this is the one thing all men are fearful of most, and they invent all kinds of words so as not to say it. And preachers come along and say you'll be born again, and you grab at the preacher and give him money, though way down deep in your heart you know he's lying. Catholic, Baptist, Methodist, Jew—I don't care what, they all know nobody's going to be born again. When you're dead, man, you're dead. That's it. That's the end. That's what this old black kept telling me, and boy, was he right. That's the one thing in all of us—you, me, and everyone else in this world—and we're scared of dying, or even thinking about it. Look at you there, almost bare-ass naked with your cousy hanging out, and you think that's going to last forever? Baby, we're all getting out. Finally. We're all getting out. Why do you think I keep coming back to you and grabbing at you to get me out? Because you always get me out for a short time, and I always know I'm coming back. And somehow, and don't ask me how because I can't explain it or understand it, you get me out for a little while and then I come back, and it makes the big getting-out easier to take. The last getting-out. Like I might come back from that, too. I don't know. I can't figure it all—but that's what I think. I want to get out so I can forget the shit I have to eat every day, but also I want to get out like it's practice for what's coming. You know? And this poor, fat, rich East Side bitch I slap around, that's what she's looking for, too. Sure, maybe it's a kick and makes us forget how much crap we wade through every day, but maybe it convinces us that every little time we die—well, then, the big time is no different, and we'll come back from that, too. Which is a laugh. Isn't that a laugh, baby?

INGRID: Yes. That is a laugh.

ANDERSON: I didn't really come here for your advice. I came to tell you what I'm going to do. I'm going to kill this Parelli guy. I don't know who he is or what he is or how bad he needs killing. But whether I do it or a bolt of lightning strikes him tomorrow or twenty years from now, it's going to be done. But I'm going to kill him because maybe I can get a few clean years out of all this. And right now I'm so charged with blood and you sitting there with all your woman hanging out and staring at me, and I can taste the moment when I put that guy down, and what I'm going to do right now is get you out . . . maybe for the first time in your life.

INGRID: And how are you going to do that?

ANDERSON: I'll do it. I don't know how, but I'll do it. You've got all this crazy stuff around for your customers, haven't you? We'll do it with that if we have to. But we'll do it. I'm going to get you out, Ingrid. I swear it. . . .

INGRID: Yes?

[37]

Xerox copy of a teletype dated 6 June, 1968.

TT-68-7946 . . . FR NYPD-PC . . . TO ALL DEP, INS, BOR AND PRNCT CMDRS, CPTS, LTS, SGTS . . . FOR POSTING . . . REPEAT, FOR POSTING . . . AS OF THIS DATE, NEW PCC (POLICE COMMUNICATIONS CENTER) IS IN FULL OPER . . . EMRGNCY NMBR 911 . . . KILL 440-1234 . . . ALL CMPLNTS TO 911 WILL BE FRWRD TO PRNCT VIA TT OR TE . . . CMD OF CARS WITH PCC . . . CNFRM . . . PC . . .

[38]

This is tape recording NYSITB-FD-15JUL68-437-6G; 15 July, 1968; 12:45 P.M.

SIMONS: Hello, Duke. Close that door quick. Let's not give any of this air conditioning a chance to escape. Good to see you again.

ANDERSON: Hello, Mr. Simons. How you been?

SIMONS: Getting by, Duke, getting by. Can I offer you something?

ANDERSON: Not right now, Mr. Simons.

SIMONS: Well . . . you don't mind if I go ahead, do you? I have a luncheon appointment in about half an hour, and I always find that a martini sharpens the appetite.

ANDERSON: You go right ahead.

SIMONS: Well, now, Duke, what have you decided?

ANDERSON: Yes. It's all right.

SIMONS: You understand completely what you must do in regards to this person from Detroit?

ANDERSON: Yes. I understand.

SIMONS: Excellent. Now then . . . let's get down to the fine print. This person from Detroit will be our responsibility. That is, any payment to him or to his heirs is our responsibility and is not part of any of the financial arrangements which, I trust, you and I will soon agree upon. Is that clear?

ANDERSON: Yes.

SIMONS: All expenses and advances will come off the top. In that connection, if these terms are agreeable to you, I have with me and am authorized to turn over to you the two thousand additional expense funds you requested. Upon approval of the operational plan, we will then turn over to you a sum sufficient for half payment of fees of the men involved which, I understand, you estimated as four to five thousand dollars. Is that correct?

ANDERSON: Yes. That's right. That's half their take.

SIMONS: Now then . . . when the final cash income is determined, all these sums—advances, expenses, and salaries—will come off the top. Clear?

ANDERSON: That includes the final payment to my staff—the other half, about four or five thousand to close them out?

SIMONS: That's correct. All such expenses will be subtracted first. We anticipate no additional expenses other than those you have outlined. In any event, we feel they will be so minor that they need not concern us at this time. Now then. . . we are down to the net income. We propose a fifty-fifty split.

ANDERSON: I asked for seventy-thirty.

SIMONS: I know you did, Duke. But under the circumstances, and considering the take may be considerably less than your most optimistic estimate, we feel a fifty-fifty split is justified. Especially in view of the moneys we have so far advanced.

ANDERSON: It's not right. Not when you figure what I'm going to do for you. I won't go for it.

SIMONS: Duke, we could sit here and argue for hours, but I know you don't want that any more than I do. I was instructed to offer you the fifty-fifty deal because we feel that is a fair and equitable arrangement, considering the risks involved and the cash outlay up to this point. Quite frankly, I must admit that Mr. Angelo—Little Pat, that is—he did not feel you would be satisfied with this. Therefore, I am authorized to propose a sixty-forty division. And that, Duke, I can tell you in all honesty is the best I can do. If that is not satisfactory, then you'll have to take up the entire matter with Mr. D'Medico or Mr. Angelo.

[Lapse of eighteen seconds.]

ANDERSON: Sixty for me, forty for you?

SIMONS: That is correct.

ANDERSON: And for this I put my cock on the line for a murder-one rap?

SIMONS: Duke, Duke . . . I wouldn't attempt to advise you, my boy. It's your decision to make, and you know the factors involved in it much better than I. All I can do is offer you the sixty-forty split. That's my job, and I'm doing it. Please don't be angry with me.

ANDERSON: I'm not angry with you, Mr. Simons. Or with Mr. D'Medico or Mr. Angelo. You got your job to do and I got mine. And I suppose you all got to answer to someone else.

SIMONS: We do indeed, Duke, we do indeed.

[Lapse of four seconds.]

ANDERSON: All right. I'll buy the sixty-forty.

SIMONS: Excellent. I'm sure you won't regret it. Here's the two thousand. Small bills. All clean. We'll make arrangements for Parelli to come in from Detroit. You'll be informed when he's available for planning. We think your idea of a hit on the Labor Day weekend is a good one. Meanwhile we'll see what we can do about getting you schedules of the two fifty-first Precinct and the Sector George cars. When you have your campaign firmed up, get in touch with me and I'll set up a meet for you with Mr. Angelo. I suggest you do this before you make a firm commitment to your staff. You understand? No use bringing them in until the whole thing is laid out. You agree?

ANDERSON: Yes.

SIMONS: Is everything clear now? I mean about money, and personnel, or anything else? If you have any questions, now is the time to ask them.

[Lapse of six seconds.]

ANDERSON: This Parelli—what did he do?

SIMONS: I don't know and I don't want to know. I suggest you cultivate the same attitude. Would you like something now?

ANDERSON: Yes. All right. A brandy.

SIMONS: Excellent, excellent. . . .

[39]

Xerox copy of a letter dated 16 July, 1968, from United Electronics Kits, Inc., 65378 Michigan Boulevard, Chicago, Illinois, addressed to Mr. Gerald Bingham, Jr., Apartment 5A, 535 East Seventy-third Street, New York, New York.

DEAR MR. BINGHAM:

In reply to your letter of the 5th inst., please be advised that we have found your suggestion of considerable merit. Accordingly, we are modifying our Amplifier Kit 57-68A so that the back plate is easily removed (via screws) rather than soldered as at present. We are sure, as you suggest, that this will aid construction and servicing of the completed unit.

We wish to express our appreciation for your interest, and we are, frankly, somewhat chagrined that our engineers did not spot this drawback to the 57-68A kit prior to its distribution. The fact that you are, as you say, fifteen years old, makes our chagrin more understandable!

In any event, to express our appreciation for your suggestion in a more tangible form, we are forwarding to you (this date) a complimentary gift of our Deluxe 32-16895 Three-Speed Stereo Tape Deck Kit (no charge).

Again—thank you for your kind interest in our products.

Sincerely,
[signed] DAVID K. DAVIDSON,
Director, Public Relations

[40]

Tape recording FBN-DA-11036. Tuesday, 16 July, 1968, 2:36 P.M.

OPERATOR: I have a person-to-person call, Detroit. From Mr. Dominick Angelo of Deal, New Jersey, to Mr. Nicola D'Agostino at three-one-one, one-five-eight, eight-nine-seven-three.

OPERATOR: Just a moment, Operator.

OPERATOR: Thank you.

[Lapse of fourteen seconds.]

OPERATOR: Is this three-one-one, one-five-eight, eight-nine-seven-three?

MALE VOICE: Yes.

OPERATOR: I have a person-to-person call for a Mr. Nicola D'Agostino from Mr. Dominick Angelo of Deal, New Jersey. Is Mr. D'Agostino there?

MALE VOICE: Just a minute, Operator.

OPERATOR: Thank you. Are you there, New Jersey?

OPERATOR: Yes, dear.

OPERATOR: Thank you. They're trying to find Mr. D'Agostino.

[Lapse of eleven seconds.]

D'AGOSTINO: Hello?

OPERATOR: Mr. Nicola D'Agostino?

D'AGOSTINO: Yes.

OPERATOR: Just a moment, please, sir. Deal, New Jersey, calling. Go ahead, New Jersey. Mr. D'Agostino is on the line.

OPERATOR: Thank you, dear. Go ahead, Mr. Angelo. Mr. D'Agostino is on the line.

ANGELO: Hello? Hello, Toast?

D'AGOSTINO: Papa—is that you? How *nice* to hear your voice! How are you, Papa?

ANGELO: Getting along. Getting along. And how was Florida?

D'AGOSTINO: Magnificent, Papa. Gorgeous. You should move there. You'd live another hundred years.

ANGELO: God forbid. And the family?

D'AGOSTINO: Couldn't be better, Papa. Angelica asked about you. I told her you'd outlive us all.

ANGELO: And the children?

D'AGOSTINO: Fine, Papa, fine. Everyone is fine. Tony fell off his bike yesterday and broke his tooth—but it's nothing.

ANGELO: My God. You need a good dentist? I'll fly him out.

D'AGOSTINO: No, no, Papa. It's a baby tooth. We

got a good dentist. He said it's nothing. Don't worry yourself.

ANGELO: Good. You have any trouble, you let me know.

D'AGOSTINO: I will, Papa, I will. Thank you for your interest. Believe me, Angelica and I, we appreciate it.

ANGELO: Toast, you remember when you were here, we discussed your problem?

D'AGOSTINO: Yes, Papa, I remember.

ANGELO: This problem, Toast—I think we can help you with it. I think we can solve it.

D'AGOSTINO: Believe me, I would appreciate that, Papa.

ANGELO: It would be a permanent solution. You understand, Toast?

D'AGOSTINO: I understand, Papa.

ANGELO: That is what you want?

D'AGOSTINO: That is what I want.

ANGELO: Good. It will work out well. You will send him to me as soon as possible. Within a week. Is that possible, Toast?

D'AGOSTINO: Of course.

ANGELO: Tell him only that it is a big job. You understand?

D'AGOSTINO: I understand, Papa. You will have him by Friday.

ANGELO: Good. Please give my love to Angelica. And to Auntie and Nick. And tell Tony I will send him a new bicycle. This one won't throw him off and break his tooth.

D'AGOSTINO [laughing]: Papa, you're too much! I love you. We all love you.

ANGELO: You keep well.

D'AGOSTINO: You too, Papa. You keep well—forever.

[41]

Transcription of tape recording POM-20JUL68-EVERLEIGH. This recording began at 1:14 P.M., 20 July, 1968, and ended at 2:06 P.M., 21 July. It was recorded at Apartment 3B, 535 East Seventy-third Street. This tape has been heavily edited to eliminate extraneous conversations, names of innocent persons, and repetition of information already obtained from other sources. During the more than twenty-four-hour period mentioned above, it is not believed that Mrs. Agnes Everleigh and John Anderson left Apartment 3B.

SEGMENT I. 20JUL-1:48PM.

ANDERSON: . . . can't. I had last weekend off.

MRS. EVERLEIGH: You can call in sick, can't you? It's not the whole weekend. It's just tonight. You can be back at work tomorrow night. You get sick leave, don't you?

ANDERSON: Yes. Ten days a year.

MRS. EVERLEIGH: Have you taken any?

ANDERSON: No. Not since I been working there.

MRS. EVERLEIGH: So take tonight off. I'll give you fifty dollars.

ANDERSON: All right.

MRS. EVERLEIGH: You'll take the fifty?

ANDERSON: Yes.

MRS. EVERLEIGH: This is the first time you've ever taken money from me.

ANDERSON: How does it make you feel?

MRS. EVERLEIGH: You know . . . don't you?

ANDERSON: Yes. Go get the fifty. I'll make a call and tell them I'm sick.

MRS. EVERLEIGH: You'll stay with me? All night?

ANDERSON: Sure.

SEGMENT II. 20JUL-2:13PM.

MRS. EVERLEIGH: I love you when you're like this—relaxed and nice and good to me.

ANDERSON: Am I good to you?

MRS. EVERLEIGH: So far. So far you've been a perfect gentleman.

ANDERSON: Like this?

MRS. EVERLEIGH: Must you? Must you do that?

ANDERSON: Sure. If I want to earn my fifty bucks.

MRS. EVERLEIGH: You're such a bastard.

ANDERSON: Honest. I'm honest.

SEGMENT III. 20JUL-5:26PM.

MRS. EVERLEIGH: . . . at least forty percent. How do you like that?

ANDERSON: Can they do it?

MRS. EVERLEIGH: You idiot, of course they can do it.

This apartment is a cooperative. I'm not on the board. After my husband moved out, our lawyers got together and I agreed to pay the maintenance and he agreed to keep paying the mortgage. The apartment is in his name. Now they're going to increase the maintenance by at least forty percent.

ANDERSON: What are you going to do?

MRS. EVERLEIGH: I haven't decided yet. I'd move out tomorrow if I could find something better. But go look for an apartment on the East Side of Manhattan. These new places charge one hundred and eighty-five dollars for one room. I'll probably give them what they want and stay right here. Roll over.

ANDERSON: I've had enough.

MRS. EVERLEIGH: No you haven't.

SEGMENT IV. 20JUL-6:32PM.

MRS. EVERLEIGH: It depends on what you want. Feraccis has barbecued chickens or short ribs—stuff like that. It's a kind of a delicatessen. If we're going to cook, we can order up from Ernesto Brothers. We can get frozen TV dinners or Rock Cornish hens or we can get a steak and pan-fry it or broil it—whatever you want.

ANDERSON: Let's have a chicken—a big chicken. Three pounds if they've got a fryer-broiler that size. We'll fry it. And maybe some French-fried potatoes and greens.

MRS. EVERLEIGH: What kind of greens?

ANDERSON: Collards? They got collards?

MRS. EVERLEIGH: What are collards?

ANDERSON: Forget it. Just get us a big chicken we can fry and a lot of cold beer. How does that sound?

MRS. EVERLEIGH: That sounds scrumptious.

ANDERSON: Order it up. I'll pay for it. Here's fifty.

MRS. EVERLEIGH: You sonofabitch.

SEGMENT V. 20JUL-9:14PM.

ANDERSON: What are you going to do in Rome?

MRS. EVERLEIGH: The usual . . . see the new fall collections . . . visit some fag boutiques . . . buy some stuff . . . it's a drag.

ANDERSON: Like I said, I wish I could travel. All you need is money. Like this apartment house. You're going to Rome. Your neighbors are going down to the Jersey shore. I bet everyone in the house will be going somewhere on the Labor Day weekend—Rome, Jersey, Florida, France . . . somewhere. . . .

MRS. EVERLEIGH: Oh, sure. The Sheldons—they're up in Four A—they're already out in their place on Montauk. The people below me, a lawyer and his wife, will be out in East Hampton. Up on top in Five B, Longene and that bitch who's living with him—they're not married, you know—are sure to be invited some place for the Labor Day weekend. So the house will probably be about half full. That fag in Two A will probably be gone, too. What are you going to do?

ANDERSON: Work, probably. I get triple-time when I work nights on a holiday. I can make a lot of loot if I work over the Labor Day weekend.

MRS. EVERLEIGH: Will you think of me?

ANDERSON: Sure. There's one drumstick left. You want it?

MRS. EVERLEIGH: No, darling. You finish it.

ANDERSON: All right. I like drumsticks and wings and the Pope's nose. More than I do the breast. Dark meat got more flavor.

MRS. EVERLEIGH: Don't you like white meat at all?

ANDERSON: Maybe. Later.

SEGMENT VI. 21JUL-6:14AM.

ANDERSON [groaning]: Mammy . . . Mammy. . . .

MRS. EVERLEIGH: Duke? Duke? What is it, Duke?

ANDERSON: Mammy?

MRS. EVERLEIGH: Hush . . . hush. You're having a nightmare. I'm here, Duke.

ANDERSON: Mammy . . . Mammy. . . .

SEGMENT VII. 21JUL-8:56AM.

ANDERSON: Shit. You got a cigarette?

MRS. EVERLEIGH: There.

ANDERSON: Filters? Christ. These places around here—they're open on Sundays?

MRS. EVERLEIGH: Ernesto's is. What do you want?

ANDERSON: Cigarettes—to begin with. You mean this place is open on Sundays?

MRS. EVERLEIGH: Sure.

ANDERSON: Holidays too?

MRS. EVERLEIGH: They're open every day in the year, twenty-four hours a day. That's their brag. They have a sign in the window that says so. If you're pregnant, you can get a dill pickle at three in the morning from Ernesto's. That's how they stay in business. They can't compete with the big supermarkets on First Avenue, like Lambreta Brothers. So they stay open every minute of the day and night.

ANDERSON: My God, don't they get held up?

MRS. EVERLEIGH: They sure do . . . about two or three times a month. But they keep open. It must pay off. Besides, doesn't insurance pay when you get robbed?

ANDERSON: I guess so. I don't know much about those things.

MRS. EVERLEIGH: Well, I'll call and have them deliver some cigarettes. It's about nine now. When do you have to go?

ANDERSON: Around two o'clock. Something like that.

MRS. EVERLEIGH: Well, suppose I order up some food for a little breakfast and some food for a dinner about noon. Like a steak and baked potatoes. How does that sound?

ANDERSON: That sounds all right.

MRS. EVERLEIGH: You're the most bubbling, enthusiastic man I've ever met.

ANDERSON: I don't understand that.

MRS. EVERLEIGH: Forget it.

[42]

The following is labeled SEGMENT 101-B of document NYDA-EHM-101A-108B, a dictated, sworn, signed, and witnessed statement by Ernest Heinrich Mann.

MANN: So . . . we are now up to twenty-sixth July. I remember it was on a Friday. On this date the man I know as John Anderson came to my shop and. . . .

QUESTION: What time was this?

MANN: It was perhaps one o'clock. Definitely after lunch. He came to my shop and asked to speak with me. So we went into the back room. There is a door there I can close and lock; we would not be disturbed. At this time, Anderson asked if I would be available for a job he had in mind.

QUESTION: What kind of a job?

MANN: He was most evasive. Very vague. Deliberately so, you understand. But I knew that it was to be in the apartment house I had already investigated for him. When I learned that, I asked him if he had determined the purpose of the cold room I had discovered in the basement of the house.

QUESTION: What did he say?

MANN: He said yes, he had discovered the purpose of the cold room.

QUESTION: Did he tell you what it was used for?

MANN: At this time, no. Later he told me. But at this meeting on July twenty-sixth he did not tell me and I did not ask further.

QUESTION: What kind of a job did John Anderson ask you to do for him?

MANN: Well . . . he did not actually ask me to do it. At this date he merely wanted to know if I was interested, if I would be available. He said the job would consist of cutting all telephone and alarm connections of the entire apartment house.

QUESTION: What else?

MANN: Well . . . of cutting the power supply to the self-service elevator.

QUESTION: What else?

MANN: Well . . . uh. . . .

QUESTION: Mr. Mann, you promised us complete cooperation. On the basis of that promise we agreed to offer you what assistance we could under the law. You understand, of course, we cannot offer you complete immunity?

MANN: Yes. I understand. Of course.

QUESTION: A great deal depends upon your attitude. What else did John Anderson ask you to do at this meeting on July twenty-six?

MANN: Well, as I told you, he did not actually ask. He was outlining a hypothetical situation, you understand. He was feeling me out, I believe you say. Determining my interest in an assignment.

QUESTION: Yes, yes, you've already said that. The assignment would include cutting all telephone and alarm connections of the apartment house in question, and perhaps cutting the power supply to the self-service elevator.

MANN: Yes. That is correct.

QUESTION: All right, Mr. Mann. You have now admitted to destruction of private property, a relatively minor offense. And perhaps breaking and entering. . . .

MANN: Oh, no! No, no, no! Not breaking and entering. The premises were to be quite open when I arrived. I was to have nothing to do with that.

QUESTION: I see. And how much money were you offered for cutting the telephone and alarm connections, and for cutting the elevator power supply?

MANN: Well . . . we came to no definite agreement. You must realize we were talking generalities. There was no definite job, no definite assignment. This man Anderson merely wished to discover if I was interested and what my charge would be.

QUESTION: And what did you tell him your charge would be?

MANN: I suggested five thousand dollars.

QUESTION: Five thousand dollars? Mr. Mann, isn't that a rather large sum for cutting a few wires?

MANN: Well . . . perhaps . . . yes. . . .

QUESTION: All right. We've got as much time as you have. We'll try again. What else were you asked to do on this hypothetical assignment?

MANN: Well, you understand it was very indefinite. No arrangement was made.

QUESTION: Yes, yes, we understand that. What else did Anderson want you to do?

MANN: Well, there were, perhaps, some doors that would require unlocking. Also, perhaps, an upright safe and perhaps a wall safe. He wanted a technically trained man who understood those things.

QUESTION: Of course, Mr. Mann. And you understood those things?

MANN: But naturally! I am a graduate of the Stuttgarter Technische Hochschule, and served as assistant professor in mechanical and electrical engineering at the Zurich Académie du Mécanique. I assure you, I am quite competent in my fields.

QUESTION: We are quite aware of that, sir. Now let's see if we've got all this straight. On July twenty-six, at about one P.M., John Anderson came to your shop at one-nine-seven-five Avenue D, New York City, and asked if you would be available for a job that might or might not materialize. This job would consist, on your part, of cutting telephone and alarm systems in a certain apartment house—location unspecified —of cutting the power supply to the self-service elevator in that house, of forcing open doors or picking the locks of doors in that house, and of opening safes of various types in the apartments of that house. Is that correct?

MANN: Well, I. . . .

QUESTION: Is that correct?

MANN: Please, may I have a glass of water?

QUESTION: Certainly. Help yourself.

MANN: Thank you. My throat is quite dry. I smoke so much. You have a cigarette perhaps?

QUESTION: Here.

MANN: Thank you again.

QUESTION: The statement I just repeated to you—is that correct?

MANN: Yes. That is correct. That is what John Anderson wanted me to do.

QUESTION: And for this you requested five thousand dollars?

MANN: Yes.

QUESTION: What was Anderson's reaction?

MANN: He said he could not pay that much, that his operating budget would not allow it. But he said, if the campaign was finalized, he was sure that he and I could get together in a mutually profitable agreement.

QUESTION: You used the term "if the campaign was finalized." Let me get this straight. Your impression is that on this date, the twenty-sixth of July, it had not yet been decided whether or not this job was actually on?

MANN: Yes, that was and is my impression.

QUESTION: Thank you. I think that's enough for today, Mr. Mann. I appreciate your cooperation.

MANN: I appreciate your kindness, sir.

QUESTION: We have much more to discuss about this affair. I'll be seeing you again, Mr. Mann.

MANN: I am at your service, sir.
QUESTION: Fine. Guard!

[43]

Xerox copy of a letter dated 29 July, 1968, from the Public Information Officer, Department of Research & Development, National Office of Space Studies, Washington, D.C. 20036, addressed to Mr. Gerald Bingham, Jr., Apartment 5A, 535 East Seventy-third Street, New York, New York.

DEAR SIR:

Re your letter of 16 May 1968, I have been instructed by the Director of the Department of Research & Development, National Office of Space Studies, to thank you for your interest in our activities, and for your suggestion of the use of solidified carbon dioxide ("dry ice") as an ablative material on the nose cones of rockets, space probes, and manned space vehicles during reentry into the Earth's atmosphere.

As you doubtlessly know, Mr. Bingham, a great deal of expensive research has been conducted in this area, and a wide variety of materials has been tested, ranging from metals and metal alloys to ceramics and ceramic-metal alloys. The material currently in use has been tested successfully in our Mercury, Gemini and Apollo programs.

I have been instructed to inform you that "dry ice" could not withstand the extremely high temperatures encountered during the reentry of heavy rockets and manned space vehicles.

However, your letter revealed a very high level of sophisticated scientific expertise, and the fact that you are, as you say, fifteen years old, is of great interest to us. As you probably know, the National Office of Space Studies has a number of college and university scholarship awards at its disposal. Within the next six months, a representative of our Scholarship Award Department will call upon you personally to determine your interest in this area.

Meanwhile, we wish to thank you again for your interest in our activities and your country's space program.

Cordially,
[signed] CYRUS ABERNATHY,
PIO, R&D

[44]

The following tape recording was made on 13 August, 1968, beginning at 8:42 P.M. The participants, Patrick Angelo and John Anderson, have been identified by voice prints. The meeting was held in the upstairs study of Angelo's home at 10543 Foxberry Lane, a few miles north of Teaneck, New Jersey.

These premises were under electronic surveillance by the Federal Trade Commission, and had been for several months, in a continuing investigation of the interlocking business holdings of Patrick Angelo. The investigation concerned possible violations of the Sherman Anti-Trust Act.

There were several time gaps during the course of this recording, which technicians were unable to explain. The tape recording mechanism checked out; the experts were inclined to believe the fault lay with the SC-7, Mk. II M-T, a relatively new device that may possibly have been affected by atmospheric conditions. It had rained heavily prior to the meeting recorded below, and during the meeting the skies were overcast and humidity was very high.

This is recording FTC-KLL-13AUG68-1701.

ANGELO: . . . like cognac?

ANDERSON: Yes. That's all I drink—brandy.

ANGELO: Then you're going to like this. It's a small importer, maybe a thousand cases a year. I must buy two hundred of them. I drink a lot of the stuff and I give it for gifts. A guy in Teaneck orders if for me. Close to twenty a bottle. There you are. Want a wash?

ANDERSON: No. This is fine.

[Lapse of four seconds.]

ANDERSON: Jesus, that's good. I don't know whether to drink it or breathe it. That's really good.

ANGELO: Glad you like it. And no head in the morning. I keep Papa supplied. He drinks maybe a bottle a month. A thimbleful before he goes to sleep.

ANDERSON: Better than pills.

ANGELO: That's for sure. You met Parelli?

ANDERSON: Yes.

ANGELO: What do you think of him?

ANDERSON: I hardly talked to him. I hardly *saw* him. We were in the steam room of that health club the Doc's got on West Forty-eighth Street.

ANGELO: I know, I know. What do you think of him?

ANDERSON: Heavy muscle. A mutt.

ANGELO: A mutt? Yeah, he's that all right. Not too much brains.

ANDERSON: I figured that.

ANGELO: Look, Duke, you're doing us a favor. So I'll do you one. The guy's crazy. Know what I mean? He likes to blast, to hurt people. He packs one of these big army automatics. What does it weigh—about ten pounds?

ANDERSON: Not that much. But it's heavy.

ANGELO: Yes, and big and mean. He loves it. You've met guys like that before. It's their cock.

ANDERSON: Yes.

ANGELO: Well, don't turn your back on him . . . you know?

ANDERSON: I know. Thanks.

ANGELO: All right . . . now what have you got for me?

ANDERSON: I got this report here. Handwritten. Just this one copy. It's how we should do it. I'm not saying it's final, but we got to start someplace. This includes what I learned since I saw you last. I've had my guys working. I know there will be changes—you'll probably want to change things—and we'll be changing things right up to the last minute . . . you know, little adjustments like. But I think the main plan is strong.

ANGELO: Did the Doctor get those police schedules to you?

ANDERSON: Yes, he did. Thanks. I had the Brodsky boys checking out the beat fuzz on my own. Everything cleared. It's all worked into this report. You want to read it now, or you want me to leave it and come back in a day or so?

ANGELO: I'll read it now. Time's getting short. We got less than three weeks.

ANDERSON: Yes.

ANGELO: Help yourself to the cognac while I read this thing. You write a nice, clear, plain hand.

ANDERSON: Thanks. Maybe my spelling ain't so great. . . .

ANGELO: It's all right. No problem. . . .

[Lapse of seven minutes twenty-three seconds, followed by sound of door opening.]

MRS. ANGELO: Pat? Oh, I'm sorry; you're busy.

ANGELO: That's all right, Maria . . . Come in, come in. Darling, this is John Anderson, a business associate. Duke, this is my wife.

MRS. ANGELO: How do you do, Mr. Anderson.

ANDERSON: Pleased to make your acquaintance, ma'am.

MRS. ANGELO: Is my husband taking care of you? I see you have a little drink. Would you like something to eat? Are you hungry? We have some cold chicken. Perhaps a sandwich?

ANDERSON: Oh, no thank you, ma'am. I'm fine.

MRS. ANGELO: Some short cookies. We have some delicious butter cookies.

ANDERSON: Ma'am, thank you kindly, I do appreciate it, but I'll just stick with this drink.

MRS. ANGELO: Pat, Stella is in bed. You want to say good night?

ANGELO: Of course. Duke, excuse me a moment, please.

ANDERSON: Sure, Mr. Angelo.

ANGELO: And when I come back, I'm bringing some of those butter cookies. My wife makes them herself. You couldn't buy them.

[Lapse of four minutes thirteen seconds.]

ANGELO: Here . . . help yourself. They're delicious. Look at the gut I got, you'll realize how many I eat.

ANDERSON: Thanks.

ANGELO: Now let's see . . . where was I. . . . Yeah, here we are. Duke, you got nice manners. I appreciate that. Now let's see. . . .

[Lapse of six minutes eighteen seconds.]

ANGELO: Duke, I got to hand it to you. Generally, I think . . . my God, no more cognac? Well, let's get rid of this dead soldier. Then we'll go over your operational plan step by step and. . . .

[Lapse of eighteen minutes nine seconds.]

ANGELO: . . . we are. Just take a sniff of that bottle.

ANDERSON: Great.

ANGELO: You're ready for another? I can see you are. So all we got is a lot of little disagreements and small details that really don't amount to much. Am I right?

ANDERSON: As long as you okay the main plan.

ANGELO: Sure. It's strong. Like I said, we can help you out with the truck. That's no problem. About the diversions—you may be right. They got these tactical squads of buttons these days—they load them into buses and before you know it, *bam!* Maybe we'd be asking for trouble. Let me talk to Papa about it.

ANDERSON: But otherwise it sounds good?

ANGELO: Yes, it sounds good. I like the idea of half the people being away on that weekend. How many on your staff?

ANDERSON: Five. With me, six. With Parelli, seven.

ANGELO: My God, you'll have them outnumbered!

ANDERSON: Just about.

ANGELO: Well, go ahead. Contact Fred Simons tomorrow and arrange to get the first half of the emolument for your personnel.

ANDERSON: Emolument?

ANGELO: It means fees or salary.

ANDERSON: Oh . . . yeah.

ANGELO: So now you can have your first real recruiting meeting. Right? You can bring them all together and get down to business. Right? This has got to include Parelli. You know how to get in touch with him?

ANDERSON: Through Simons or the Doctor. Not directly.

ANGELO: That's right. Fred will keep you in touch with him. I would also like to talk to you about once a week, at least, until D-Day. Out here. Is that a problem?

ANDERSON: I rented a car. I shouldn't be leaving the state, but I don't figure the risk is too much.

ANGELO: I agree. All right. You get the money from Simons. At the same time you contact Parelli through him and set up a meet with your other people. I'll start working on the truck. I'll talk to Papa about the diversions. You get that map to me—the one the Brodsky boys made. Come on . . . let's get rolling on this thing!

ANDERSON: Yes. We're coming down to the line. . . .

ANGELO: Jesus Christ, I'm really getting excited! Duke, I think you can pull it off.

ANDERSON: Mr. Angelo, I've been living with this thing for four months now, and I just can't see what could go wrong.

[45]

Tape SEC-16AUG68-IM-11:43AM-198C. New York City. This is a telephone interception.

ANDERSON: Hello? Ingrid?

INGRID: Yes. Duke? Is that you?

ANDERSON: Can I talk?

INGRID: Of course.

ANDERSON: I got your card.

INGRID: It was a silly idea. A little-girl idea. You will laugh at me.

ANDERSON: What is it?

INGRID: Tomorrow, Saturday, do you work?

ANDERSON: Yes.

INGRID: You must be there by four o'clock you said?

ANDERSON: About.

INGRID: I would like . . . what I would like. . . . You will laugh at me, Duke.

ANDERSON: For Jesus' sake, will you tell me what it is?

INGRID: I would like us to go on a picnic.

ANDERSON: A *picnic?*

INGRID: Yes. Tomorrow. In Central Park. If the weather is nice. The radio states the weather will be nice. I will bring some cold fried chicken, potato salad, tomatoes, peaches, grapes—things like that. You will bring a bottle of wine for me and perhaps a bottle of brandy for yourself, if you so desire. Duke? What do you think?

[Lapse of five seconds.]

INGRID: Duke?

ANDERSON: That's fine. A good idea. Let's do it. I'll bring the stuff to drink. When should I pick you up—about eleven?

INGRID: Excellent. Yes, about eleven. Then we can

stay in the park and have our lunch until you must leave. You know a good place?

ANDERSON: Yes. There's a little spit of land that sticks out into the lake at Seventy-second Street. Not too crowded but easy to get to. It's really a turn-around for cars, but the grass slopes down to the lake. It's nice.

INGRID: Good. Duke, if you bring a bottle of wine for me, I would like something chilled.

ANDERSON: All right.

INGRID: And please, do not forget the corkscrew.

ANDERSON: And please, do not forget the salt.

INGRID [laughing]: Duke, it will be fun for us. I have not been on a picnic in many years.

ANDERSON: Yes. I'll see you tomorrow at eleven.

[46]

Acting on internal evidence contained in the preceding recording, the SEC requested the cooperation of the New York Parks, Recreation and Cultural Affairs Administration. With the help of this agency, a Borkgunst Telemike Mk. IV (a telescopic microphone) was concealed in wooded high ground overlooking the site of the proposed picnic of John Anderson and Ingrid Macht on 17 August, 1968.

The following recording is SEC-17AUG68-#146-37A. It has been heavily edited to eliminate extraneous material and evidence currently under adjudication.

SEGMENT I. 17AUG-11:37AM.

ANDERSON: This was a great idea. Beautiful day. Clear for a change. Not too hot. Look at that sky! Looks like someone washed it and hung it out to dry.

INGRID: I remember a day like this. I was just a little girl. Eight, perhaps, or nine. An uncle took me on a picnic. My father was dead. My mother was working. So this uncle offered to take me to the country for the day. A Saturday, just like this. Sunshine. Blue sky. Cool breeze. Sweet smells. He gave me some schnapps, and then he pulled my pants down.

ANDERSON: Some uncle.

INGRID: He was all right. A widower. In his late forties. Perhaps fifty. He had a great Kaiser Wilhelm mustache. I remember it tickled.

ANDERSON: Did you like it?

INGRID: It meant nothing to me. Nothing.

ANDERSON: Did he give you something, a gift, so you wouldn't talk?

INGRID: Money. He gave me money.

ANDERSON: Was that his idea or yours?

INGRID: That was my idea. My mother and I, we were always hungry.

ANDERSON: Smart kid.

INGRID: Yes. I was a smart kid.

ANDERSON: How long did that go on?

INGRID: A few years. I took him for much.

ANDERSON: Sure. Did your mother know?

INGRID: Perhaps. Perhaps not. I think she did.

ANDERSON: What happened?

INGRID: To my uncle?

ANDERSON: Yes.

INGRID: A horse kicked him and he died.

ANDERSON: That's funny.

INGRID: Yes. But it made no difference. I was then ten, perhaps eleven. I knew then how it was done. There were others. *Schatzie,* the wine! It will be getting warm.

SEGMENT II. 17AUG-12:02PM.

ANDERSON: What then?

INGRID: You will not believe.

ANDERSON: I'll believe it.

INGRID: For an example, there was this man in Bavaria. Very rich. Very important. If I said his name, you would recognize it. Once a month, on a Friday night, his butler would assemble perhaps six, perhaps ten young girls. I was just thirteen. We would be naked. The butler would put feathers in our hair and tie belts of feathers about our waists and make us wear bracelets of feathers around our wrists and ankles. Then this man, this very important man, would sit on a chair, quite naked, and he would play with himself. You understand? And we would dance around him in a circle. We would flap our arms and caw and make bird sounds. Like chickens. You understand? And this funny butler with gray whiskers would clap his hands to mark time and chant, "One and two, and one and two," and we would dance around and caw, and this old man would look at us and our feathers and play with himself.

ANDERSON: Did he ever touch you?

INGRID: Never. When he was finished with himself, he rose and stalked out. We would remove our feathers, and we would dress. The butler stood by the door and paid us our money as we walked out. Very good money. The next month we'd be back again. Perhaps the same girls, perhaps a few new ones. Same thing.

ANDERSON: How do you figure his hang-up?

INGRID: I don't. I gave up trying many years ago. People are what they are. This I can accept. But I cannot accept what they pretend to be. This man who fondled himself while I pranced about him clad in chicken feathers, this man attended church every Sunday, contributed to charities, and was—still is—considered one of the leading citizens of his city and his country. His son is also now very important. At first it all sickened me.

ANDERSON: The chicken feathers?

INGRID: The filth! The filth! Then I learned how the world is run. Who has the power. What money can do. So I declared war on the world. My own personal war.

ANDERSON: Have you won?

INGRID: I am winning, *Schatzie*.

SEGMENT III. 17AUG-12:41PM.

ANDERSON: It could have been different.

INGRID: Perhaps. But we are mostly what has happened to us, what the world has done to us. We cannot always make the choice. By the time I was fifteen I was an accomplished whore. I had stolen, blackmailed, had been terribly beaten several times, and I had marked a pimp. Still, I was a child. I had no education. I tried only to survive, to have food, a place to sleep. At that time I wanted very little. Perhaps that is why we are so *simpatico*. You were poor also . . . *nein?*

ANDERSON: Yes. My family was white niggers.

INGRID: Understand, *Schatzie,* I make no excuses. I did what I had to do.

ANDERSON: Sure. But after you got older . . . ?

INGRID: I learned very quickly. As I told you, I learned where the money was and where the power was. Then there was nothing I would not do. It was war—total war. I hit back. Then I hit first. That is very important. The only crime in this world is to be poor. That is the only crime. If you are not poor, you can do anything.

SEGMENT IV. 17AUG-12:08PM.

ANDERSON: Sometimes you scare me.

INGRID: Why is that, *Schatzie?* I mean no bad to you.

ANDERSON: I know, I know. But you never get out. You live with it every minute.

INGRID: I have tried everything—alcohol, drugs, sex. Nothing works for me. I must live with it every minute—so I do. Now I live quietly. I have a warm home. Food. I have money invested. Safe money. Men pay me. You know that?

ANDERSON: Yes.

INGRID: I have stopped wanting. It is very important to know when to stop wanting.

ANDERSON: Don't you ever want to get out?

INGRID: It would be nice—but if I cannot, I cannot.

[Lapse of seven seconds.]

ANDERSON: You're some woman.

INGRID: It is my occupation, *Schatzie*. It is not my sex.

SEGMENT V. 17AUG-2:14PM.

INGRID: It has been a beautiful afternoon. Are you drunk?

ANDERSON: A little.

INGRID: We must go soon. You must go to work.

ANDERSON: Yes.

INGRID: Are you sleeping?

ANDERSON: Some. . . .

INGRID: Shall I talk to you . . . the way you like?

ANDERSON: Yes. Do *you* like it?

INGRID: Of course.

SEGMENT VI. 17AUG-3:03PM.

INGRID: Please, *Schatzie,* we must go. You will be late.

ANDERSON: Sure. All right. I'll clean up. You finish the wine; I'll finish the brandy.

INGRID: Very well.

ANDERSON: I would like to tell you what I am doing.

INGRID: Please . . . no.

ANDERSON: You're the smartest woman I ever knew. I'd like to get your opinion, what you think of it.

INGRID: No . . . nothing. Tell me nothing. I do not wish to know.

ANDERSON: It's big.

INGRID: It is always big. It will do no good to tell you to be careful, I know. Just do what you must do.

ANDERSON: I can't pull out now.

INGRID: I understand.

ANDERSON: Will you kiss me?

INGRID: Now? Yes. On the lips?

[47]

Tape BN-DT-TH-0018-98G; 19 August, 1968; 11:46 A.M.

HASKINS: Was that what you wanted?

ANDERSON: Fine. It was fine, Tommy. More than I expected.

HASKINS: Good. Some day I'll tell you how I got those floor plans. It was a gas!

ANDERSON: You want in?

HASKINS: In? On the whole hype?

ANDERSON: Yes.

[Lapse of five seconds.]

HASKINS: How much?

ANDERSON: A fee. Two big ones.

HASKINS: Two? That's a bit skimpy, isn't it, darling?

ANDERSON: It's what I can go. I got six guys to think about.

HASKINS: Are you including Snapper?

ANDERSON: No.

HASKINS: I don't know . . . I don't know. . . .

ANDERSON: Make up your mind.

HASKINS: Are you anticipating . . . well, you know . . . violence?

ANDERSON: No. More than half will be out of the house.

HASKINS: You don't want me to carry . . . ?

ANDERSON: No. Just to spot for me. Finger what to take and what to leave. The paintings, the rugs, the silver–shit like that.

[Lapse of four seconds.]

HASKINS: When would I be paid?

ANDERSON: Half before, half after.

HASKINS: I've never done anything like this before.

ANDERSON: A piece of cheese. Nothing to worry about. We'll take our time. The whole fucking place will be ours. Two, three hours . . . whatever it takes.

HASKINS: Will we wear masks?

ANDERSON: Are you in?

HASKINS: Yes.

ANDERSON: All right. I'll let you know later this week when we all get together. It's going to be all right, Tommy.

HASKINS: Oh, God. Oh, Jesus.

[48]

21 August, 1968; 12:15 P.M. Tape NYSNB-49B-767 (continuing).

ANDERSON: You want in?
JOHNSON: Who do I bash and what's the cash?
ANDERSON: Two big ones, half in advance.
JOHNSON: Gimme your han' 'cause you're my man.
ANDERSON: I'll be in touch to tell you where and when. Keep clean for the next two weeks. Can you do that?
JOHNSON: You gotta know. Like the driven snow.
ANDERSON: Don't fuck me up, Skeets. Or I'll have to come looking for you. You know?
JOHNSON: Aw, now, Massa Anderson, you wouldn't be trying to skeer this pore, ignorant ole nigguh, would you now?

[49]

Transcription NYPD-JDA-154-11; 22 August, 1968; 1:36 P.M. A telephone interception.

ANDERSON: Ed?

BRODSKY: Duke?

ANDERSON: Yes.

BRODSKY: Was everything all right? Was that what you wanted?

ANDERSON: Fine, Ed. Just right. The map was great.

BRODSKY: Jesus, that's good to hear. I mean we worked, Duke. We really sweat.

ANDERSON: I know you did, Ed. I liked it. The man liked it. Everything is set. You want in?

BRODSKY: Me? Or me and Billy?

ANDERSON: Both of you. Two G's. No shares. Just a fee. Half in advance.

BRODSKY: Yes. Christ, yes! I need it, Duke. You got no idea how I need it. The sharks are at me.

ANDERSON: I'll be in touch.

BRODSKY: Thank you very much, Duke.

[50]

Anderson's apartment; an interior conversation. Transcription NYPD-JDA-155-23; 23 August, 1968. Participants John Anderson and Vincent "Socks" Parelli have been identified by voice prints.

PARELLI: Jesus Christ, a guy could get a heart attack climbing those fucking stairs. You really live in this shit-house?

ANDERSON: That's right.

PARELLI: And you got to make a meet here? It couldn't be a nice restaurant in Times Square? A hotel room maybe?

ANDERSON: This place is clean.

PARELLI: How do you know? How does anyone know? Maybe one of your rats is wired. Maybe your cockroaches been trained. Hey! How about that! Trained bugs! Not bad, huh?

ANDERSON: Not bad.

PARELLI: What I'm saying is, why have me drag my ass all the way over here? What's so important?

ANDERSON: This is the way I wanted it.

PARELLI: All right, all right. So you're the boss. Big

deal. We agreed. I take orders. Okay, boss, what's the setup?

[Lapse of six seconds.]

ANDERSON: We have our first meet tomorrow night, eight thirty. Here's the address. Don't lose it.

PARELLI: Tomorrow? Eight thirty? For Christ's sake, tomorrow's Saturday. Who the hell works on Saturday?

ANDERSON: We meet tomorrow, like I said.

PARELLI: Not me, buster. I can't make it. I'm getting a blow-job at eight. Include me out.

ANDERSON: You want out of the whole thing?

PARELLI: No, I don't want out of the whole thing. But I. . . .

ANDERSON: I'll tell Mr. Angelo you can't make the meet tomorrow because some quiff is going to give you head. Okay?

PARELLI: You suck, you bastard. When this is all over, you and me, we'll have our own meet. Somewhere. Someday.

ANDERSON: Sure. But you be at that meet tomorrow.

PARELLI: All right, all right . . . I'll be there.

ANDERSON: I got five guys, plus you and me. There's a smart fag who can finger the good stuff. He knows paintings and jewelry and silver. His name's Haskins. I got a tech named Ernest Mann. He'll cut off the telephones and alarms, open the doors and boxes—whatever we need. Then there's a spade named Johnson, a muscle, but smart. He's no hooligan. Then there's two brothers—Ed and Billy Brodsky. Ed is an all-around man, a good driver. His young brother

Billy, he's a wet-brain but he's a powerhouse. We need a guy for lifting and carrying. Billy will do what he's told.

PARELLI: Any of them panic guys?

ANDERSON: Tommy Haskins maybe. The others are solid—real pros.

PARELLI: I'll keep my eye on Haskins.

ANDERSON: You do that. Socks, I don't want no blasting. There's no need. Half the families will be gone. No one left but old women and kids. We got a plan that's been figured four ways from the middle. You'll hear it tomorrow. Everything will go like silk.

PARELLI: I carry a stick. That's definite.

ANDERSON: All right, you carry a stick. Just don't use it—that's all I'm saying.

PARELLI: I hear you work clean.

ANDERSON: That's right.

PARELLI: I still carry.

ANDERSON: I told you, that's up to you—but you'll have no call to use it. You won't need it.

PARELLI: We'll see.

ANDERSON: Another thing—I don't want these people slammed around. You understand?

PARELLI: Oh, I'll be very polite, boss.

[Lapse of five seconds.]

ANDERSON: And I don't like you, prick-nose. But I'm stuck with you. I needed another body and they gave me a sack of shit like you.

PARELLI: You fuck! You fuck! I could burn you! I should burn you right now!

ANDERSON: Go ahead, prick-nose. You're the guy

who carries a stick. I got nothing. Go ahead, burn me.

PARELLI: Oh, you lousy fuck! You piece of funk! I swear to Christ, when this is over I'll get you good. But good! Nice and slow. That's what you'll get, cracker. Something nice and slow, right through the balls. Oh, are you going to get it! I can taste it. I can taste it!

ANDERSON: Sure, you can taste it. You got a big, fucking mouth—and that's all you've got. Just you be at that meet tomorrow, and at the other meets until next Saturday.

PARELLI: And after that, white trash, it'll be you and me . . . just you and me.

ANDERSON: That's right, prick-nose. How many women you screwed with that snout? Now get your ass out of here. Be careful getting a cab. We got some punks in this neighborhood—oh, maybe ten years old or so—who might take your piece away from you.

PARELLI: You mother. . . .

[51]

The driveway outside Patrick Angelo's home, 10543 Foxberry Lane, Teaneck, New Jersey; 25 August, 1968; 8:36 P.M. On this date, Angelo's "personal" car (he owned three) was under electronic surveillance by an investigative agency of the U.S. government, which cannot be named at this time, using a device which cannot be revealed. The car was a black Continental, license LPA-46B-8935K. Patrick Angelo and John Anderson sat in the back seat of the parked car.

ANGELO: Sorry I can't ask you into the house, Duke. The wife's got some neighbors in tonight for bridge. I figured we could talk better out here.

ANDERSON: Sure, Mr. Angelo. This is okay.

ANGELO: But I brought out some of this cognac you like and a couple of glasses. We might as well be comfortable. Here you are. . . .

ANDERSON: Thanks.

ANGELO: Success.

ANDERSON: Luck.

[Lapse of four seconds.]

ANGELO: Beautiful. Jesus, that's like music on the tongue. Duke, I heard you leaned on our boy the other day.

ANDERSON: Parelli? Yes, I leaned on him. He tell you?

ANGELO: He told D'Medico. The Doc told me. What are you doing—setting him up?

ANDERSON: Something like that.

ANGELO: You figured he's got a short fuse as it is—and not too much brains—so you'll psych him. Now he's so sore at you he's not even using the little brains he's got. So you're that much more on top of him.

ANDERSON: I guess that's it.

[Lapse of seven seconds.]

ANGELO: Or was it you wanted to hate his guts so it would be easier to spoil him?

ANDERSON: What difference does it make?

ANGELO: None, Duke. None at all. I'm just running off at the mouth. You had your first meet yesterday?

ANDERSON: That's right.

ANGELO: How did it go?

ANDERSON: It went fine.

ANGELO: Any weak spots?

ANDERSON: The faggot, Tommy Haskins, has never done a hard job before. He's been on the con or hustling his ass or pulling paper hypes. But his job is easy. I'll keep an eye on him. Johnson—he's the dinge—and the two Brodsky boys are true blue. Hard. The tech, Ernest Mann, is so money hungry he'll do what I tell him. If he's caught, he'll spill, of course. All they'll have to do is threaten to take his cigarettes away.

ANGELO: But he's not going to be caught . . . is he?

ANDERSON: No. Parelli is stupid and vicious and kill-crazy. A bad combination.

ANGELO: You'll have to play that guy by ear. I told you . . . don't turn your back.

ANDERSON: I don't figure to. I gave my boys their advances.

ANGELO: Do they know what everyone is getting?

ANDERSON: No. I gave them sealed envelopes separately. I told each guy he was getting more than the others and to keep his mouth shut.

ANGELO: Good.

ANDERSON: Did you ask about the diversions?

ANGELO: Papa says forget it. Keep it as simple as possible. He says it's tricky enough as it is.

ANDERSON: He's right. I'm glad about that. Can you tell me about the truck now?

ANGELO: Not now. When we meet on Thursday.

ANDERSON: All right. The Brodsky boys will pick it up wherever you say. It'll be in New York, won't it?

ANGELO: Yes. In Manhattan.

ANDERSON: Fine. Then we can figure out our final timing. What about the drop?

ANGELO: I'll give you that on Thursday, too. How many men will make the drop?

ANDERSON: I was figuring on me and the Brodsky boys.

ANGELO: All right. Now let's see . . . what else did I want to ask. . . . Oh, yes . . . do you need a piece?

ANDERSON: I can get one. I don't know how good it will be.

ANGELO: Let me get you a good one. Right off the docks. When your boys pick up the truck, it'll be in the glove compartment or taped under the dash. Loaded. How does that sound?

ANDERSON: That sounds all right.

ANGELO: A .38 okay?

ANDERSON: Yes.

ANGELO: I'll see it's taken care of. Now let's see . . . oh, yes, the masks. You got all that fixed? Gloves . . . shit like that?

ANDERSON: It's all arranged, Mr. Angelo.

ANGELO: Good. Well, I can't think of anything else. I'll see you on Thursday, then. Your second meet is on Wednesday and your last on Friday?

ANDERSON: Yes.

ANGELO: How do you feel?

ANDERSON: I feel great. I'm hot with this thing but I got no doubts.

ANGELO: Duke . . . remember one thing. This is like war. Your reconnaissance and intelligence and operations plan can be the best in the world. But things go wrong. Unexpected things come up. Somebody screams. A rabbit becomes a lion. The fuzz drops by unexpected because one of them has to take a pee. Sometimes crazy things happen—things you never counted on. You know?

ANDERSON: Yes.

ANGELO: So you've got to stay loose in there. You got a good plan, but be ready to improvise, to deal with these unexpected things as they come up. Don't get spooked when something happens you didn't figure on.

ANDERSON: I won't get spooked.

ANGELO: I know you won't. You're a pro, Duke. That's why we're going along with you on this. We trust you.

ANDERSON: Thanks.

[52]

Dictated, signed, sworn, and witnessed statement by Timothy O'Leary, 648 Halverston Drive, Roslyn, New York. This is transcription NYPD-SIS-#146-11, dated 7 September, 1968.

"On the night of thirty-one August of this year—that is, the night it was between the last day of August and the first of September, with Labor Day to come, it was that weekend—I come on duty at 535 East Seventy-third Street where I am doorman from midnight until eight in the morning.

"Being my usual custom, I arrived on the premises about ten minutes early, stopped to exchange the time of night with Ed Bakely, the lad I was relieving, and then I went down into the basement. There we have three lockers in the hallway that leads from the super's apartment to the back basement rooms where are the boilers and such. I changed to my uniform which, in the summer, is merely a tan cotton jacket, and as I was wearing black pants, white shirt, and a black bow tie, the time was nothing.

"I come back upstairs and Ed goes down, to change back. Whilst he was gone, I took a look at the board where it is we keep messages and such.

I saw that Dr. Rubicoff, he's One B, was in his office and working late. And also there would be two friends of Eric Sabine, he's Two A, staying in his apartment for the Labor Day weekend. Ed, then, came up—he was carrying his bowling ball in a little bag—and said he was off to his alleys and would be able to get in a few games with his mates before the alleys closed.

"No sooner was he gone, with me out on the street taking a breath of air, when a truck come slowly down the street—yes, from East End Avenue since that is how the street runs. Much to my surprise it made a slow turn and pulled into our service entrance, going all the way to the back where it stopped, and turned off motor and lights. As it went past me I saw it was a moving van of some kind—I remember seeing the word 'moving' painted on the side and surmised it either had the wrong address or perhaps some of my tenants was moving or was expecting a furniture delivery of some kind which struck me as strange considering the time of night it was and also, you understand, we would have it on the board if some tenant was expecting a night delivery.

"So I strolled back to where the truck was now parked and dark, and I says, 'And what the hell do you think you are doing in my driveway?'

"No sooner was these words out of my mouth when I felt something on the back of my neck. Cool it was, metal and round. It could have been a piece of pipe, I suppose, but I surmised it was a gun. I was twenty years on the Force, and I am no stranger to guns.

"At the same time I felt the muzzle on my neck—a crawly feeling it was—the man holding the gun says, very cool, 'Do you want to die?'

" 'No,' I tells him, 'I do not want to die.' I was calm, you understand, but I was honest.

" 'Then you will do just what I tell you,' he says, 'and you will not die.'

"With that he walks me back to the service door, kind of prodding me with the muzzle of the gun, if that's what it was, and I think it was, but not hurting me, you understand. All this time the truck was dark and quiet and I saw no other men. In fact, up to this time I had actually seen no one. Just felt the gun and heard the voice.

"He had me stand pressed face-up against the wall by the service door, the muzzle of the gun still in the middle of my neck. 'Not a sound from you,' he says.

" 'Not a sound you'll get,' I whispers to him.

" 'All right,' he calls, and I hear the doors of the truck opening. Two doors open. In a minute I hear a rattle of chain and the sound of a tailgate flopping down. I saw nothing, nothing at all. I stared at the wall and said 'Hail, Marys.' I had the feeling others were standing about, but I turned my head neither to the right nor to the left. I heard footsteps walking away. All was quiet. No one spoke. In a moment I heard the buzzer and knew that someone inside the lobby was pressing the button that released the lock on the service door.

"I was prodded forward into the service entrance, the gun still at my neck, and told to lay on the concrete floor, which I did although I was sorry for soiling my uniform jacket and my trousers which my wife Grace had pressed that very afternoon. I was told to cross my ankles and cross my wrists behind me. I did all this, just as I was told, but at this time I switched to 'Our Father, Who art in Heavens. . . .'

"They used what I guess was a wide strip of adhesive tape. I could hear that sound of sticking as it came off the reel. They taped my ankles and my wrists, and then a strip was put across my mouth.

"At this time, the man—I think he was the man with the gun—he says to me, 'Can you breathe okay? If you can breathe okay, nod your head.'

"So I nodded my head and blessed him for his consideration."

[53]

The following is from a dictated, sworn, signed, and witnessed statement by Ernest Heinrich Mann. This is Segment NYDA-EHM-105A.

MANN: So . . . now we are at the night of August

thirty-first and the morning hours of September first. The truck picked me up at the appointed place and I. . . .

QUESTION: Pardon me a moment. I believe you told us previously that the truck was to pick you up on the southeast corner of Lexington Avenue and Sixty-fifth Street. Is that correct?

MANN: Yes. Correct.

QUESTION: And that was, in fact, where you joined the others?

MANN: Yes.

QUESTION: What time was this?

MANN: It was eleven forty P.M. This was the time agreed upon. I was on time and so also was the truck.

QUESTION: Will you describe this truck for us.

MANN: It was, I would say, a medium-sized moving van. In addition to the doors to the cab, there were two large rear doors fastened with a chained tailgate, as well as a door in the middle of each side. It was by one of these doors that I entered the truck, the men inside assisting me to climb up.

QUESTION: How many men were in the truck at this time?

MANN: Everyone was there—everyone I have described to you who was at the planning meetings. The man I know as Anderson and the two men I know as Ed and Billy were in the cab. Ed was driving. The others were in the body of the truck.

QUESTION: What was painted on the side of the

truck? Did you notice any words or markings?

MANN: I saw only the word "Moving." There were also several markings that appeared to be license numbers and maximum load weights—things of that sort.

QUESTION: After you boarded the truck, what happened?

MANN: The truck began to move. I assumed we were heading for the apartment house.

QUESTION: Were you standing inside the truck or were you seated?

MANN: We were seated, but not on the floor. A rough wooden bench had been provided on one side of the truck. We sat on that. Also, there was a light inside the truck body.

QUESTION: What happened then?

MANN: The man I know as John Anderson opened the sliding wooden panel between the cab and the body of the truck. He told us to put on our masks and gloves.

QUESTION: These had been provided for you?

MANN: Yes. There was a set for each of us, plus two extra sets in case of accident . . . in case the stocking masks might perhaps tear while we were putting them on.

QUESTION: And you all put them on?

MANN: Yes.

QUESTION: The men in the cab, too?

MANN: That I do not know. Anderson closed the sliding panel. I could not see what was happening up there.

QUESTION: Then what?

MANN: We drove. Then we stopped. I heard the cab door open and slam. I assumed that was Anderson getting out. As I told you, the plan required him to be waiting across the street from the apartment house when the truck arrived.

QUESTION: And then?

MANN: The truck drove on. We went around a few blocks to give Anderson time to get into position.

QUESTION: What time was this?

MANN: It was perhaps ten minutes after midnight, give or take a minute either way. Everything was precisely timed. It was an admirable plan.

QUESTION: Then what?

MANN: The truck picked up a little speed. We were all quiet. We made a very sharp turn, up a small rise. I knew we were then pulling into the driveway of the apartment house. The truck engine was switched off and the lights also.

QUESTION: Including the light in the body of the truck, where you were?

MANN: Yes. There were no lights whatsoever. In addition, we did not speak. This had been made very clear. We made no noise whatsoever.

QUESTION: Then what happened?

MANN: I heard voices outside the truck, but so low that I could not hear what was being said. Then, in a minute or two, Anderson called, "All right." At this time the side door of the truck was opened, and we all got out. Also Ed and Billy from the cab. I was assisted to descend from the truck by the man I know as Skeets, the Negro. He was very polite and helpful.

QUESTION: Go on.

MANN: The one named Tommy, the slight, boyish one, went immediately around to the front of the building. I watched him. He paused a moment to make certain there was no one on the street, no one observing—he was wearing mask and gloves, you understand—and then he slipped around to the front entrance. In a moment the release button sounded on the outside service door, and the man I know as Socks—the uncouth man I described to you before—entered first, his hand in his jacket pocket. I believe he was carrying a weapon. He went directly down to the basement. I waited until Anderson had bound and gagged the doorman, then I followed Socks down into the basement, as we had planned. Every move had been planned.

QUESTION: What was the purpose of your waiting until the doorman was tied up before following Socks down to the basement?

MANN: I don't know precisely why I was to wait, but this is what I was told to do—so I did it. I think perhaps it was to give Socks time to immobilize the superintendent. Also, it was to give Anderson time to follow me and check on my work. In any event, as I went down into the basement, Anderson was right behind me.

QUESTION: Then what?

MANN: As we entered the basement, Socks came toward us from the superintendent's apartment. He said, "What a pigsty. The slob is out cold. The place smells like a brewery. He won't wake up till Monday." Anderson said, "Good." Then he turned to me. "All right, Professor," he said. So I set to work.

QUESTION: The lights in the basement were on at this time?

MANN: One dim overhead light, yes. But it was insufficient, and flashlights and a flood lantern were used in the area of my work.

QUESTION: You had brought your tools with you.

MANN: That is correct. My own personal hand and power tools. The heavy equipment, as I explained to you—the torches and the gas cylinders—had been provided and were still inside the body of the truck. So . . . I set to work on the schedule we had planned. Anderson and Socks held the lights. First of all, I cut all telephonic communication, isolating the entire building. I then bridged the alarms in a manner which I have described to your technician, Mr. Browder. This was in case the alarm would sound if the current was interrupted. I then cut the power to the self-service elevator. This was simply a matter of throwing a switch. Finally, I cut the alarm to the cold box and picked the lock. I opened the door. At this time the men I know as Ed and Billy had joined us. Anderson motioned at the furs hanging inside the cold box and said to Ed and Billy, "Start loading. Everything. Clean it out. And don't forget the super's apartment." I then went back to the service entrance on the ground level and picked the lock of the door connecting the service entrance with the lobby. The Negro, Skeets, and Anderson went into the lobby. Myself and Tommy, we waited. We watched Ed and Billy carry up armloads of fur coats and put them in the truck.

[54]

Dictated, signed, sworn, and witnessed statement by Dr. Dmitri Rubicoff, Suite 1B, 535 East Seventy-third Street, New York City. NYPD-SIS-#146-8, dated 6 September, 1968.

"It had been my intention to spend the entire Labor Day weekend with my wife and my daughter, her husband and child, at our summer home in East Hampton. However, early Friday morning I realized the press of work facing me was so great that I could not afford the luxury of taking four or five days off away from my desk.

"Accordingly, I sent my family on ahead—they took the station wagon, my wife driving—and I told them I would be out late Saturday night or perhaps early Sunday morning. I said I would keep them informed by phone as to my plans.

"My secretary I allowed to leave early on Friday as she was planning a five-day holiday at Nassau. I worked alone in the office all day Saturday, but realized I was too tired to drive out Saturday night in the Corvair. So I determined to work late Saturday night and sleep at home—I live on East Seventy-ninth Street—and then drive out on Sunday morning. I called my wife and informed her of my plans.

"I had a sandwich sent in at noon on Saturday. In the evening I dined at a nearby French restaurant, the Le Claire. I had an excellent poached filet of sole that was, perhaps, a trifle too salty. I returned to my office at about nine in the evening to finish up as much as I could. As usual when I am working alone in the office at night, I locked the door to the lobby and put on the chain. I then turned on my hi-fi. I believe it was something by Von Weber.

"It was perhaps twelve thirty or a little later when the lobby door chimed. I was in the process of straightening my desk and packing a briefcase with professional journals I wished to take to East Hampton with me. I went to the door and opened the peephole. The man standing there was off to one side; all I could see was his shoulder and half of his body.

" 'Yes?' I said.

" 'Doctor Rubicoff,' he said, 'I'm the relief doorman for the Labor Day weekend. I have a special delivery, registered letter for you.'

"I must admit I reacted foolishly. But in my own defense, I should tell you this: First—I was ready to leave, I was about to unlock the door, and it seemed ridiculous to ask this man to slide the letter under the door. Second—frequently, you understand, on holidays and during vacations, we have relief doormen take the place of our regular employees. So I was not concerned that, on the Labor Day weekend, this was a man whose voice I did not recognize. Third—the fact that he had a special delivery, registered letter for me—or claimed he had—did not alarm me. You understand, psychiatrists are quite used to receiving letters, telegrams, and phone calls from patients, in unusual forms and at unusual hours.

"I suspected nothing. I slipped the chain and unlocked the door.

"The two men who pushed the door forcibly aside and entered were both wearing head coverings that appeared to be semiopaque women's stockings. The bottom half of the stocking had been cut off. The top half was pulled over the man's head and tied in a knot at the top. Presumably so it could not slip down or be pulled down. One of the men, I should say, was slightly under six feet tall. The other was perhaps three inches taller, and I had the feeling this man was a Negro. It was extremely difficult to judge, as only a vague shape of their features came through their masks, and both men wore white cotton gloves.

" 'Is your secretary here?' the shorter man asked me. This was the first thing he said.

"I am quite used to dealing with disturbed people, and I think I handled the situation quite calmly.

" 'No,' I told him. 'She has left for a five-day vacation. I am alone.'

" 'Good,' the man said. 'Doctor, we don't want

to hurt you. Please lay down on the floor, your wrists and ankles crossed behind you.'

"Frankly, I was impressed by his air of quiet authority. I knew at once of course that this was a robbery. I thought perhaps they had come for my drugs. I had been the victim twice before of robberies in which the thieves only wanted my drugs. Incidentally, I keep an extremely small supply of narcotics in my safe. I did as the man requested. My ankles and wrists were taped, and then a strip of wide tape was put across my mouth. Very painful to remove later, I might add, because of my mustache. The man asked me if I could breathe comfortably, and I nodded. I was quite impressed with him—in fact, with the whole operation. It was very professional."

[55]

NYPD-SIS recording #146-83C; interrogation of Thomas Haskins; Segment IA, dated 4 September, 1968. The following tape has been heavily edited to avoid repetition of material already presented and to eliminate material currently under adjudication.

QUESTION: Mr. Haskins, my name is Thomas K.

Brody, and I am a detective, second grade, in the Police Department of the City of New York. It is my duty. . . .

HASKINS: Thomas! My name is Thomas, too. Isn't that sweet?

QUESTION: It is my duty to make absolutely certain that you are aware of your rights and privileges, under the laws of the United States of America, as a person accused of a crime constituting a felony under the laws of the State of New York. Now, you are. . . .

HASKINS: Oh, I'm aware, Tommy. I'm really aware! I know all that jazz about lawyers and such. You can skip it.

QUESTION: You are not required at this time to answer any questions whatsoever that may be put to you by law enforcement officials. You may request legal counsel of your choice. If you are unable to afford legal counsel, or if you have no personal counsel of your own, the court will suggest such counsel, subject to your approval. In addition, you. . . .

HASKINS: All right already! I'm willing to spiel. I want to talk! I know my rights better than you. Can't we just start talking—just you and me, two Tommies?

QUESTION: Whatever statements you may make at this time, without the presence of counsel, are of your own free will and volition. And anything you say—I repeat, *anything* you say—even that which may seem to you of an innocent nature—may possibly, in the future, be used against you.

Do you understand?

HASKINS: Of course I understand.

QUESTION: Is everything clear to you?

HASKINS: Yes, Tommy baby, everything is clear to me.

QUESTION: In addition. . . .

HASKINS: Oh, Jesus Christ!

QUESTION: In addition, I have this printed statement I would like you to sign in the presence of Policewoman Alice H. Hilkins, here as witness, that you fully understand your rights and privileges as an accused person under the laws already cited, and that whatever statements you make are made with full and complete comprehension of those rights and privileges.

HASKINS: Look, Dick Two, I want to talk, I'm willing to talk, I'm eager to talk. So let's. . . .

QUESTION: Will you sign this statement?

HASKINS: Gladly, gladly. Gimme the goddamn thing.

[Lapse of four seconds.]

QUESTION: In addition, I have a second statement that. . . .

HASKINS: Oh, oh, oh. Tommy, I just. . . .

QUESTION: This second printed statement declares that you have not been physically threatened into signing the first statement, that you signed it of your own free will and desire, that no promises have been made to you as to the extent or punishment for the accused crime. In addition, you do say, affirm, and swear that. . . .

HASKINS: Tommy, how the fuck does a guy confess these days?

[Lapse of seven minutes thirteen seconds.]

HASKINS: . . . so that the one thing that really stuck in my mind was something Duke said at our last meeting. He said crime was just war during peacetime. He said the most important thing we could learn from war was that no matter how good a plan was, it was just not humanly possible to plan *everything*. He said things can go wrong or unexpected things happen, and you must be ready to cope with them. He said—this is Duke talking, you understand—he said that he and others—that's what he said, "Others"—had made our plan as foolproof as they could, but he knew unexpected things would happen they hadn't counted on. Maybe a squad car would stop by. Maybe a beat fuzz would come into the lobby to rap a little with the doorman. Maybe one of the tenants would pull a gun. He said to expect the unexpected and not get spooked by it. He said the plan was good, but things could happen that hadn't been planned for. . . .

So after we got there, I went around into the lobby and pressed the release button for the outside service door. It was right where Duke had told me it would be. While I was there, I took a look at a clipboard the doormen keep. It tells them what deliveries to expect and what tenants were away for the weekend—things like that. I saw right away that the headshrinker was in his office and working late. Also, there were two guests staying in Two A. Those were two of the unexpected things Duke had warned us about. So the moment he came through the opened door to the service entrance, I told him about them. He patted my arm. That's the first time he ever touched me. . . .

So he and the smoke took care of the doctor, just like that, and we went ahead with the plan. You see, we knew there would be several tenants still in the building who hadn't gone away for the Labor Day weekend. The idea was, instead of tying them all up in their apartments or keeping a watch on them, which we didn't have enough people to do, the idea was to assemble everyone in the building in Apartment Four B where the old widow Mrs. Hathway lived with her housekeeper. These were two really ancient dames, and Duke didn't want to risk taping them up. So it was decided we'd bring everyone in the building to Apartment Four B, scare the hell out of them, and Skeets or Socks would keep an eye on them all together. After all, what could they do? The phones were cut. They didn't know if we had guns or knives or whatever. And we had them all in one place and one guy could keep them quiet while the rest of us cleaned out the whole fucking apartment house.

It was a marvelous plan. . . .

[56]

The following is a portion of a lengthy letter addressed to the author from Ernest Heinrich Mann, dated 28 March, 1969.

My Dear Sir:

I wish to thank you for your kind inquiries as to my physical health and mental stamina, as expressed in your recent missive. I am happy to tell you that, God willing, I am in good health and spirits. The food is plain but plentiful. The exercise—outdoors, that is—is sufficient, and my work in the library I find very rewarding.

You may be interested to learn that I have recently taken up the Yoga regimen, insofar as it relates to physical exercise. The philosophy does not concern me. But the physical program interests me as it requires no equipment, so that I am able to practice it in my cell, at any time. Needless to say, this is much to the amusement of my cellmate whose main exercise is turning the pages of the latest comic book, detailing the adventures of Cosmic Man!

I thank you for your recent gift of books and cigarettes which arrived in good order. You ask if there is any special printed matter which you may supply that is not available in the prison library. Sir, there is. Some months ago, in an issue of the New York *Times,* I read that, for the first time, scientists had succeeded in the synthetic reproduction of an enzyme in the laboratory. This is a subject that interests me greatly, and I would be much obliged if you could obtain for me copies of the scientific papers describing this discovery. I thank you.

Now then . . . you ask me about the personality and the character traits of the man I called John Anderson.

I can tell you he was a most complex man. As you may have surmised, I had several dealings with him prior to the events of 31 August–1 September, 1968. In all our dealings, I found him a man of the highest probity, of exceptional honesty, trustworthiness, and steadfastness. I would never hesitate in giving him a character reference, if such was requested of me.

A man of very little education and very much intelligence. And the two have little in common as, I am certain, you recognize. In all our personal and business relations he radiated strength and purposefulness. As is understandable in such a relationship, I was, perhaps, a little frightened of him. Not because he ever threatened me physical harm. Not at all! But I was frightened as we all poor mortals become frightened in the presence of one we feel and sense and know is of, perhaps, almost superhuman strength and resolve. Let me say only that I felt inferior to him.

I believe that, directed into more constructive

channels, his intelligence and native wit could have taken him very far. Very far indeed. Let me give you an example. . . .

Following our second planning meeting—I believe it was on August 28th—I walked with him to the subway after the meeting was concluded. Everything had gone very well. I congratulated him on the detailed planning, which I thought was superb. I told him I thought it must have taken much thought on his part. He smiled, and this is what he said—as nearly as I can remember. . . .

"Yes, I have been living with this thing for some months now, thinking of it every waking minute and even dreaming of it. You know, there is nothing like thinking. You have a problem that worries you and nags you and keeps you awake. The thing to do then is to get to the very rock bottom of that problem. First, you figure out *why* it is a problem. Once you have done that, it is half solved. For instance, what do you think was the most difficult problem in making up the plan you heard tonight?"

I suggested it might be how to handle the doorman when the truck first pulled into the driveway.

"No," he said, "there are several good ways we could handle that. The big problem, as I saw it, was how to handle the tenants who were still at home. That is, how could we get into their apartments? I figured they all had locked doors and chains also. In addition, it would be after midnight and I could figure most of them—particularly the old ladies in Four B and the family with the crippled boy in Five A—would be asleep. I thought of our possibilities. We could force the doors, of course. But even if their phones were cut, they could still scream before we broke in and maybe alert the people in the house next door. I could ask you to pick the locks—but I had no guarantee that *everyone* would be asleep at that hour. They might hear you working and start screaming. It was a problem to know exactly what we should do. I wrestled with this thing for three days, coming up with a dozen solutions. I threw them all out because they didn't *feel* right to me. So then I went to the rock-bottom basic of the problem, just like I told you. I asked myself, Why do all these people have locks and chains on their doors? The answer was easy—because they were scared of guys like me—crooks and burglars and muggers. So then I thought, if they keep their doors locked from *fear,* what can make them open up? I remembered from the first time I was in that house that the doors above the lobby floor didn't have peepholes. The doctors' offices on the lobby floor did, but the doors above were blind. Who needs peepholes when they have twenty-four-hour doorman service and a locked service door and all that shit? So then I thought, if *fear* makes them keep their doors locked, then a *bigger* fear will make them unlock them. And what's a bigger fear than being robbed? That was easy. It was fire."

And that, my dear sir, is something I can tell you about the man I knew as John Anderson and how intelligent he was at his job, although he was, as I have told you, uneducated. . . .

[57]

Following the events related herein, attempts were made to obtain sworn statements from all the principals involved as soon as possible, while the details were fresh in their minds. Individuals interrogated included the victims and the alleged lawbreakers. It soon became apparent that the key to the proposed plan to loot the apartment house at 535 East Seventy-third Street was Apartment 4B, owned by Mrs. Martha Hathway, widow, and occupied by her and her companion-housekeeper, Miss Jane Kaler, a spinster.

Mrs. Hathway was ninety-one at the time of the crime. Miss Kaler was eighty-two. Both ladies refused to be interviewed or to make statements individually; each insisted the other be present—a rather surprising request in view of the results of their interrogation.

In any event, the statements of both ladies were taken at the same time. The following is an edited transcription of NYPD-SIS recording #146-91A.

MRS. HATHWAY: Very well. I will tell you exactly

what happened. Are you taking all this down, young man?

QUESTION: The machine is, ma'am. It's recording everything we say.

MRS. HATHWAY: Hmph. Well . . . it was the morning of September first. Sunday morning. I'd say it was about one o'clock in the morning.

MISS KALER: It was about fifteen minutes to one.

MRS. HATHWAY: You shut your mouth. I'm telling this.

MISS KALER: You're not telling it right.

QUESTION: Ladies. . . .

MRS. HATHWAY: It was about one o'clock. We had been asleep for, oh, about two hours or so.

MISS KALER: You might have been asleep. I was wide awake.

MRS. HATHWAY: Oh, you were indeed! I could hear the snores!

QUESTION: Ladies, please. . . .

MRS. HATHWAY: Suddenly I woke up. There was this pounding on our front door. A man was shouting, "Fire! Fire! There is a fire in the building and everyone must vacate the premises!"

QUESTION: Were those the exact words you heard?

MRS. HATHWAY: Something like that. But of course all I heard was "Fire! Fire!" so I immediately rose and donned my dressing gown.

MISS KALER: Naturally, being awake, I was already suitably clad and standing near the front door. "Where is the fire?" I asked through the door. "In the basement, ma'am," this man said, "but it is spreading rapidly throughout the entire building and we must ask you to leave the premises until the fire is under control." So I said to him, "And who might you be?" And he said, "I am Fireman Robert Burns of the New York Fire Department, and I would—"

MRS. HATHWAY: Will you stop gabbling for just a minute? I own this apartment, and it is my right to tell what happened. Isn't that correct, young man?

QUESTION: Well, ma'am, we'd like to get both. . . .

MISS KALER: "And I would like all the occupants of this apartment to leave immediately," he said. So I said, "Is it serious?" And he said—all this was through our locked door, you understand—he said, "Well, ma'am, we hope it won't be, but for your own safety we suggest you come down to the lobby while we get the fire under control." So I said, "Well, if you're—"

MRS. HATHWAY: Will you shut your mouth, you silly, blathering creature? Just be quiet and let me tell this nice young man what happened. So, seeing we were both perfectly covered in our dressing gowns and we had on our carpet slippers, I told the girl to open the door. . . .

MISS KALER: Mrs. Hathway, I've asked you times without end not to refer to me as "the girl." If you remember, you promised to. . . .

MRS. HATHWAY: So she opened the door. . . .

QUESTION: It was locked at the time?

MRS. HATHWAY: Oh, my, yes. We have the regular lock, always double-locked whenever we're in the apartment. Then we have a chain lock which allows the door to be opened slightly but held with a powerful chain. And we also have something called a policeman's lock which had been recommended to me by Sergeant Tim Sullivan, retired now but formerly of the Twenty-first Precinct. Do you know him?

QUESTION: I'm afraid not, ma'am.

MRS. HATHWAY: A wonderful man—a very good friend of my late husband's. Sergeant Sullivan was forced to retire at an early age because of a hernia. After we had so many robberies on the East Side, I called him and he suggested we have this policeman's lock installed, which is really a steel rod that fits into the floor and is shoved against the door, and it's impossible to break in.

MISS KALER: Ask her how this "wonderful man" got his hernia.

MRS. HATHWAY: That is of no importance, I'm sure. So the man outside kept shouting, "Fire! Fire!" and naturally we were quite upset, so we opened the three locks and threw open the door. And much. . . .

MISS KALER: And there he was! A monster! He must have been seven feet tall, with this terrible mask and a big gun in his hand. And he snarled at us, "If you—"

MRS. HATHWAY: He was, perhaps, six feet tall, and he had no gun that I could see, although I believe one hand was in his pocket so he might have had a weapon. But really, he was quite polite and said, "Ladies, we must use your apartment for a short while, but if you are quiet and offer us no resistance, then we can—"

MISS KALER: And right behind him were two other monsters—sex fiends, all of them! And they had masks and revolvers. And they pushed us back into the apartment, and I said, "Then there is no fire?" And the first man to come in said, "No, ma'am, there is no fire, but we must request the use of your apartment for a while. And if you don't scream or carry on, it won't be necessary to tie you up or tape your mouth shut. And we will not tape your mouth shut if you act intelligently." And I said, "I will act intelligently." And then the first man said, "Keep an eye on them, Killer, and if they scream or act up, you may destroy them." And the second man—who, I am sure, was a darkie—he said, "Yes, Butch, if they scream or act up, I will destroy them." And then the darkie stayed and watched us through his mask, and the other two men. . . .

MRS. HATHWAY: Will you shut up? Will you just shut your mouth?

QUESTION: Ladies, ladies. . . .

[58]

Recording NYDA-#146-98B. See NYDA-#146-98BT for corrected and edited transcription.

QUESTION: The recorder has now started, Mrs. Bingham. My name is Roger Leibnitz. I am an assistant in the office of the District Attorney, County of New York, State of New York. It is the eleventh day of September, 1968. I wish to question you about events occurring during the period August thirty-first to September first of this year at your residence. If for any reason you do not wish to make a statement, or if you wish counsel of your choice to be present during this interview, or if you wish the court to appoint such counsel, will you please so state at this time?

MRS. BINGHAM: No . . . that's all right.

QUESTION: Very well. You understand, it is my duty to notify you of your rights under law?

MRS. BINGHAM: Yes. I understand.

QUESTION: For the record, will you please identify yourself—your full name and your place of residence.

MRS. BINGHAM: My name is Mrs. Gerald Bingham, and I live in Apartment Five A, five-three-five East Seventy-third Street, Manhattan, New York.

QUESTION: Thank you. Before we get started—may I inquire about your husband's condition?

MRS. BINGHAM: Well . . . I feel a lot better now. At first they thought he might lose the sight of his right eye. Now they say he will be able to see, but the sight may be impaired. But he's going to be all right.

QUESTION: I'm very happy to hear that, ma'am. Your husband is a very brave man.

MRS. BINGHAM: Yes. Very brave.

QUESTION: Are you all right, Mrs. Bingham?

MRS. BINGHAM: Yes . . . I'm all right.

QUESTION: If you wish to put this questioning over to another day, or if you'd like to rest at any time, please tell me. Would you like coffee . . . a cup of tea?

MRS. BINGHAM: No . . . I'll be all right.

QUESTION: Fine. Now I want you to state in your own words exactly what happened during the period in question. I'll try to avoid interrupting. Just take your time and tell me what happened in your own words. . . .

MRS. BINGHAM: It was the thirty-first of August. Most of the people in the house had left for the Labor Day weekend. We very rarely go away because of my son. His name is Gerry—Gerald junior. He is fifteen years old. He was in an accident at the age of ten—he was hit by a truck—and he has lost the use of his legs. The doctors say there is no hope he will ever walk normally again. He is a good boy, very intelligent, but he must be helped. He uses a wheelchair and sometimes crutches for short periods. From the waist up he is very strong, but he can't walk without help. So we very rarely go anywhere.

QUESTION: You have no other children?

MRS. BINGHAM: No. On the night of August thirty-first, my son went to bed about midnight. He read a while, and I brought him a Coca-Cola, which he dearly loves, and then he turned out his bed lamp and went to sleep. My husband

and I were in the living room. I was working on a petit point cover for a footstool, and my husband was reading something by Trollope. He dearly loves Trollope. I think it was about fifteen minutes after one. I'm not sure. It could have been fifteen minutes either way. Suddenly there was a pounding at the front door. A man's voice shouted, "Fire! Fire!" It was a very cruel thing to do.

QUESTION: Yes, Mrs. Bingham, it was.

MRS. BINGHAM: My husband said, "My God!" and jumped to his feet. He dropped his book on the floor. He rushed over to the door and unlocked it and took off the chain and opened it. There were two men standing there with masks on their faces. I could see them from where I sat. I was still in the easy chair. I hadn't reacted as fast as my husband. I could see these two men. The one in front had his hand in his jacket pocket. They were wearing these strange masks that came to a knot on the tops of their heads. I didn't know at first, but later I realized they were stockings—women's stockings. My husband looked at them and he said again, "My God!" Then he . . . he struck at the man in front. He reacted very quickly. I was so proud of him, thinking about it later. He knew at once what it was and he reacted so quickly. I was just sitting there, stunned.

QUESTION: A very brave man.

MRS. BINGHAM: Yes. He is. So he hit out at this man, and this man laughed and moved his head so that my husband didn't really hit him. Then this man took a gun out of his pocket and hit my husband in the face with it. He just smashed him with it. We found out later it had broken the bones above and below my husband's right eye. My husband fell to the floor and I saw the blood. The blood just gushed out. Then this man kicked my husband. He kicked him in the stomach and in the . . . in the groin. And I just sat there. I just sat there. . . .

QUESTION: Please, Mrs. Bingham . . . please. . . . Would you like to put this over to another day?

MRS. BINGHAM: No . . . no . . . that's all right . . . no. . . .

QUESTION: Let's take a little break. What I would like you to do, if you feel you are capable of it at this time, is to come with me downstairs to another office. There we have an exhibit of many types of guns used by lawbreakers. I would like you, if you can, to identify the gun the man used when he hit your husband. Will you do that for us?

MRS. BINGHAM: It was a very big gun, very heavy. I think it was black or maybe. . . .

QUESTION: Just come with me, and let's see if you can identify the gun from our collection. I'll take the machine with us.

[Lapse of four minutes thirty-eight seconds.]

QUESTION: This is NYDA Number one-four-six, nine-eight-B, two. We are now in the gun room. Now, Mrs. Bingham, as you can see, these are cases of weapons that have been used in crimes.

What I would like you to do is to examine these weapons—take all the time you need; don't hurry—and try to pick out the weapon you think that first masked man used to strike your husband.

MRS. BINGHAM: There are so many!

QUESTION: Yes . . . many. But take your time. Look at all of them and try to identify the gun the man used.

[Lapse of one minute thirty-seven seconds.]

MRS. BINGHAM: I don't see it.

QUESTION: Take your time. No hurry.

MRS. BINGHAM: It was black, or maybe dark blue. It was square.

QUESTION: Square? Come over to this case, ma'am. Something like this?

MRS. BINGHAM: Yes . . . these look more like it . . . Yes . . . yes . . . there it is! That's the one.

QUESTION: Which one is that?

MRS. BINGHAM: There it is . . . that second one from the top.

QUESTION: You're sure of that, ma'am?

MRS. BINGHAM: Absolutely. No question about it.

QUESTION: The witness has just identified a U.S. pistol, caliber .45, 1917, Colt automatic, Code Number nineteen seventeen, C-A, three-seven-one-B. Thank you, Mrs. Bingham. Shall we go upstairs now? Perhaps I'll order in some coffee or tea?

MRS. BINGHAM: A cup of tea would be nice.

QUESTION: Of course.

[Lapse of seven minutes, sixteen seconds.]

MRS. BINGHAM: I feel better now.

QUESTION: Good. This is NYDA Number one-four-six, nine-eight-B, three. Ma'am, do you think you'd like to finish up today—or should we put it off?

MRS. BINGHAM: Let's finish now.

QUESTION: Fine. Now then . . . you said your husband hit out at the masked man. The masked man drew a weapon from his pocket and struck your husband. Your husband fell to the floor. The masked man then kicked him in the stomach and in the groin. Is that correct?

MRS. BINGHAM: Yes.

QUESTION: Then what happened?

MRS. BINGHAM: It's all very hazy. I'm not sure. I think I was out of my chair by this time and moving toward the door. But I distinctly saw the second masked man push the first one aside. And the second man said, "That's enough." I remember that very clearly because it was exactly what I was thinking at the time. The second masked man shouldered the first one aside so he couldn't kick my husband anymore, and he said, "That's enough."

QUESTION: And then?

MRS. BINGHAM: I'm afraid I don't remember in what sequence things took place. I'm very hazy about it all. . . .

QUESTION: Just tell it in your own words. Don't worry about the sequence.

MRS. BINGHAM: Well, I ran over to my husband. I think I got down on my knees alongside him. I could see his eye was very bad. There was a lot of blood, and he was groaning. One of the men said, "Where's the kid?"

QUESTION: Do you remember which man said that?

MRS. BINGHAM: I'm not sure, but I think it was the second one—the one who told the first man to stop kicking my husband.

QUESTION: He said, "Where's the kid?"

MRS. BINGHAM: Yes.

QUESTION: So he knew about your son?

MRS. BINGHAM: Yes. I asked him please, not to hurt Gerry. I told him Gerry was asleep in his bedroom and that he was crippled and could only move in his wheelchair or for short distances on crutches. I asked him again, please not to hurt Gerry, and he said he wouldn't hurt him.

QUESTION: This is still the second man you're talking about?

MRS. BINGHAM: Yes. Then he went into my son's bedroom. The first man, the one who kicked my husband, stayed in the living room. After a while the second man came out of the bedroom. He was pushing my son's empty wheelchair and carrying his aluminum crutches. The first man said to him, "Where's the kid?" The other one said, "He's pretending he's asleep, but he's awake all right. I told him if he yelled I'd come back and break his neck. As long as we've got his chair and crutches, he can't move. He's a gimp. We checked this out." And the first man said, "I think we should take him." And then the second man said, "The elevator is stopped. You want to carry him down? How we going to get him down?" And then they argued a while about whether they should take the boy. Finally they agreed they would leave him in bed but they would gag him and look in on him every ten minutes or so. I asked them please not to do that. I told them that Gerry has sinus trouble, and I was afraid if they'd gag him, perhaps he wouldn't be able to breathe. The second man said they were taking my husband and me down to Mrs. Hathway's apartment on the fourth floor, and they couldn't take the chance of leaving Gerry alone in the apartment, even if he couldn't move. I told them I would make Gerry promise to keep quiet if they would let me talk to him. They argued about this for a while, and then the second man said he would come into the bedroom with me and listen to what I said to Gerry. So we went into the bedroom. I snapped on the light. Gerry was lying on his back, under the covers. His face was very white. His eyes were open. I asked him if he knew what was going on, and he said yes, he had heard us talking. My son is very intelligent.

QUESTION: Yes, ma'am. We know that now.

MRS. BINGHAM: I told him they had taken his chair and crutches, but if he promised not to yell or make any sounds, they had agreed not to tie him up. He said he wouldn't make any sounds. The man went over to the bed and looked down at Gerry. "That's a bad man out there, boy," he said to Gerry. "I think he's already put your pappy's eye out. You behave yourself or I'll have to turn him loose on your pappy again. You understand?" Gerry said yes, he understood. Then the man said there would be someone looking in on him every few minutes so not to get wise-ass. That was the expression he used. He said, "Don't get wise-ass, kid." Gerry nodded. Then we went back into the living room.

QUESTION: Did you leave the light on in the bedroom?

MRS. BINGHAM: Well, I turned it off, but the masked man turned it on again and said to leave it on. So we went back into the living room. My husband was on his feet, swaying a little. He had gotten a towel from the bathroom and was holding it to his eye. I don't know why I hadn't thought of that before. I'm afraid I wasn't behaving very well.

QUESTION: You were doing just fine.

MRS. BINGHAM: Well . . . I don't know. . . . I don't think I'm very brave. I know I was crying. I started crying when I saw my husband on the floor and the man was kicking him, and somehow I just couldn't stop. I couldn't stop. . . . I tried to stop but I just. . . .

QUESTION: Let's leave the rest of this for another day, shall we? I think we've done enough for one day.

MRS. BINGHAM: Yes . . . all right. Well, they just took us down the service staircase to the fourth floor, to Mrs. Hathway's apartment. I imagine you know what happened after that. I helped support my husband on the way down the stairs; he was still very shaky. But in Mrs. Hathway's apartment we could take care of him. They had brought everyone there, including Dr. Rubicoff, and he helped me bathe my husband's eye and put a clean towel on it. Everyone was very . . . everyone was very . . . everyone . . . oh, my God, my God!

QUESTION: Yes, Mrs. Bingham . . . yes, yes. Just relax a moment. Just sit quietly and relax. It's all over. It's all completely over.

[59]

The following is a personal letter to the author, dated 3 January, 1969, from Mr. Jeremy Marrin, 43-580 Buena Vista Drive, Arlington, Virginia.

DEAR SIR:

In reply to your letter of recent date, requesting my personal recollections and reactions to what happened in New York City last year on the Labor Day weekend, please be advised that both myself and John Burlingame have made very complete statements to the New York City police anent these events, and I'm sure our statements are a matter of public record and you may consult them. However, as a matter of common courtesy (called common, no doubt, because it is so *un*common) I will pen this very short note to you as you say it is of importance to you.

John Burlingame, a chum of mine, and I planned to spend the Labor Day weekend in New York, seeing a few shows and visiting companions. We wrote to Eric Sabine, a very dear friend of ours, who occupies Apartment 2A at 535 East Seventy-third Street, hoping to spend some time with him and his very groovy circle of acquaintances. Eric wrote back that he would be out of the city for the weekend. Fire Island, I believe he said. But he put his gorgeous apartment completely at our disposal, mailed us the key, and said he would leave instructions with the doormen that we would be staying for the weekend. Naturally, we were delighted and very grateful to kind-hearted Eric.

We started out very early Saturday morning, driving up, but with one thing and another, we did not arrive until 10:30 or so, quite worn out with the trip. The traffic was simply murder. So we bought the Sunday papers and just locked ourselves in for the night. Dear Eric had left a full refrigerator (fresh salmon in aspic, no less!) and, of course, he's got the best bar in New York —or anywhere else, for that matter. Some of his liqueurs are simply incredible. So John and I had a few drinks, soaked a while in a warm tub, and then went to bed—oh, I'd say it was 12:15, 12:30, around then. We were awake, you understand, just lying in bed and drinking and reading the papers. It was a very groovy experience.

It was about—oh, I'd say fifteen minutes after

one o'clock or so, when we heard this terrible banging on the front door, and a man's voice shouted, "Fire! Fire! Everybody out! The whole house is on fire!"

So naturally, we just leaped out of bed. We had brought pj's, but neither of us had thought to bring robes. Fortunately, dear Eric has this groovy collection of dressing gowns, so we borrowed two of his gowns (I had this lovely thing in crimson jacquard silk), put them on, rushed into the living room, unlocked the door . . . and here were these two horrid men with masks over their heads. One was quite short and one quite tall. The tall one, whom I am absolutely certain was a jigaboo, said, "Let's go. You come with us and no one get hurt."

Well, we almost fainted, as you can well imagine. John shouted, "Don't hurt my face, don't hurt my face!" John is in the theater, you know—a very handsome boy. But they didn't hurt us or even touch us. They had their hands in their pockets and I suspect they had weapons. They took us up the service stairway at the back of the building. We went into Apartment 4B where there were several other people assembled. I gathered that everyone in the building, including the doorman, had been brought there. One man was wounded and bleeding very badly from his eye. His wife, the poor thing, was weeping. But as far as I could see, no one else had been physically harmed.

We were told to make ourselves comfortable, which was a laugh as this was the most old-fashioned, campy apartment I have ever seen in my life. John said it would have made a perfect set for *Arsenic and Old Lace.* They told us not to scream or make any noise or attempt to resist in any way, as they merely wished to rob the apartments and not to hurt anyone. They were polite, in a way, but still you felt that if the desire came over them, they would simply slit your throat wide open.

After a while they all left except for the man who was, I'm sure, a spade. He stood by the door with his hand in his pocket, and I believe he was armed.

I'm sure you know the rest better than I can tell it. It was a very shattering experience, and in spite of the many groovy times I have had in New York, I can assure you it will be a long time before I visit Fun City again.

I do hope this may be of help to you in assembling your account of what happened, and if you're ever down this way, do look me up.

Very cordially,
[signed] JEREMY MARRIN

[60]

Statement NYDA-EHM-106A.

MANN: It was now twenty minutes after one. Perhaps one thirty. Everything was going very well.

Everyone had been assembled in Apartment Four B except for the superintendent, drunk and asleep in his basement apartment, and the crippled boy in Apartment Five A. So then, the building secured, we moved into the second phase of the operation in which we were divided into three teams.

QUESTION: Teams?

MANN: Yes. The man I knew as John Anderson and I constituted the first team. We worked from the basement upward. He had a checklist. We would move to an apartment. I would unlock the door and. . . .

QUESTION: Pick the lock?

MANN: Well . . . ah . . . my assignment was purely technical, you understand. Then we would enter the apartment. Anderson, who carried the checklist, would point out to me what he wished me to do.

QUESTION: What did that entail?

MANN: Well . . . you understand . . . perhaps a box safe, a wall safe. Perhaps a locked closet or cabinet. Things of that sort. Then, as we left the apartment, the second team would enter. This was the very short man, Tommy—effeminate, I believe—and the two men I knew as Ed and Billy. Tommy, who apparently knew the value of things, carried a copy of Anderson's checklist. He would direct the two brothers as to what should be removed and carried down to the truck. They were merely laborers, you understand.

QUESTION: What did they remove and carry to the truck?

MANN: What did they *not* remove! Furs, the triptych from the super's apartment, a small narcotics safe from one of the doctor's offices, jewelry, paintings, silver, unset gems, *objets d'art,* even rugs and small pieces of furniture from the decorator's apartment in Two A. One unexpected treasure was discovered in the medical doctor's suite on the lobby floor. There, this man Anderson, after I had opened the door, went directly to a closet in the doctor's office and there, on a back shelf of the closet, he discovered a cardboard shoe box containing a great deal of cash. I would say at least ten thousand dollars. Perhaps more. The Internal Revenue Service will be interested in that . . . *nein?*

QUESTION: Perhaps. You had no problems opening the doors or safes?

MANN: None. Very inferior. After we gained the third floor, I was confident I would have no need for the torches and tanks in the truck. Quite frankly, it was not a challenge to me. Simple. Everything went well.

QUESTION: You mentioned three teams. Who were on the third team?

MANN: They were the Negro and the uncouth man. They were detailed to guard the people assembled in Apartment Four B, and to look in on the sleeping super in the basement and the crippled boy in Apartment Five A. They were what is called muscle. They took no actual part in removing objects from the house—and, of course, I didn't either, you understand. Their duties were merely to keep the building quiet while it was being emptied.

QUESTION: And everything went well?

MANN: Beautiful. It was beautiful! A remarkable job of organization. I admired the man I knew as John Anderson.

[61]

The following is a portion of a statement dictated to a representative of the District Attorney's Office, County of New York, by Gerald Bingham, Jr., a minor, resident of Apartment 5A, 535 East Seventy-third Street, New York, New York. His entire statement is on recordings NYDA-#145-113A-113G, and as transcribed (NYDA-#146-113AT-113GT) consists of forty-three typewritten pages.

The following is an excerpt covering the most crucial period of the witness' activities. Material covered in previous testimony, and that to be covered in following testimony, has been deleted.

WITNESS: I heard the front door close, and I looked at my watch on the bedside table. It was nine minutes, thirty-seven seconds past one. My watch was an Omega chronometer. I never got it back. It was a very fine machine. Very accurate. I don't believe it gained more than three minutes a year. That's very good for a wristwatch, you know. In any event, I noted the time. Of course, I wasn't certain both the thieves had left the apartment with my parents. But my hearing is very acute—possibly because of my physical debility. That is an interesting avenue for research—whether paralyzed legs might affect other senses, the way a blind man hears and smells with such sensitivity. Well, some day. . . .

I judged they would come back to check on me within ten minutes. Actually, I heard the living room door open about seven minutes after they had left. A masked man came into the apartment, came into my bedroom, and looked at me. He was not the man who had spoken to me before. This man was somewhat shorter and heavier. He just looked at me, without saying anything. Then he saw my Omega chronometer on the bedside table, picked it up, put it in his pocket, and walked out. This angered me. I was already resolved to foil their plans, but this gave me an added incentive. I do not like people to touch my personal belongings. My parents know this and respect my wishes.

I heard the living room door close, and I began counting, using the professional photographers' method of ticking off seconds: "One hundred and one, one hundred and two . . ." and so forth. While I was counting, I picked up my bedside phone extension. As I suspected, it was completely dead, and I judged they had cut the main trunk line in the basement. This did not alarm me.

I judged they would check me every ten minutes or so for one or two times. Then, when they saw I was making no effort to escape or to raise an alarm, their visits would become more infrequent. Such proved to be the case. Their first visit, as I have said, occurred about seven minutes after their initial departure from the apartment. The second visit, by the same man, was eleven minutes and thirty-seven seconds after the first. The third visit—this was by a taller, more slender, masked man—came sixteen minutes and eight seconds after the second visit.

I judged the fourth visit would be approximately twenty minutes after the third. I estimated that, conservatively speaking. I had ten minutes in which I would not be disturbed. I did not wish to take the full twenty minutes as I did not wish to endanger my parents or the other tenants of the building who endeavor to be pleasant to me.

You must understand that although the lower half of my body is paralyzed and without control, I am very well developed from the waist up. My father takes me to a private health club three times a week. I am a very good swimmer, I can perform on the horizontal bars, and Paul—he's the trainer—says he has never seen anyone as fast as I am on the rope climb. My shoulders and arms are very well muscled.

The moment I heard the outside door close, after the third visit by one of the miscreants, I threw back the sheet and began to slide to the floor. Naturally, I wanted to be as quiet as possible. I didn't want to make any heavy thumps that might alert the thieves if they happened to be in Apartment Four A, directly below. So I got my upper body onto the floor and then, lying on my shoulders and back, I lifted my legs down with my hands. All this time I was counting, you understand. I wished to accomplish everything within the ten minutes I had allotted myself and be back in bed before the next inspection.

I moved by reaching out my arms, placing my forearms flat on the floor, and dragging my body forward with my biceps and shoulder muscles. I weigh almost one hundred and seventy-five pounds, and it was slow going. I remember trying to estimate the physical coefficients involved—angles, muscles involved, power required, the friction of the rug—things like that. But that's of no importance. Within three minutes I had reached the door of my closet—the walk-in closet on the north side of my bedroom, not the clothes closet on the south side.

After I became interested in electronics, my father had the walk-in closet cleared of hooks, hangers, and poles. He had a carpenter install shelves and a desk at the right height for me when I was seated in my wheelchair. It was in this closet that I installed all my electronic equipment. This not only included my shortwave transmitter and receiver, but also hi-fi equipment wired to speakers in my bedroom and in the living room and in my parents' bedroom. I had two separate turntables so my parents could listen to one LP while I listened to another, or we could even listen to separate tapes, if so desired. This was a wise arrangement as they enjoy Broadway show tunes—original-cast recordings—while I like Beethoven, Bach, and also Gilbert and Sullivan.

You may be interested to know that I had personally assembled every unit in that closet from do-it-yourself kits. If I told you how many junctions I had soldered, you wouldn't believe me. But not only were the savings considerable—over what the cost of the completed units would be—but as I went along I was able to make certain improvements—minor ones, to be sure—that gave us excellent stereo reproduction from tape and LP's and FM radio. I am currently assembling a cassette player on the work table to the left of the control board. Well, enough of that. . . .

I opened the closet door by reaching up. However, the work table and controls of my shortwave transmitter seemed impossibly high. But fortunately, the carpenter who installed the table had built sturdily, and I was able to pull myself up by fingers, wrists, arms, and shoulders.

It was somewhat painful but not unendurable. I should mention here that my antenna was on the roof of the building next door. It is an eighteen-story apartment house and towers over our five-story building. My father paid for the installation of an antenna and also pays ten dollars a month fee. The lead-in comes down the side of the tall building and into my bedroom window. It is not a perfect arrangement, but obviously better than having the antenna on our terrace, blocked by surrounding buildings.

Supporting myself on my arms, I turned on my equipment and waited patiently for the warm-up. I was still counting, of course, and figured five minutes had elapsed since I crawled out of bed. About thirty seconds later I began broadcasting. I gave my call signal, of course, and stated that a robbery was taking place at five-three-five East Seventy-third Street, New York, New York, and please, notify the New York Police Department. I didn't have time to switch on my receiver and wait for acknowledgments. I merely broadcast steadily for two minutes, repeating the same thing over and over, hoping that someone might be on my wavelength.

When I calculated that seven minutes had elapsed from the time I got out of bed, I switched off my equipment, let myself drop to the floor, closed the closet door, dragged myself back to my bed, hauled myself up, and got beneath the sheet. I was somewhat tired.

I was glad I had not taken the full twenty

minutes I had estimated I had before the fourth visit because one of the thieves came into my bedroom sixteen minutes and thirteen seconds after the third visit. It was the same tall, slender man who had made the previous inspection.

"Behaving yourself?" he asked pleasantly. Actually, he said, "Behavin' yoself," from which I judged he was colored. "Yes," I said, "I can't move, anyhow." He nodded and said, "We all got troubles." Then he left and I never saw him again.

I lay there and thought back on what I had just done. I tried to analyze the problem to see if there was anything more I could do, but I couldn't think of what it might be—without endangering my parents or the other tenants. I hoped someone had heard me, and I felt that, with luck, someone had. Luck is very important, you know. In many ways I know I am very lucky.

Also, to be quite frank, I thought these robbers were very stupid. They had obviously investigated our apartment house very well, but they had missed the one thing that might possibly negate all their efforts.

I could plan a crime much better than that.

[62]

NYPD-SIS recording #146-83C.

HASKINS: "Oh, God, Tommy, it was beautiful. Beautiful! It's about two o'clock now, maybe a little later. The first team is working the third floor. The second team, with me in charge, is finishing up Two A and Two B. And what we got in those places you wouldn't believe! From the fruit's apartment we took his paintings, small rugs, a few small pieces of antique furniture, his collection of unset gemstones, two original Picassos, and a Klee. From Two B, from the wall safe the tech had opened, we got a gorgeous tiara, a pearl necklace, and also a very chaste ruby choker I slipped into my pocket, figuring Snapper would flip over it. After all, she worked on this thing, too—even if the orders were that everything went into the truck. I knew we were already over our estimate when we hit the third floor. That retired jeweler in Three A had bags and bags of unset diamonds—most of them industrial but some very nice rocks as well. His little hedge against inflation. It took the tech less than three minutes to open the can—and without a torch. I was sure we'd hit a quarter of a mil at least. Maybe more. From the third, we were going to move up to the fifth, clean that out, and then come back down to the fourth where all the tenants were being held. But already I knew it was going to be great—much better than we had estimated. I knew the old biddies' apartment, Four B, would be a treasure-house. I was thinking we might hit half a million. Jesus, what luck! Everything was coming up roses!

[63]

The following are the introductory paragraphs of an article appearing in *The New York Times,* Tuesday, 2 July, 1968. The story was published on the first page of the second section of that day's newspaper, was by-lined by David Burnham, and is copyrighted by *The New York Times.*

The article was entitled "Police Emergency Center Dedicated By Mayor."

> Mayor Lindsay yesterday dedicated a $1.3-million police communications center that cuts in half the average time it takes the police to dispatch emergency help to the citizen.

"The miraculous new electronic communication system we inaugurate this morning will affect the life of every New Yorker in every part of our city, every hour of the day," Mr. Lindsay said during a ceremony staged in the vast, windowless, air-conditioned communications center on the fourth floor of the ponderous old Police Headquarters building at 240 Centre Street.

"This is, perhaps, the most important event of my administration as Mayor," Mr. Lindsay said. "No longer will a citizen in distress risk injury to life or property because of an archaic communications system."

The Mayor dedicated the new system about four weeks after it went into operation.

In that period the police response time to emergency calls was reduced to 55 seconds from about two minutes through a number of complex inter-related changes in the police communication change.

First, the time it takes to dial the police has been shortened by changing the old seven-digit emergency number—440-1234—to a new three-digit number, 911.

Second, the time it takes the police to answer an emergency call has been reduced by increasing the maximum number of policemen receiving calls during critical periods to 48 from 38 and by putting them in one room where all are available to handle any emergency that might occur in one area. Under the old system, when a citizen dialed 440-1234, his call went to a separate communications center situated in the borough from which he was calling.

[64]

The following section—and those of a similar nature below—are excerpts from the twenty-four-hour tape kept during the period 12:00 midnight, 31 August, 1968, to 12:00 midnight, 1 September, 1968, at the New York Police Communications Center at 240 Centre Street, Manhattan.

Tape NYPDCC-31AUG-1SEP. Time: 2:14:03 A.M.

OFFICER: New York Police Department. May I help you?

OPERATOR: Is this the New York City Police Department?

OFFICER: Yes, ma'am. May I help you?

OPERATOR: This is New York Telephone Company Operator four-one-five-six. Will you hold on a moment, please?

OFFICER: Yes.

[Lapse of fourteen seconds.]

NEW YORK OPERATOR: I have the New York City Police Department for you, Maine. Will you go ahead, please.

MAINE OPERATOR: Thank you, New York. Hello? Is this the New York City Police Department?

OFFICER: Yes, ma'am. May I help you?

MAINE OPERATOR: This is the operator in Gresham, Maine. I have a collect call for anyone in the New York City Police Department from Sheriff Jonathon Preebles of County Corners, Maine. Will you accept the charges, sir?

OFFICER: Pardon? I didn't get that.

MAINE OPERATOR: I have a call for anyone in the New York City Police Department from Sheriff Jonathon Preebles of County Corners, Maine. It is a collect call. Will you accept the charges, sir?

OFFICER: What's it about?

MAINE OPERATOR: Will you accept the charges, sir?

OFFICER: Can you hang on a minute?

MAINE OPERATOR: Yes, sir.

[Lapse of sixteen seconds.]

O'NUSKA: Sergeant O'Nuska.

OFFICER: Sarge, this is Jameson. I've got a collect call from a sheriff up in Maine. They want to know if we'll accept the charges.

O'NUSKA: A collect call?

OFFICER: That's right.

O'NUSKA: What's it about?

OFFICER: They won't tell unless we accept the charges.

O'NUSKA: Jesus Christ. Hang on a minute—I'll be right over.

OFFICER: Okay, Sarge.

[Lapse of forty-seven seconds.]

O'NUSKA: Hello? Hello? This is Sergeant Adrian O'Nuska of the New York Police Department.

Who's calling?

MAINE OPERATOR: Sir, this is the operator in Gresham, Maine. I have a collect call for anyone in the New York City Police Department from Sheriff Jonathon Preebles of County Corners, Maine. Will you accept the charges, sir?

O'NUSKA: What's it about?

MAINE OPERATOR: Will you accept the charges, sir?

O'NUSKA: Hang on a minute. . . . Jameson, what can it cost to call from Maine?

JAMESON: A couple of bucks maybe. Depends on how long you talk. I call my folks down in Lakeland, Florida, every month. Costs me maybe two—three bucks, depending on how long we talk.

O'NUSKA: I'll never get it back. I'll get stuck for it. You mark my words, I'll get stuck for it. . . . Okay, Operator, put the sheriff on the line.

OPERATOR: Go ahead, sir. Sergeant Adrian O'Nuska of the New York City Police Department is on the line.

SHERIFF: Hello there! You there, Sergeant?

O'NUSKA: I'm here.

SHERIFF: Well . . . good to talk to you. What kind of weather you folks been having?

O'NUSKA: Sheriff, I. . . .

SHERIFF: I tell you, we had a rainy spell last week. Four solid days like a cow pissing on a flat rock. Let up yesterday though. Sky nice and clear tonight. Stars out.

O'NUSKA: Sheriff, I. . . .

SHERIFF: But that ain't what I called to tell you about.

O'NUSKA: I'm glad to hear that, Sheriff.

SHERIFF: Sergeant, we got a boy down the road. Smart as a whip. Willie Dunston. He's the son—the second son—of old Sam Dunston. Sam's been farming in these parts for two hundred years. His folks has, anyways. Well, Willie is the smartest kid we've had in these parts since I can remember. We're right proud of Willie. Wins all the prizes. Had a writing of his published in this here scientific journal. The kids these days—I tell you!

O'NUSKA: Sheriff, I. . . .

SHERIFF: Willie's in his last year in high school over in Gresham. He's interested in all things scientific like. He's got himself this telescope, and I saw with my own eyes this little weather station he built with his own hands. You want to know what kind of weather you'll have tomorrow down there in New York, you just ask Willie.

O'NUSKA: I'll do that. I'll surely do that. But Sheriff, I. . . .

SHERIFF: And Willie's got this ham radio setup he built in a corner of the barn old Sam let him have. You know about this shortwave radio, Sergeant?

O'NUSKA: Yes, I know. I know.

SHERIFF: Well, maybe about fifteen–twenty minutes ago, I got this call from Willie on the telephone. He said on account of it was Saturday night and he could sleep late Sunday morning, he said he was out there in his corner there in the barn, listening in and talking to folks. You know how these shortwave radio folks do.

O'NUSKA: Yes. Go on.

SHERIFF: Willie said he picked up a call from New York City. He said he logged it in real careful and he figures it was about two minutes after two o'clock. You got that, Sergeant?

O'NUSKA: I got it.

SHERIFF: He said it was from a real smart kid in New York City he had talked to before. This kid said a robbery was going on right then and there in the apartment house where he lived. The address is five-three-five East Seventy-third Street. You got that, Sergeant?

O'NUSKA: I've got it. It's five-three-five East Seventy-third Street.

SHERIFF: That's right. Well, Willie said the kid wasn't receiving and didn't answer any questions. All he said was that there was a robbery going on in his house and if anyone heard him they should call the New York City Police and tell them. So then Willie called me. Got me up. I'm standing here in my skin. I figure it's probably nothing. You know how kids like to fun. But I figured I better call you anyhow and let you know.

O'NUSKA: Sheriff, thank you very much. You did exactly right, and we appreciate it.

SHERIFF: Let me know how it comes out, will you?

O'NUSKA: I'll surely do that. Thanks, Sheriff. Good-bye.

SHERIFF: Good-bye. You take care now.

[Lapse of six seconds.]

JAMESON: For God's sakes.

O'NUSKA: Were you listening in on that?

JAMESON: I sure was. That's pretty nutty—to have a Maine sheriff call us and tell us we got a crime in progress.

O'NUSKA: I think it's a lot of shit, but with all this stuff on tape, who can take a chance? Send a car. That's Sector George, isn't it? Tell them to cruise five-three-five East Seventy-third Street. Tell them not to stop—just cruise the place, take a look, and call back.

JAMESON: Will do. That was some long-winded sheriff . . . wasn't he, Sarge?

O'NUSKA: Was he? I guess so. Toward the end there he was getting to me.

2:23:41AM.

DISPATCHER: Car George Three, car George Three.

GEORGE THREE: George Three here.

DISPATCHER: Proceed five-three-five East Seventy-three. Signal nine-five. Proceed five-three-five East Seventy-three. Signal nine-five. Extreme caution. Report A-sap.

GEORGE THREE: Rodge.

2:24:13AM.

OFFICER: New York Police Department. May I help you?

VOICE: This is the Wichita, Kansas, Police Department Crime Communications Center. We got a phone call from a ham radio operator stating that he tuned in a call from New York stating that a robbery. . . .

2:25:01AM.

OFFICER: New York Police Department. May I help you?

VOICE: My name is Everett Wilkins, Junior. I live in Tulsa, Oklahoma, where I'm calling from. I'm a ham radio operator, and a little while ago I got a. . . .

2:27:23AM.

OFFICER: New York Police Department. May I help you?

VOICE: Hiya, there! This here's the chief of police down in Orange Center, Florida. We got this little old boy here who's like a nut about electronics and shortwave radio, and he says. . . .

2:28:12AM.

SERGEANT O'NUSKA: Jesus Christ!

2:34:41AM.

GEORGE THREE: Car George Three reporting.

DISPATCHER: Go ahead, Three.

GEORGE THREE: On your signal nine-five. Five-story apartment house. Lobby is lighted but we couldn't see anyone in it. There's a truck pulled up in the service alley. We saw two men loading what appeared to be a rug into the truck. The men appeared to be wearing some kind of masks.

DISPATCHER: Stand by. Out of sight around the corner or some place.

GEORGE THREE: Will do.

2:35:00AM.

JAMESON: Sarge, the car says it's a five-story apartment house. No one in the lobby. Truck parked in the service entrance. Two men, maybe masked, loading what appeared to be a rug into the truck.

O'NUSKA: Yes. Who's on duty—Liebman?

JAMESON: No, Sarge, his son was Bar-Mitzvahed today—or yesterday rather. He switched with Lieutenant Fineally.

O'NUSKA: Better get Fineally down here.

JAMESON: I think he went across the street to Ready's.

O'NUSKA: Well, get him over here, God damn it! And call the phone company. Get the lobby number of that address.

2:46:15AM.

OFFICER: New York Police Department. May I help you?

VOICE: My name is Ronald Trigere, and I live at four-one-three-two East St. Louis Street, Baltimore, Maryland. I am a ham radio operator, and I heard. . . .

2:48:08AM.

OFFICER: New York Police Department. May I help you?

VOICE: This is Lieutenant Donald Brannon, Chicago. We picked up a call from New York that stated. . . .

2:49:32AM.

JAMESON: Sarge, the phone company says the lobby number of that apartment house is five-five-five, nine-oh-seven-eight.

O'NUSKA: Call it.

JAMESON: Yes, sir.

2:49:53AM.

LIEUTENANT FINEALLY: What the fuck's going on here?

[65]

NYPD-SIS recording #146-83C.

HASKINS: Now it's a quarter to three. Maybe a smidgen before. We were all in Five B. The second team had caught up with the first. The tech was having trouble with a wall safe. This was the apartment of Longene, the theatrical producer. We already had his collection of gemstones, and the brothers had taken a very nice Kurdistan down to the truck. We figured the wall safe for Longene's cash and his wife's jewels —if she *was* his wife which I, for one, am inclined to doubt. Then Ed Brodsky came running in, breathing hard. He had just pounded up all the stairs. He told Duke a squad car had cruised by, just as he and his brother were loading the rug into the truck. Duke cursed horribly and said the cruise car for that street was supposed to be in the coop at that hour.

QUESTION: Is that the term he used—"In the coop?"

HASKINS: Yes, Tommy, it was. Definitely. Duke then asked Brodsky if he thought the fuzz had seen him. Brodsky said he couldn't tell for sure, but he thought they had. Just as the car came past, Ed and his brother were carrying the rug out the service entrance. The inside of the service staircase was lighted. We had to keep the lights on so the brothers wouldn't break their necks coming downstairs with the stuff. Brodsky said he thought he saw a white blur as the face of the driver turned toward him. Ed and his brother were still wearing their masks, of course.

QUESTION: What did Anderson say to this?

HASKINS: He just stood there a while, thinking. Then he called me over to a corner, and he said he had decided to cut the whole thing short. We would just hit the things we were sure of. So he and I went over our checklists together. We decided to do the wall safe in Five B, which the tech was still working on. We'd skip Five A completely. This was where the crippled boy was in his bedroom, but there was really nothing worth risking our necks for. Then we'd go down to Four A and get Sheldon's coin collection and also spring his wall safe. That's all we'd do there. Then we'd move all the tenants from Four B to Four A, and then we'd do as much as we could in Mrs. Hathway's Four B apartment as I anticipated a veritable treasure trove there. So we agreed on this, and Duke told everyone to move faster—we were getting out. About this time he also sent the spade down to the lobby and told him to stay there, out of sight, but to report any police activity in the street outside. That maniac from Detroit would guard the people in Four A. Just then the tech sprung Longene's wall safe, and we got a nice box of ice, some bonds, and at least twenty G's in cash. I took this as a good omen, although I didn't like the idea of a prowl car going by outside.

[66]

Continuing excerpts from twenty-four-hour tape, NYPDCC-31AUG-1SEP.

2:52:21AM.

JAMESON: Sir, there's no answer from the lobby

phone at five-three-five East Seventy-third Street. It's not even ringing.

LIEUTENANT FINEALLY: Get back to the phone company. Ask them if they know what's wrong. Sergeant.

O'NUSKA: Sir?

FINEALLY: The captain picked a good weekend to go to Atlantic City.

O'NUSKA: Yes, sir.

FINEALLY: Who's the standby inspector?

O'NUSKA: Abrahamson, sir.

FINEALLY: Get him up. Tell him what's happening. We'll call him as soon as we know.

O'NUSKA: Yes, sir.

FINEALLY: You . . . what's your name?

OFFICER: Bailey, sir.

FINEALLY: Bailey, get out the block map for the Two fifty-first Precinct. Find out what address is back-to-back with five-three-five East Seventy-third Street. That's on the north side of Seventy-third, so the house backing it will be on the south side of Seventy-fourth. Probably five-three-four or five-three-six. Get a description of it.

BAILEY: Yes, sir.

2:52:49AM.

FINEALLY: You want me?

JAMESON: The phone company says the lobby line is completely dead, sir. They don't know why. And they get no answer from any other phone at that address.

FINEALLY: Who told them to try the other numbers at that address?

JAMESON: I did, sir.

FINEALLY: What's your name?

JAMESON: Marvin Jameson, sir.

FINEALLY: College?

JAMESON: Two years, sir.

FINEALLY: You're doing all right, Jameson. I won't forget it.

JAMESON: Thank you, sir.

2:59:03AM.

BAILEY: Lieutenant, the house backing on five-three-five East Seventy-third Street is five-three-six East Seventy-fourth Street. It's a ten-story apartment house with a small open paved space in back.

FINEALLY: All right. Who talked to the car that saw the masked men—or thought they saw masked men?

JAMESON: I talked to the dispatcher, sir.

FINEALLY: You again? What number was it?

JAMESON: George Three, sir.

FINEALLY: Where are they now?

JAMESON: I'll find out, sir.

FINEALLY: Fast. Sergeant.

O'NUSKA: Sir?

FINEALLY: You think we ought to bring in the inspector?

O'NUSKA: Yes, sir.

FINEALLY: So do I. Call him and alert his driver.

3:01:26AM.

JAMESON: Lieutenant.

FINEALLY: Yes?

JAMESON: Car George Three is standing by on East Seventy-second Street.

FINEALLY: Tell them to proceed to five-three-six East Seventy-fourth Street. No siren. Get on the roof or any floor where they can see down onto five-three-five East Seventy-third Street. Tell them to report any activity A-sap. You got that?

JAMESON: Yes, sir.

O'NUSKA: Lieutenant, the inspector's on his way. But he's got to come in from Queens. It'll be half an hour at least.

FINEALLY: All right. It may still be nothing. Better call the Two fifty-first and talk to the duty sergeant. Tell him what's going on. Find out where his nearest beat men are. You better send three more cars. Have them stand by on East Seventy-second Street. No sirens or lights. Tell the duty sergeant of the Two fifty-first that we'll pull in two cars from Sector Harry to fill in. You take care of it. And we'll keep him informed. Now let's see—have we forgotten anything?

O'NUSKA: Tactical Patrol Force, sir?

FINEALLY: God bless you. But what have they got on for tonight? It's a holiday weekend.

O'NUSKA: One bus. Twenty men. I put them on Blue Alert.

FINEALLY: Good. Good.

O'NUSKA: And I didn't even go to college.

[67]

The following is an additional portion of the statement dictated to a representative of the District Attorney's Office, County of New York, by Gerald Bingham, Jr., a minor, resident of Apartment 5A, 535 East Seventy-third Street, New York, New York, excerpted from recordings NYDA-#146-113A-113G, and as transcribed (NYDA-#146-113AT-113GT).

WITNESS: I estimated it was now approximately three in the morning. I heard voices and sounds of activity coming from across the hall. I judged that the thieves were ransacking Apartment Five B and would soon be into our apartment. This caused me some trepidation, as I felt certain they would discover the electronic equipment in the closet in my bedroom. However, I took comfort from the fact that it might be possible they would not recognize the nature of the equipment. They would not realize it was a shortwave transmitter. Perhaps I could convince them it was part of our hi-fi system.

In any event, you understand, although I felt some fear—I realized that my body was covered with perspiration—I did not really care what they did to me. They could not know I had used the equipment. And I did not really believe they would kill me. I felt they might hurt me if they recognized the equipment and thought I might have used it. But I am no stranger to pain, and the prospect did not alarm me unduly. But I was disturbed by the realization that they might hurt my mother and father.

However, all my fears were groundless. For reasons I did not comprehend at the time, they skipped our apartment completely. The only man who came in was the tall, slender one who had removed my wheelchair and crutches earlier. He came in, stood alongside my bed and said, "Behaving yourself, boy?"

I said, "Yes, sir."

As soon as I said it, I wondered why I called him Sir. I do not call my father Sir. But there was something about this masked man. I have thought a great deal about him since the events of that night, and I have decided that somehow—I don't know quite how—he had an air and bearing of authority. Somehow, I don't know how, he demanded respect.

In any event, he nodded and looked about. "Your room?" he asked me.

"Yes," I said.

"All yours." He nodded again. "When I was your age, I lived in a room not much bigger than this with my mammy and pappy and five brothers and sisters."

"The late John F. Kennedy said that life is unfair," I told him.

He laughed and said, "Yes, that is so. And anyone over the age of four who don't realize it ain't got much of a brain in him. What you want to be, boy?"

"A research scientist," I said promptly. "Perhaps in medicine, perhaps in electronics, maybe in space technology. I haven't decided yet."

"A research scientist?" he asked, and by the way he said it, I knew he didn't have a very clear idea of what that was. I was going to explain to him but then I thought better of it.

"A research scientist?" he repeated. "Is there money in it?"

I told him there was, that I'd already had offers from two companies and that if you discovered something really important, you could become a multimillionaire. I don't know why I was telling him these things except that he seemed genuinely interested. At least, that's the impression I received.

"A multimillionaire," he repeated. He said, "Mult-*eye*."

Then he looked around the room—at my books, my work table, the space maps I had pinned to the walls.

"I could—" he started to say, but then he stopped and didn't go on.

"Sir?" I said.

"I could never understand any of this shit," he said finally and laughed. Then he said, "You keep behaving yourself, y'hear? We'll be out of here soon. Try to get some sleep."

He turned around and walked out. I only saw him once after that, very briefly. I felt that if he. . . . I felt that maybe I could have been a good. . . . I felt that maybe he and I might. . . . I am afraid I am not being very precise. I do not know exactly what I felt at that moment.

[68]

Continuing excerpts from the twenty-four-hour tape, NYPDCC-31AUG-1SEP.

3:14:32AM.

O'NUSKA: Lieutenant, we have a report from Officer Meyer in car George Three. He got onto the roof of the building at five-three-six East Seventy-fourth Street. He says shades are drawn in all the apartments at five-three-five East Seventy-third. Lights are on in several apartments. The service staircase in the rear of the building is also lighted. There is an unshaded window on the service staircase at each floor. Meyer says he saw masked men carrying objects down the stairs and placing them in the truck parked in the service alley.

FINEALLY: How many men did he see?

O'NUSKA: He says at least five different men, maybe more.

FINEALLY: Five men? My God, what's this going to be—the shoot-out at the O.K. Corral? Get the tactical squad moving. Red Alert. Tell them to park on Seventy-second near the river and wait further instructions. You got those three other cars?

O'NUSKA: Yes, sir. Standing by, within a block or so.

FINEALLY: Seal off East Seventy-third Street. Put one car across the street at East End Avenue and another at York Avenue.

O'NUSKA: Got it.

FINEALLY: Tell George Three to stay where they are. Send the third car around to join them.

O'NUSKA: Right.

FINEALLY: Let's see now—there's got to be tenants in there.

O'NUSKA: Yes, sir. It's the holiday weekend and some of them'll be gone, but there's got to be someone—the super, the doorman, the kid who sent out the shortwave call. Others probably.

FINEALLY: Get me the duty sergeant at the Two fifty-first. You know who he is?

O'NUSKA: Yes, sir. He's my brother.

FINEALLY: You kidding?

O'NUSKA: No, sir. He really is my brother.

FINEALLY: What kind of a precinct is it?

O'NUSKA: Very tight. Captain Delaney lives right next door in a converted brownstone. He's in and out all the time, even when he's not on duty.

FINEALLY: Don't tell me that's "Iron Balls" Delaney?

O'NUSKA: That's the man.

FINEALLY: Well, well, well. Will wonders never cease? Get him for me, will you? We need a commander on the scene.

O'NUSKA: Right away, Lieutenant.

3:19:26AM.

DELANEY: I see. . . . What is your name?

FINEALLY: Lieutenant John K. Fineally, sir.

DELANEY: Lieutenant Fineally, I shall now repeat what you have told me. If I am incorrect in any detail, please do not interrupt but correct me when I have finished. Is that understood?

FINEALLY: Yes, sir.

DELANEY: You have reason to believe that a breaking and entering, and a burglary and/or armed robbery is presently taking place at five-three-five East Seventy-third Street. A minimum of five masked men have been observed removing objects from this residence and placing them in a truck presently located in the service alleyway alongside the apartment house. Four Sector George cars are presently in the area. One is blocking Seventy-third Street at East End Avenue, and one is blocking the street at York Avenue. Two cars with four officers are on Seventy-fourth Street, in the rear of the building in question. The duty sergeant of this precinct has alerted two patrolmen to stand by their telephones and await further instructions. The

Tactical Patrol Force bus is presently on its way with a complement of twenty men, under Red Alert, and has been instructed to stand by on Seventy-second Street to await further orders. Inspector Walter Abrahamson has been alerted and is on his way to the scene of the suspected crime. I will proceed to the scene and take command of the forces at my disposal until such time as the inspector arrives. I will enter the premises with the forces at my disposal and, with proper care for the life and well-being of innocent bystanders, forestall the alleged thieves from escaping, place them under arrest, and recover the reportedly stolen objects. Is that correct in every detail?

FINEALLY: You've got it right, sir. In every detail.

DELANEY: Is a tape being made of this conversation, Lieutenant?

FINEALLY: Yes, sir, it is.

DELANEY: This is Captain Edward X. Delaney signing off. I am now departing to take command of the forces available to me at the scene of the reported crime.

[Lapse of six seconds.]

FINEALLY: Jesus Christ. I don't believe it. I heard it but I don't believe it. Were you listening to that, Sergeant?

O'NUSKA: Yes, sir.

FINEALLY: I've heard stories about that guy but I never believed them.

O'NUSKA: They're all true. He's had more commendations than I've had hangovers.

FINEALLY: I still don't believe it. He's something else again.

O'NUSKA: That's what my brother says.

[69]

The following is a typed transcription (NYDA-#146-121AT) from an original recording (NYDA-#146-121A) made on 11 September, 1968, at Mother of Mercy Hospital, New York City. The witness is Gerald Bingham, Sr., resident of Apartment 5A, 535 East Seventy-third Street, New York, New York.

QUESTION: Glad to see you looking better, Mr. Bingham. How do you feel?

BINGHAM: Oh, I feel a lot better. The swelling is down, and I received some good news this morning. The doctors say I won't lose the sight of my right eye. They say the sight may be slightly impaired, but I'll be able to see out of it.

QUESTION: Mr. Bingham, I'm glad to hear that . . . real glad. I can imagine how you felt.

BINGHAM: Yes . . . well . . . you know. . . .

QUESTION: Mr. Bingham, there are just a few details in your previous statement we'd like to get cleared up—if you feel you're up to it.

BINGHAM: Oh, yes. I feel fine. As a matter of fact, I welcome your visit. Very boring—just lying here.

QUESTION: I can imagine. Well, what we wanted to clear up was the period around three thirty on the morning of 1 September, 1968. According to your previous statement, you were at that time in Apartment Four B with the other tenants and the doorman. You were being guarded by the man who struck you in the face and kicked you earlier in your own apartment. This man was carrying a weapon. Is that correct?

BINGHAM: Yes, that's right.

QUESTION: Do you know anything about handguns, Mr. Bingham?

BINGHAM: Yes . . . a little. I served with the Marines in Korea.

QUESTION: Can you identify the weapon the man was carrying?

BINGHAM: It looked to me like a government issue Colt .45 automatic pistol of the 1917 series.

QUESTION: Are you certain?

BINGHAM: Fairly certain, yes. I had range training with a gun like that.

QUESTION: At the time in question—that is, three thirty on the morning of first September—what was your physical condition?

BINGHAM: You mean was I fully conscious and alert?

QUESTION: Well . . . yes. Were you?

BINGHAM: No. My eye was quite painful, and I was getting this throbbing ache from where he had kicked me. They had put me on the couch in Mrs. Hathway's living room—it was really a Victorian love seat covered with red velvet. My wife was holding a cold, wet towel to my eye, and Dr. Rubicoff from downstairs was helping also. I think I was a little hazy at the time. Perhaps I was in mild shock. You know, it was the first time in my life I had been struck in anger. I mean, it was the first time I had ever been physically assaulted. It was a very unsettling experience.

QUESTION: Yes, Mr. Bingham, I know.

BINGHAM: The idea that a man I didn't know had struck me and injured me, and then had kicked me . . . to tell you the truth, I felt so ashamed of myself. I know this was probably a strange reaction to have, but that's the way I felt.

QUESTION: You were ashamed?

BINGHAM: Yes. That's the feeling I had.

QUESTION: But why should you feel ashamed? You had done all you could—which was, incidentally, much more than many other men would have done. You reacted very quickly. You tried to defend your family. There was no reason why you should have been ashamed of yourself.

BINGHAM: Well, that's the way I felt. Perhaps it was because the man with the gun treated me—and the others, too—with such utter, brutal contempt. The way he waved that gun around. The way he laughed. I could see he was enjoying it. He shoved us around. When he wanted the doorman to get away from the window, he didn't tell him to get away; he shoved him so that poor Tim O'Leary fell down. Then the man laughed again. I think I was afraid of him. Maybe that's why I felt ashamed.

QUESTION: The man was threatening you with a loaded gun. There was good reason to be frightened.

BINGHAM: Well . . . I don't know. I was in action in Korea. Small-scale infantry action. I was frightened then, too, but I wasn't ashamed. There's a difference but it's hard to explain. I knew this man was very sick and very brutal and very dangerous.

QUESTION: Well, let's drop that and get on. . . . Now, you said that at about three thirty—maybe a bit later—four of the others came in and moved all of you to Apartment Four A across the hall.

BINGHAM: That's correct. I was able to walk, supported by my wife and Dr. Rubicoff, and they got us all out of Apartment Four B and into Four A.

QUESTION: Did they tell you why they were moving you?

BINGHAM: No. The man who seemed to be the leader just came in and said, "Everyone across the hall. Make it fast. Move." Or something like that.

QUESTION: He told you to make it fast?

BINGHAM: Yes. Perhaps I was imagining things—I was still shaky, you understand—but I thought there was a tension there. They prodded us to move faster. They seemed to be in a big hurry now. When they first came to my apartment earlier in the evening they were more controlled, more deliberate. Now they were hurrying and pushing people.

QUESTION: Why did you think that was?

BINGHAM: I thought they seemed frightened, that something was threatening them and they wanted to wind up everything and get out in a hurry. That's the impression I got.

QUESTION: You thought *they* were frightened? Didn't that make you feel better?

BINGHAM: No. I was still ashamed of myself.

[70]

The following section (and several below) is excerpted from the final report of Captain Edward X. Delaney—a document that has become something of a classic in the literature of the New York Police Department, and that has been reprinted in the police journals of seven countries, including Russia. Its official file number is NYPD-EXD-1SEP1968.

"I arrived at the corner of East Seventy-third Street and York Avenue at approximately 3:24 A.M. I had driven over from the 251st Precinct house. My driver was Officer Aloysius McClaire. I immediately saw the squad car that had been parked across Seventy-third Street, supposedly blocking exit from the street. However, it was improperly situated. This was car George Twenty-four (See

Appendix IV for complete list of personnel involved.) After identifying myself, I directed that the car be parked slightly toward the middle of the block at a point where private cars were parked on both sides of the street, thus more effectively blocking exit from the street.

"There is a public phone booth located on the northwest corner of East Seventy-third Street and York Avenue. My investigation proved this phone to be out of order. (N.B. Subsequent investigation proved all the public phone booths within a ten-block area of the crime had been deliberately damaged, apparent evidence of the careful and detailed planning of this extremely well-organized crime.)

"I thereupon directed Officer McClaire to force open the door of a cigar shop located on the northwest corner of East Seventy-third Street and York Avenue. He did so, without breaking the glass, and I entered, switched on the lights, and located the proprietor's phone. (I was careful to respect his property, although recompense should be made by the City of New York for his broken lock.)

"I then called Communications Center and spoke to Lieutenant John K. Fineally. I informed him of the location of my command post and requested that the telephone line on which I was speaking be kept open and manned every minute. He agreed. I also requested that Inspector Walter Abrahamson, on his way in from Queens, be directed to my command post. Lieutenant Fineally acknowledged. I then directed my driver, Officer

McClaire, to remain at the open phone line until relieved. He acknowledged this order.

"I was dressed in civilian clothes at this time, being technically off duty. I divested myself of my jacket and carried it over one arm, after rolling up my shirt sleeves. I left my straw hat in the cigar store. I borrowed a Sunday morning newspaper from one of the officers in the car blockading Seventy-third Street. I placed the folded newspaper under my arm. Then I strolled along the south side of East Seventy-third Street, from York Avenue to East End Avenue. As I passed 535 East Seventy-third Street, across the street, I could see, without turning my head, the truck parked in the service entrance. The side doors of the truck were open, but there was no sign of human activity.

"I saw immediately that it was a very poor tactical situation for a frontal assault. The houses facing the beleaguered building offered very little in the way of cover and/or concealment. Most were of the same height as 535, being town houses or converted brownstones. A frontal assault would be possible, but not within the directives stated in NYPD-SIS-DIR-#64, dated 19 January, 1967, which states: 'In any action, the commanding officer's first consideration must be for the safety of innocent bystanders and, secondly, for the safety and well-being of police personnel under his command.'

"When I reached the corner of East Seventy-third Street and East End Avenue, I identified myself to the officers in car George Nineteen, blocking the street at this corner. Again, the car was improperly parked. After pointing out to the driver how I wished the car to be placed, I had him drive me around the block, back to my command post on York Avenue, and then directed him to return to his original post and block the street at that end in the manner in which I had directed. I then returned the newspaper to the officer from whom I had borrowed it.

"In the short drive around the block to my command post, I had formulated my plan of attack. I contacted Lieutenant Fineally at Communications Center via the open telephone line in the cigar store. (May I say at this time that the cooperation of all personnel at Communications Center during this entire episode was exemplary, and my only suggestion for improvement might be a more formalized system of communication with more code words and numbers utilized. Without these, communications tend to become personalized and informal, which just wastes valuable time.)

"I ordered Lieutenant Fineally to send to my command post five more two-man squad cars. I also requested an emergency squad—to be supplied with at least two sets of walkie-talkies; a weapons carrier, with tear gas and riot guns; two searchlight cars; and an ambulance. Lieutenant Fineally stated he would consult his on-duty roster and supply whatever was available as soon as possible. At this time—I estimate it was perhaps 3:40 or 3:45 A.M.—I also asked Lieutenant Fineally to inform Deputy Arthur C. Beatem, the standby deputy of that date, of what was going on and leave it to Deputy Beatem's judgment as to whether or not to inform the commissioner and/or the mayor.

"I then began to organize my forces. . . ."

[71]

NYPD-SIS recording #146-83C.

HASKINS: About this time, Duke told. . . .

QUESTION: What time was it?

HASKINS: Oh, I don't know exactly, Tommy. It was getting late—or rather early in the morning. I thought the sky was getting light, or perhaps I was imagining it. In any event, I had pointed out to the Brodsky brothers what was to be taken from Apartment Four B. As I had suspected, it was a veritable treasure trove. The tech sprung a huge old-fashioned trunk, brass-bound, with a hasp and padlock on it. And he also opened a few odds and ends like jewel boxes, file cases, and even a GI ammunition box that had been fitted with a hasp and padlock. It was really hilarious what those old biddies had squirreled away. Quite obviously, they did not trust banks! There was one diamond pendant and a ruby choker—all their jewels were incredibly filthy, incidentally—and I judged those two pieces alone would bring close to fifty G's. In addition, there was cash—even some of the old-style large bills that I hadn't seen for years and years. There were negotiable bonds, scads and scads of things like Victorian tiaras, bracelets, "dog collars," headache bands, pins, brooches, a small collection of jeweled snuffboxes, loops and loops of pearls, earrings, men's stick pins—and all of it good, even if it did need a cleaning. My God, Tommy, it was like being let loose in Tiffany's about seventy-five years ago. There were also some simply yummy original glass, enamel, and cloisonné pieces that I couldn't bear to leave behind. Duke had told us to hurry it up, so we disregarded the rugs and furniture, although I saw a Sheraton table—a small one—that any museum in the city would have given an absolute fortune for, and there was a tiny little Kurdistan, no bigger than three by five, that was simply exquisite. I just couldn't bear to leave that behind, so I had Billy Brodsky—the one who had the wet brain—tuck it under his arm and take it down to the truck.

QUESTION: Where was Anderson while all this was going on?

HASKINS: Oh, he was—you know—here, there, and everywhere. He checked on the crippled boy in Apartment Five A, and then he went out on the terrace of Five B to look around. Then he checked how that monster from Detroit was doing with the tenants who had been moved across the hall to Four A, and then he helped the Brodsky boys carry some things down to the truck, and then he prowled through some of the empty apartments. Just checking, you know. He was very good, very alert. Then, after I had finished in Apartment Four B, he told me to go down to the basement and see if the super was still sleeping and also check with the spade who had been stationed in the lobby. So I went down to the basement, and the super was still snoring.

QUESTION: Did you take anything from his apartment?

HASKINS: Oh no. It had been cleaned out earlier. The only thing we got was an antique triptych.

QUESTION: The super claims he had just been paid, he had almost a hundred dollars in his wallet, and this money was taken. Did you take it?

HASKINS: Tommy, that hurts! I may be many things, but I am not a cheap little sneak thief.

QUESTION: When they searched you at the station house you had about forty dollars in a money clip. And you also had almost a hundred dollars folded into a wad and tucked into your inside jacket pocket. Was that the super's money?

HASKINS: Tommy! How could you?

QUESTION: All right. What happened next—after you checked on the super and found he was still sleeping?

HASKINS: Duke had told me to check with Skeets Johnson in the lobby on the way up. He was in the doormen's booth in the rear of the lobby so no one could see him from the street. I asked him if everything was all right.

QUESTION: And what did he say?

HASKINS: He said he hadn't seen any beat fuzz or squad cars. He said the only person he had seen was a man carrying a newspaper with his jacket over his arm go humping by on the other side of the street. He said the man hadn't turned his head when he went by so he didn't think that was anything. But I could tell something was bothering him.

QUESTION: Why do you say that?

HASKINS: Well, everything he had said up to now had been in rhymes, some of them quite clever and amusing. The man was obviously talented. But now he was speaking normally, just as you or I, and he didn't seem to have the high spirits he had earlier in the evening. Like when we were in the truck, on the way to the apartment house, he kept us laughing and relaxed. But now I could tell he was down, so I asked him why. And he said he didn't know why he was down, but he said—and I remember his exact words—he said, "Something don't smell right." I left him there and went back upstairs and reported to Duke that Skeets hadn't seen any fuzz or cars but that he was troubled. Duke nodded and hurried the Brodsky boys along. We were about ready to leave. I figured another half hour at the most and we'd be gone. I wasn't feeling down. I was feeling up. I thought it had been a very successful evening, far beyond our wildest hopes. Even though I was working for a fixed fee, I wanted the whole thing to come off because it was very exciting—I had never done anything like that before—and I thought Duke might give me some more work. Also, you know, I had pocketed a few little things—trinkets . . . really nothing of value—but the whole evening would prove very profitable for me.

[72]

Excerpt from the final report of Captain Edward X. Delaney, NYPD-EXD-1SEP1968.

"See my memorandum No. 563 dated 21 December, 1966, in which I strongly urged that every commanding officer of the NYPD of the rank of lieutenant and above be required to attend a course in the tactics of small infantry units (up to company strength), as taught at several bases of the U.S. Army and at Quantico, Virginia, where officer candidates of the U.S. Marine corps are trained.

"During my service as patrolman in the period 1946-49, the great majority of crimes were committed by individuals, and the strategy and tactics of the NYPD were, in a large part, directed toward thwarting and frustrating the activities of individual criminals. In recent years, however, the nature of crime in our city (and, indeed, the nation—if not the world) has changed radically.

"We are now faced, not with individual criminals, but with organized bands, gangs, national and international organizations. Most of these are paramilitary or military-type organizations, be they groups of militant college students or hijackers in the garment center. Indeed, the organization variously known as Cosa Nostra, Syndicate, Mafia, etc., even has military titles for its members—don for general or colonel, *capo* for major or captain, soldier for men in the ranks, etc.

"The realization of the organized military character of crime today led to my memo cited above in which I urged that police officers be given military training in infantry tactics, and also be required to take a two-week refresher course each year to keep abreast of the latest developments. I myself have taken such courses on a volunteer basis since my appointment as lieutenant in 1953.

"Hence, I saw the situation at 535 East Seventy-third Street, in the early morning hours of 1 September, 1968, as a classic military problem. My forces, gathered and gathering (it was now approximately 3:45 A.M.), occupied the low ground—on the street—while the enemy occupied the high ground—in a five-story apartment house. ('War is geography.') Of particular relevance to such a situation are the U.S. Army handbooks—USA-45617990-416 (*House-to-House Combat*) and USA-917835190-017 (*Tactics of Street Fighting*).

"I decided that, although a direct, frontal assault was possible (such an assault is *always* possible if casualties may be disregarded), the best solution would be vertical envelopment. This is a technique developed by the Germans in World War II with the dropping of paratroopers behind the enemy's lines. It was further refined during the Korean Police Action by the use of helicopters. Attack, up to this time, had been largely a two-dimensional problem. It now became three-dimensional.

"During my reconnaissance along East Seventy-third Street, I had noted that the building immediately adjacent to 535 was what I judged to be a 16- to 18-story apartment house. It was flush against the east side of the beleaguered building. I realized at once that a vertical envelopment was possible. That is, I could have combat personnel lowered from the roof of the higher building or, with luck (a very important consideration in all human activities), I could have police officers exit through the windows of the higher building at perhaps the sixth or seventh floor and merely drop or jump to the terraces of the building occupied by the enemy.

"With a noisy display of force, I judged, the police personnel on the top floors of 535 could 'spook' the criminals and drive them down onto the street. I did not desire the police personnel on the upper floor (I estimated five would be an adequate number) to enter into combat with the enemy. Their sole duty would be to frighten the criminals down to the street level without endangering any tenants of the building who might be present.

"At that time the enemy would no longer enjoy the advantage of holding the upper ground. By careful, calculated timing, I would then have emplaced in a semicircle about the front of 535, four two-man squad cars and two searchlight cars, all personnel instructed to keep behind the cover and concealment offered by their vehicles as much as possible, and not to fire until fired upon. In addition, I intended to position a force of six men in the rear of 535—that is, in the cemented open space in the rear of the Seventy-fourth Street building that backed onto 535 East Seventy-third Street. This force, I felt, would be sufficient to block a rearward escape by the enemy. The fact that one, indeed, by his extraordinary ability and good fortune, did escape (temporarily), does not, in my opinion, negate the virtues of my plan of operations.

"By this time, the tactical squad (Tactical Patrol Force) had reported to me at my command post. This unit consisted of twenty men, in a bus, commanded by a Negro sergeant. There were two additional Negroes in the squad.

"The following comments may be considered by some to be unnecessary—if not foolhardy—considering the current state of ethnic and racial unrest in New York City. However, I feel my judgments—based on twenty-two years of service in the NYPD—may be of value to other officers faced with a comparable situation, and I am determined to make them. . . .

"It is said that all men are created equal—and this may be correct, in the sight of God and frequently—but not always—under the law. However, all men are *not* created equal as to their ethnic and racial origins, their intelligence, their physical strength, and their moral commitment. Specifically, ethnic and racial groups, whatever they may be—Negro, Irish, Polish, Jewish, Italian, etc.—have certain inborn characteristics. Some of these characteristics can be an advantage to a commanding officer; some may be a disadvantage. But if the commanding officer disregards them—through a misguided belief in total equality—he is guilty of dereliction of duty, in my opinion, since his sole duty is to solve the problem at hand, using the best equipment and personnel under his command, with due regard to the potential of his men.

"It has been my experience that Negro personnel are particularly valuable when the situation calls for a large measure of élan and derring-do. And they are especially valuable when they operate as units—that is, when several Negro officers are operating together. Hence, I ordered the Negro sergeant commanding the tactical squad to select the two other Negroes in his squad, augment them by two white officers, and execute the vertical envelopment. This would be the unit that would drop onto the terrace of 535 and flush the enemy down to the street.

"He acknowledged my order, and after a short discussion we agreed his men would be armed with one Thompson submachine gun, two riot guns, service revolvers, smoke, and concussion grenades. In addition, his squad of five men (including himself) would carry a walkie-talkie radio, and they would inform me the moment they had made their drop onto the terrace of 535. The officer's name is Sergeant James L. Everson, Shield 72897537, and

I hereby recommend him for a commendation. (See attached form NYPD-RC-EXD-109FGC-1968.)"

[73]

From the official report of Sergeant James L. Everson, Shield 72897537. This is coded NYPD-JLE-1SEP68.

"I received my orders from Captain Edward X. Delaney at his command post in a cigar store on the corner of East Seventy-third Street and York Avenue. I selected the four additional officers from my squad and proceeded to the corner of East Seventy-third Street and East End Avenue. Transportation was by squad car, as directed by Captain Delaney.

"Upon arrival at the aforesaid corner, I determined it would be best if we went one at a time into the building adjoining 535 East Seventy-third Street. Therefore I ordered my men to follow me at counted intervals of sixty seconds. I went first.

"I entered the lobby of the adjoining building and found the man on duty was not the regular doorman but was the super filling in for the doorman because of the holiday weekend. He was sleeping. I awakened him and explained the situation. By the time the other four men of my squad had joined me, he had told me he thought we could drop onto the terrace of 535 by going out the windows of Apartment 6C which overlooked the apartment house where the criminals were located and operating. We had service revolvers, a submachine gun, riot guns, and grenades. The super escorted us to Apartment 6C.

"This apartment was occupied by Irving K. Mandelbaum, a single man. At the time, there was also present in the apartment a single female, Gretchen K. Strobel. I believe, if desired, a charge of unlawful fornication could be brought against Irving K. Mandelbaum under the civil laws of the City of New York. But because of the cooperation Mr. Mandelbaum offered and provided to officers of the New York Police Department, I do not suggest this.

"Miss Strobel went into the bathroom, and me and the squad went through the bedroom window which directly overlooks the terrace at 535. It was only a two- or three-foot drop. The moment we were all on the terrace, I contacted Captain Delaney via walkie-talkie. Reception was very good. I told him we were in position, and he told me to wait two minutes, then go ahead."

[74]

From Captain Edward X. Delaney's report NYPD-EXD-1SEP1968.

"It was approximately 4:14 A.M. when Sergeant

Everson got through to me. I should mention here that the operation of the new 415X16C radios was excellent. Everson said he and his squad were on the terrace of 535 East Seventy-third Street. We agreed he would wait two minutes before commencing his spooking operation.

"Not all the men and equipment I had requisitioned had arrived by this time. However, I felt it better to proceed with what I had rather than await optimum conditions which rarely, if ever, seem to arrive. Hence, I directed cars George Six and George Fourteen (two officers each) to approach from York Avenue toward 535, and cars George Twenty-four and George Eight to approach from East End Avenue. Leading the two approaching from East End would be Searchlight Car SC-147 (the single one that had arrived by this time). The five vehicles would then park in a semicircle around the entrance of 535. The searchlight car would illuminate the building after all personnel had taken cover behind their vehicles. The arrival of additional squad cars, provided by the efficiency of Lieutenant John K. Fineally, NYPDCC, enabled me to station blocking cars at the exits from East Seventy-third Street at York Avenue and East End Avenue. Car George Nineteen was stationed at East End Avenue, and car George Thirty-two at York Avenue.

"I was in the first car (George Six) approaching the apartment house from York Avenue. My order, repeated several times, was that there was to be no firing until I gave the command."

[75]

Recording NYDA-#146-114A-114G. Interrogation of Gerald Bingham, Jr.

QUESTION: What time was it then?

WITNESS: I don't know exactly. It was after four in the morning.

QUESTION: What happened then?

WITNESS: Suddenly five policemen burst into my bedroom. They came in through the French doors leading to the terrace. Three of them were colored. The man in front was colored. They were all carrying weapons. The first man had a machine gun in his hands, and he said to me, "Who are you?"

I said, "I am Gerald Bingham junior, and I live in this apartment."

He looked at me and said, "You the kid that sent out the report?"

"Yes," I said, "I sent out a shortwave transmission."

He grinned at me and said, "You get yourself out on that terrace."

I told him I was crippled and couldn't move

because they had taken away my wheelchair and my crutches.

He said, "Okay, you stay right where you're at. Where *they* at?"

"Down on the fourth floor," I told him. "I think they're all on the fourth floor, right below us."

"Okay," he said, "we'll take care of them. You stay right where you're at and don't make no noise."

They all started out of the apartment. I called after them, "Please don't kill him," but I don't think they heard me.

[76]

NYPD-SIS recording #146-83C.

HASKINS: We were finishing up Apartment Four B. We were close to finishing. God, we were so *close!* Then everything came apart. Shouts from upstairs. Noise. Gunshots. A big explosion. Smoke pouring down the stairway. Men shouting, "You're surrounded! Hands up! Throw down your guns! You're dead! We've got you!" Silly things like that. I wet my pants. Yes, Tommy, I admit it freely—I soiled myself. Then we started moving. The tech went pounding down the back stairs, then the two Brodsky boys, and then me following. But before I left I saw the Detroit hooligan rush to the front window of Four A and fire his gun through the glass.

QUESTION: Was there return fire?

HASKINS: No. Well . . . I don't know for sure. I had turned away from the foyer between the two apartments. I was on my way down the service staircase. I saw and heard him fire through the window of Four A. But I didn't see or hear any return fire from the street.

QUESTION: Where was Anderson while all this was going on?

HASKINS: He was standing there in the foyer between the two apartments. He was just standing still. He just didn't move.

[77]

From the final report of Captain Edward X. Delaney, NYPD-EXD-1SEP1968.

"My assault forces were in position. The moment I heard the envelopment squad start their mission, the searchlight car—as per my previous orders—illuminated the front of the building. We were almost immediately fired upon from a fourth-floor window. I shouted to my men to hold their fire."

[78]

NYDA-EHM-108B, dictated, sworn, signed, and witnessed statement by Ernest Heinrich Mann.

"The moment the noise began, I realized it was all over. Therefore I walked slowly and quietly down the service staircase, took the door into the lobby, removed my mask and gloves, and seated myself on the marble floor, well out of range of the front doors. I then put my back against the wall, raised my arms above my head, and waited. I detest violence."

[79]

From the final report of Captain Edward X. Delaney, NYPD-EXD-1SEP1968.

"We still had not yet fired a shot. Then suddenly a masked man burst through the front doors of the house, firing a revolver at the assembled cars. I thereupon gave the command to open fire, and he was cut down in short order."

[80]

Excerpt from NYPD-SIS recording #146-83C, interrogation of Thomas Haskins by Thomas K. Brody, detective, second grade.

HASKINS: When we got down to the ground floor, the two Brodsky boys headed out to the truck through the back entrance. I took the door into the lobby. And there was the tech, sitting on the floor against the wall, without his mask, his hands raised over his head. I felt sick. Then I saw the smoke draw his gun and dash out through the front doors. I heard him say "Shit," and then he was gone out through the doors. Then I heard the guns and I knew he was dead. Frankly, I didn't know what to do. I believe I might have been somewhat hysterical. You understand, don't you, Tommy?

QUESTION: Yes. But what *did* you do?

HASKINS: Well, silly as it may seem—I wasn't thinking quite right, you understand—I turned and went back to the service staircase and started to go up. And there, at the second-floor landing, was Duke Anderson.

QUESTION: What was he doing?

HASKINS: Just standing there. Very calm. I said, "Duke, we've got—" And he said, very quiet, "Yes, I know. Don't do a thing right now. Stay right where you are. Just stand here. I've got something to do, but I'll be right down and we'll be getting out together."

QUESTION: Are those his exact words?

HASKINS: As near as I can remember.

QUESTION: And what did you do then?

HASKINS: I did exactly what he told me. I just stood there on the stairs.

QUESTION: What did he do?

HASKINS: Duke? He turned around and went back up the stairs.

[81]

From the final report of Captain Edward X. Delaney, NYPD-EXD-1SEP1968.

"We were still receiving intermittent fire from the fourth-floor window from what, I judged, was a single gunman. I instructed my men not to return his fire. Discipline, I should say at this time, under these difficult and aggravating circumstances was excellent. At approximately three minutes after the start of the action, two men dashed from the rear service entrance, climbed aboard the truck, and began to back the truck from the service alley at high speed.

"This was, of course, a move of desperation, doomed to failure as I had arranged my cordon of squad cars to forestall such a move. As the truck backed, one man leaned from the window and fired a revolver at us as the other drove. We returned his fire.

"The truck crashed into car George Fourteen and stopped there. In the crash, Officer Simon Legrange, Shield 67935429, suffered a broken leg, and Officer Marvin Finkelstein, Shield 45670985, was slightly wounded in the upper arm by a bullet fired by the gunman in the truck. Up to this time, this was the extent of our casualties.

"When I ordered, 'Cease fire!', we determined that the gunman in the truck was dead (later certified as Edward J. Brodsky) and the driver of the truck (later certified as William K. Brodsky) suffered a broken shoulder as a result of the crash."

[82]

NYPD-SIS-#146-92A.

MRS. HATHWAY: Well, we were all across the hall in Apartment Four A when suddenly the shooting started. I would say it was about fifteen minutes after four in the morning.

MISS KALER: Closer to four thirty.

MRS. HATHWAY: I had my brooch watch, you silly thing, and it was almost four fifteen.

MISS KALER: Four thirty.

QUESTION: Ladies, please. What happened then?

MRS. HATHWAY: Well, this masked man who had been so mean and cruel rushed to the window and began firing his weapon. He broke the glass —and what a mess it made on the rug. And he fired his gun down into the street. And then. . . .

MISS KALER: And then there were these terrible explosions on the stairs and men shouting and everyone wondered what was happening. So I said we should all sit right where we were and not move, and that would be the best thing, and this ruffian kept shooting his gun out the window, and I was thankful we were not in our own apartment as I feared the policemen might fire an atomic rocket through the window and destroy just everything. And just about then this other masked man came through the door and he was drawing a gun from his pocket and I thought he would also fire down through the window but he didn't. . . .

[83]

NYDA-#146-121AT.

BINGHAM: When the firing started, I suggested everyone get down on the floor. We all did except for the old ladies from across the hall who said they wouldn't—or perhaps they couldn't. In any event, they slumped in their chairs. The man who was guarding us fired his pistol out the window.

QUESTION: Was there any return fire, Mr. Bingham?

BINGHAM: No, sir, I do not believe there was. None that I was aware of. The man just kept firing his gun and cursing. I saw him reload at least once from a clip he took from his pocket. And then a few minutes later another masked man came into the apartment. I recognized him as the second man who had been in my apartment.

QUESTION: The man who told the first masked man to stop kicking you?

BINGHAM: Yes, that's the one. Well, he came into the apartment right then and he was drawing a gun from his pocket.

QUESTION: What kind of a gun? Did you recognize it?

BINGHAM: It was a revolver, not a pistol. Big. I'd guess a .38. I couldn't recognize the make.

QUESTION: All right. Then what?

BINGHAM: The second man, the man with the revolver who came in the door, said, "Socks."

QUESTION: Socks? That's all he said?

BINGHAM: Yes. He said, "Socks," and the man at the window turned around. And the second man shot him.

QUESTION: Shot him? How many times?

BINGHAM: Twice. I was watching this very closely and I'm sure of this. He came through the door, taking his gun from his pocket. He said, "Socks," and the man at the window turned around. And then the man coming in walked toward him and shot him twice. I could see the bullets going in. They plucked at his jacket. I think he shot him in the stomach and the chest. That's where it looked to me where the bullets went in. The man at the window dropped his own gun and went down. He went down very slowly. As a matter of fact, he grabbed at the drapes at the window and pulled down a drape and the rod. I think he said "What?"—or maybe it was something else. It sounded like "Wha" or something like that. Then he was on the floor and this maroon drape was across him and he was bleeding and twisting. Jesus. . . .

QUESTION: Shall we take a break for a few minutes, Mr. Bingham?

BINGHAM: No. I'm all right. And then my wife was sick; she up-chucked. And one of the old ladies from across the hall fainted and one screamed, and the two faggots I didn't know and had never see before hugged each other, and Dr. Rubicoff looked like someone had sapped him. Holy God, what a moment that was.

QUESTION: And what did the killer do then?

BINGHAM: He looked at the man on the floor for a very brief moment. Then he put the gun back in his pocket, turned around, and walked out of the apartment. I never saw him again. Strange you should call him a killer.

QUESTION: That's what he was—wasn't he?

BINGHAM: Of course. But at the moment I got the feeling he was an executioner. That's the feeling I got—this man is an executioner, doing his job.

QUESTION: Then what happened?

BINGHAM: After he left? Dr. Rubicoff went over and knelt by the man who had been shot and examined his wounds and felt his pulse. "Alive," he said, "but not for long. This is very bad."

QUESTION: Thank you, Mr. Bingham.

BINGHAM: You're welcome.

[84]

NYPD-SIS recording #146-83C.

HASKINS: It was a lifetime, an eternity. All that noise and gunfire and confusion. But I did what Duke told me and stood there on the second-floor landing.

QUESTION: You trusted him?

HASKINS: Of course, you silly! If you can't trust a man like Duke, who can you trust? So of course he came back down from the fourth floor, as I knew he would, and he said to me, "Better take your mask off, put your hands up, and go down slowly out the front door."

QUESTION: Why didn't you do that? It was good advice.

HASKINS: I know it was, I know it was. I knew it was then. But I can't explain to you how this man Anderson made me feel. He made me forget caution and made me willing to take a chance. Do you understand?

QUESTION: I'm afraid not.

HASKINS: Oh, Tommy, Tommy—he gave me balls! Well, anyway, when I didn't move, I could see him grin, and he said, "Out the back." So we took off our masks and gloves, dashed down the stairs, out the service entrance, started climbing the back wall . . . and suddenly there were eighteen million screws with flashlights in our faces and guns firing, and then I had my hands in the air as far as I could reach and I was screaming, "I surrender! I surrender!" Oh, God, Tommy, it was so *dramatic!*

QUESTION: And what happened to Anderson?

HASKINS: I really don't know. One moment he was there beside me, and the next moment he was gone. He just simply disappeared.

QUESTION: But you trusted him?

HASKINS: Of course.

[85]

NYDA-#146-113A-114G, interrogation of Gerald Bingham, Jr.

WITNESS: The noise suddenly stopped. There was no more gunfire or shouts. It was very quiet. I thought it was all over. I was still lying in bed. I was very wet, sweating. . . . Then suddenly the front door slammed. He came running through the apartment, through my bedroom, and out onto the terrace. He didn't say anything. He didn't even look at me. But I knew it was him . . . .

[86]

Statement of Irving K. Mandelbaum, resident of Apartment 6C, 537 East Seventy-third Street, New York, New York. This transcription is coded NYPD-#146-IKM-123GT.

WITNESS: What a night. What a *night!* I mean, we didn't go away for the weekend. We'll stay in the city, I figured. We'll have a nice, quiet weekend. No traffic. No hang-ups. No crowds. Everything will be nice and quiet. So we're in bed. You understand? Five cops armed like the invasion of Normandy come through the bedroom and go out the window. Okay. I'm a good, law-abiding citizen. I'm with them. We get out of bed. Gretch, she goes into the bathroom while the cops pile through the window. At least one of the *shvartzes* has the decency to say, "Sorry about this, pal." So then Gretch comes out of the bathroom and says, "Back to bed." So then the fireworks start. Guns, lights, screams—the whole thing is right out of a Warner Brothers' movie of the late 1930's, which I really dig—you know, something with James Cagney and Chester Morris. We get out of bed. We're watching all this from the front windows, you understand. It's very exciting. What a weekend! Then everything dies down. No more guns. No more yells. So Gretch says, "Back to bed!" So we go. About five minutes later a guy comes through the bedroom window, hoisting himself up and climbing in. He's got a gun in his hand. Gretch and I get out of bed. He says, "One word out of you and you're dead." So naturally I didn't even agree with him. A second later and he's gone. Gretch says, "Back to bed?" And I said, "No, dear. I think at this moment I will drink a quart of Scotch." Oh boy.

[87]

Statement of Officer John Similar, Shield 35674262, driver of car George Nineteen. Document NYPD-#146-332S.

"I was stationed with my partner, Officer Percy H. Illingham, 45768392, in car George Nineteen closing the exit at East Seventy-third Street and East End Avenue. We had been ordered to place our car across Seventy-third Street to prevent exit from or entrance to the street. We had been informed of the action that was taking place.

"At approximately thirty minutes after four A.M. on the morning of 1 September, 1968, a male (white, about six feet, 180 pounds, black jacket and pants) approached us, walking on the sidewalk, the south sidewalk of East Seventy-third Street. Percy said, 'I better check him out.' He opened the door on his side of the car. As he emerged onto the street, the man drew a weapon from his pocket and fired directly at Officer Illingham. Officer Illingham dropped to the pavement. Later investigation proved that he had been killed.

"I thereupon got out of the car on my side and fired three times at the suspect with my service revolver (Serial Number 17189653) as he fired one shot at me which hit me in the thigh and caused me to fall to the pavement. He then began to run, and while I was trying to line up another shot at him, he disappeared around the corner of Seventy-third Street and East End Avenue.

"I did what I could."

[88]

The following manuscript has been made available through the cooperation of its author, Dr. Dmitri Rubicoff, psychiatrist, with offices at 535 East Seventy-third Street, New York City. It is a portion of a speech Dr. Rubicoff delivered on the evening of 13 December, 1968, at a meeting of the Psychopathology Society of New York. This is an informal association of psychiatrists and psychologists in the New York area, which meets at irregular intervals to dine at one of the larger Manhattan hotels, to exchange "shop talk," and to hear an address by one of its members which then becomes the subject of a round-table discussion.

The speech from which the following remarks are excerpted (with the permission of Dr. Rubicoff) was delivered by him at the meeting of the society held in the Hunt Room of the President Fillmore Hotel. It is quoted exactly from the typed transcript of the speech made available to the author by Dr. Rubicoff.

"Madam Chairman—although I have long thought that title something of a sexual anomaly!

(Pause for laughter)

"Fellow members, and ladies and gentlemen. After such a dinner, a belch might be more in order than a speech!

(Pause for laughter)

"May I interject at this time that I feel we all owe a vote of thanks to the Entertainment Committee which arranged such a Lucullan feast.

(Pause for applause)

"Indeed, I'm certain you'll sympathize with me if I question whether their motive was to feed you well or to dull your sensibilities to my remarks that follow!

(Pause for small laughter)

"In any event, it is now my turn to offer the intellectual dessert to such a delightfully physical meal, and I shall do my best.

"As some of you, I'm sure, are aware, I was recently one of the victims of a crime which took place in the City of New York during the late evening and early morning of August 31 and September 1 of this year. My remarks this evening shall concern my thoughts about that crime, about crime in general, and what our profession can contribute to the amelioration of crime in our society.

"I can assure you my remarks will be brief—very brief!

(Possible pause for applause)

"These thoughts I offer to you are pure theory.

I have done no research on the subject. I have consulted no hallowed authorities. I merely offer them as what I feel are original ideas—reactions to my experience, if you will—that will serve as subject for the discussion to follow. Needless to say, I shall be extremely interested in your reactions.

"First, let me say that it is hardly new to suggest that sexual aberrations are the underlying motivations for criminal behavior. What I would like to suggest at this time is a much closer relationship between sex and crime. In fact, I suggest that crime—in modern society—has become a substitute for sex.

"What is crime? What is sex? What have they in common? I suggest to you that both share a common characteristic—a *main* characteristic—of penetration. The bank robber forces his way into a vault. The housebreaker forces his way into a house or apartment. The mugger forces his way into your wallet or purse. Is it his intention to penetrate your body—your privacy?

"Even the more complex crimes include this motive of penetration. The confidence man invades his victim's wealth—be it wall safe or savings account. The criminal accountant rapes the firm for which he works. The public servant bent on fraud invades the body of society.

"Indeed, a term used for the most common of crimes—breaking and entering—is a perfect description of the deflowering of a virgin.

"So I suggest to you this evening that the commission of a crime is a substitute for the sexual act, committed by persons who consciously, unconsciously, or subconsciously derive extreme pleasure from this quasisexual activity.

"The crime having been committed—what then? The sex act having been finished—what then? In both cases, what follows the penetration is similar. Escape and withdrawal. Getting out. Frantic departure and sometimes a difficult disentangling, be it physical or emotional.

"I suggest to you that the *commission* of the sex crime—and I am convinced that *all* crimes are sex crimes—is easiest for the disturbed protagonist. The *withdrawal,* the escape, is much more difficult.

"For, considering the puritanical hang-up of most Americans, the withdrawal or escape involves recognition of guilt, an emotional desire for punishment, a terrible, nagging wish to be caught and publicly exposed.

"Sex and crime. Penetration and withdrawal. It seems to me they are all ineradicably wedded. Now, if you will allow me, I would like to expand upon. . . ."

[89]

From the final report of Captain Edward X. Delaney, NYPD-EXD-1SEP1968.

"It was now, I would judge, approximately 4:45 A.M. We were no longer under fire from the fourth-floor window. Suddenly we heard the sound of several gunshots from the vicinity of East Seventy-third Street and East End Avenue. I immediately dispatched officers Oliver J. Kronen (Shield 76398542) and Robert L. Breech (Shield 92356762) to investigate. Officer Kronen returned in a few moments to report that an officer had been slain, another wounded in the thigh. Both had been in car George Nineteen, blocking exit from Seventy-third Street at that corner.

"I thereupon contacted my command post via walkie-talkie. I instructed my driver, Officer McClaire, to send the standby ambulance around to the East End Avenue corner. He acknowledged. I also instructed him at this time to report the situation to Communications Center and request them to pass on the information to Inspector Abrahamson and Deputy Beatem. He acknowledged.

"I immediately led a squad of six armed men into the building at 535 East Seventy-third Street. We passed the body of the masked man who had been killed while trying to escape. Later investigation proved him to be Samuel 'Skeets' Johnson, a Negro. We then entered the lobby where we found a white man seated on the floor of the lobby, his back against the wall, his hands raised. He was taken into custody. Later investigation proved him to be Ernest Heinrich Mann.

"At that time my squad joined forces with the men from the Tactical Patrol Force coming down from the terrace and the men who had been stationed at the rear of the building. These men had taken an additional suspect, Thomas J. Haskins, into custody.

"We searched the building thoroughly and found the super asleep in his basement apartment. We also found some of the tenants and the doorman present in Apartment 4A. One of the tenants, Gerald Bingham, Sr., was wounded and apparently in shock. His right eye was bleeding badly. In addition to the people who had been held captive in this apartment, there was also a masked man lying on the floor, seriously wounded. I was told by eyewitnesses that he had been shot twice by another masked man.

"I thereupon instructed an officer to go outside and call for three more ambulances to facilitate the removal of the dead and wounded—officers, criminals, and innocent victims.

"Preliminary questioning of the victims revealed there had been another man (later identified as John 'Duke' Anderson) who had been present during the crime and had apparently escaped. I judged he was the man responsible for the killing of Officer Illingham and the wounding of Officer Similar of car George Nineteen at the corner of Seventy-third Street and East End Avenue. I thereupon left the apartment house and, using a walkie-talkie, dictated an alert to Officer McClaire for relay to Communications Center. I described the suspect as the witnesses had described him to me. Officer McClaire acknowledged, and I stayed on the radio until he could report that Communications Center—Lieutenant Fineally in command—had acknowledged and was alerting all precincts and sectors.

"When the ambulances arrived, I sent off the wounded immediately—and later the dead. It so happened that Gerald Bingham, Sr., the wounded tenant, and the wounded suspect (later identified as Vincent 'Socks' Parelli, of Detroit) shared the ambulance going to Mother of Mercy Hospital.

"I then returned to my command post at the corner of York Avenue and East Seventy-third Street. Via Communications Center, I alerted Homicide East, the Police Laboratory, the Manhattan District Attorney's Office, and the Public Relations Division. At this time—it was shortly after 5:00 A.M.—there had been no reports on the whereabouts of the escaped suspect, John Anderson."

[90]

The following is a transcription of a personal tape recording made by the author on 6 November, 1968. To my knowledge, the testimony it contains is not duplicated in any official recording, statement, or transcription now on record.

AUTHOR: This will be recording GO-2B. Will you identify yourself, please, and state your place of residence.

WITNESS: My name is Ira P. Mayer and I live at twelve hundred sixty East Second Street, New York.

AUTHOR: Thank you. Mr. Mayer, as I explained to you previously, this recording will be solely for my own use in preparing a record of a crime that occurred in New York City on the night and morning of August thirty-first to September first, 1968. I am not an officer of any branch of the government—city, state, or federal. I shall not ask you to swear to the testimony you are about to give, nor will it be used in a court of law or in any legal proceeding. The statement you make will be for my personal use only, and will not be published without your permission which can only be granted by a signed statement from you, giving approval of such use. In return, I have paid you the sum of fifty dollars, this sum paid whether or not you agree to the publication of your statement. Is all that understood?

WITNESS: Yes.

AUTHOR: Good. Now then, Mr. Mayer, where were you at about five o'clock on the morning of September first, 1968?

WITNESS: I was driving home. Down East End Avenue.

AUTHOR: And where had you been prior to this time?

WITNESS: Well, I was working. Ordinarily I wouldn't be working a holiday weekend, you understand, but so many of the men were off or on vacation—taking the Labor Day weekend off, you understand—that the boss asked me to work the night shift. I'm a master baker, and I work in the Leibnitz Bakery at one-nine-seven-four-oh East End Avenue. That's at One hundred fifteenth Street. My wife was expecting her seventh, and my second-youngest daughter—there was this big dental bill for her. So I needed the money, you understand, so I said I'd work. The union says we get triple-time for working nights on a holiday, and also the boss said he'd slip me an extra twenty. So that's why I was working from four o'clock on August thirty-first to four o'clock the next morning.

AUTHOR: You say you're a master baker. What do you bake?

WITNESS: Bagels, bialies, onion rolls—things like that.

AUTHOR: And what did you do after you got off work at four on the morning of September first?

WITNESS: I got cleaned up and changed into my street clothes. I stopped for a beer with the boys in the locker room. No bars are open at that time, you understand, but we got a refrigerator and we keep beer in there. In the locker room. We chip in a dollar a week a man. The boss knows about it, but he don't care providing nobody gets loaded. Nobody ever does. We just have a beer or two before heading home. To relax like. You understand? So then I had one beer and got into my car and headed south on East End Avenue. I usually take First Avenue when I go uptown to work, and East End when I go downtown after work.

AUTHOR: And what happened at approximately five A.M. on the morning of September first?

WITNESS: I stopped for a red light on the corner of Seventy-fourth Street. I started to light a cigar. Then suddenly the door opened on the passenger side, and a guy was standing there. He had a gun, and he poked this gun at me. He held the gun in his right hand, and his left arm was across the front of him, like he was holding his belly.

AUTHOR: Can you describe this man?

WITNESS: Maybe six feet tall. Thin. No hat. His hair was short—like a crew cut. Sharp features. Mean looking. You understand?

AUTHOR: What was he wearing?

WITNESS: It was mostly black. A black jacket, black turtleneck sweater, black pants, black shoes. But he was a white man. You understand?

AUTHOR: And he opened the door on the passengers' side of the front seat and shoved a gun at you?

WITNESS: That's right.

AUTHOR: This was on the corner of Seventy-fourth Street and East End Avenue, while you were stopped for a light?

WITNESS: That's right. I was just lighting a cigar.

AUTHOR: And what was your reaction?

WITNESS: My reaction? Well, right away I thought it was a stickup. Why else would a guy jerk open the door of my car and point a gun at me?

AUTHOR: And how did you react?

WITNESS: How did I react? I felt sick. I had just been paid. With triple-time and the bonus I had almost four hundred bucks on me. I needed that dough. It was spent already. And I thought this guy was going to take it away from me.

AUTHOR: Would you have given it to him? If he had asked for your money?

WITNESS: Sure, I'd have given it to him. What else?

AUTHOR: But he didn't ask for your money?

WITNESS: No. He got in alongside of me and poked

the gun in my side. With his left hand he slammed the door on his side, then went back to holding his belly.

AUTHOR: What did he say?

WITNESS: He said, "When the light changes, you drive south just the way you're going. Don't drive too fast and don't jump any lights. I'll tell you when to turn off." That's what he said.

AUTHOR: And what did you say?

WITNESS: I said, "You want my money? You want my car? Take them and let me go." And he said, "No, you gotta drive. I can't drive. I'm hurt." And I said, "You wanta go to a hospital? Mother of Mercy is back only five blocks. I'll drive you there." And he said, "No, you just drive where I tell you." And I said, "You gonna kill me?" And he said, "No, I won't kill you if you do what I say."

AUTHOR: And did you believe him?

WITNESS: Of course I believed him. What else am I going to do in a situation like that? You understand? Sure I believed him.

AUTHOR: What happened then?

WITNESS: I did like he said. When the light changed I headed south. I drove at the legal limit so we made all the lights.

AUTHOR: I don't imagine there was much traffic at that time on a Sunday?

WITNESS: Traffic? There was no traffic. We had the city to ourself.

AUTHOR: Did he say anything while you were driving?

WITNESS: Once. It was maybe around the Sixties. He asked me what my name was and I told him. He asked me if I was married, and I told him I was and had six kids and one on the way. I thought maybe he'd feel sorry for me and wouldn't kill me. You understand?

AUTHOR: That's all he said?

WITNESS: Yes, that's all he said. But once he kinda groaned. I looked sideways at him, just for a second, and blood was coming out from between his fingers. Where he had his left hand clamped across his belly. I could see blood coming out from between his fingers. I knew he was hurt bad, and I felt sorry for him.

AUTHOR: Then what happened?

WITNESS: At Fifty-seventh Street he told me to take a right and drive west on Fifty-seventh Street, so I did.

AUTHOR: Was his voice steady?

WITNESS: Steady? Sure, it was steady. Low, maybe, but steady. And that gun in my ribs was steady, too. So we drove across town on Fifty-seventh Street. When we got to Ninth Avenue he told me to take a left and drive downtown. So I did.

AUTHOR: What time was this?

WITNESS: Time? Oh, five thirty. About. Something like that. It was getting light.

AUTHOR: What happened then?

WITNESS: I drove very, very carefully, so I made all the signals. He told me to stop at Twenty-fourth Street.

AUTHOR: Which side?

WITNESS: The west side. On the right. I pulled over to the curb. It was on his side. He opened the door using his right hand, the hand with the gun in it.

AUTHOR: You didn't think of jumping him at this moment?

WITNESS: You crazy? Of course not. He got out, closed the door. He leaned through the window. He said, "Just keep driving. I will stand here and watch to make sure that you keep driving."

AUTHOR: And what did you do then?

WITNESS: What do you think? I kept driving. I went on south to Sixteenth Street, and I figured he couldn't see me anymore. So I stopped and went into a corner phone booth on the sidewalk. There was a sign saying you could call nine-one-one, the police emergency number, without putting a dime in. So I called the cops. When they answered, I told them what had happened. They asked me for my name and address, which I gave them. They asked where I was, which I told them. They told me to stay right where I was and a car would be right there.

AUTHOR: Then what?

WITNESS: I went back to my car. I figured I'd sit in my car and try to calm down until the cops came. I was shaky—you understand? I tried to light my cigar again—I never had got it lighted—but then I saw the seat where he had been. There was a pool of blood on the seat and it was dripping down onto the mat. I got out of the car and waited on the sidewalk. I threw my cigar away.

[91]

Vincent "Socks" Parelli was admitted to Emergency at Mother of Mercy Hospital, Seventy-ninth Street and East End Avenue, at 5:23 A.M., 1 September, 1968. He was first declared DOA (Dead On Arrival) but a subsequent examination by Dr. Samuel Nathan revealed a faint pulse and heartbeat. Stimulants and plasma were immediately administered, and Parelli was taken to the Maximum Security Ward on the second floor. After further examination, Dr. Nathan declared the prognosis was negative. Parelli had been shot twice, one bullet apparently entering the lungs and the other rupturing the spleen.

By 5:45 A.M., the bed occupied by Parelli was surrounded by screens. In this enclosure, in addition to Dr. Nathan, were Dr. Everett Brisling (intern) and Nurse Sarah Pagent, both of the

Mother of Mercy staff; Assistant District Attorney Ralph Gimble of the New York District Attorney's Office; Detective, First Grade, Robert C. Lefferts of Homicide East; Detective, Second Grade, Stanley Brown of the 251st Precinct; Officer Ephraim Sanders (no relation to the author) of the 251st Precinct; and Security Guard Barton McCleary, also of the Mother of Mercy staff.

The following recording, made by the New York District Attorney's Office, is coded NYDA-VP-DeBeST. It is dated 6:00 A.M., 1 September, 1968.

GIMBLE: What's happening?

NATHAN: He's dying. By all rights he should be dead now.

LEFFERTS: Can you do anything?

NATHAN: No. We've already done all we can.

GIMBLE: Will he regain consciousness?

NATHAN: Brisling?

BRISLING: Maybe. I doubt it.

GIMBLE: We've got to question him.

NATHAN: What do you want from me? I'm not God.

BRISLING: Let the man die in peace.

BROWN: No, goddamn it. An officer was killed. Get him up. Get him awake. We've got to find out what all this was about, why he was shot. This is important.

BRISLING: Doctor?

[Lapse of seven seconds.]

NATHAN: All right. Nurse?

PAGENT: Yes, Doctor?

NATHAN: Fifty cc's. You've got it?

PAGENT: Yes, Doctor.

NATHAN: Administer it.

[Lapse of twenty-three seconds.]

NATHAN: Pulse?

BRISLING: Maybe a little stronger. Heart is still fluttering.

GIMBLE: His eyelids moved. I saw them move.

LEFFERTS: Parelli? Parelli?

NATHAN: Don't shove him.

BROWN: He's dying, isn't he?

NATHAN: Just don't touch him. He's a patient in this hospital under my care.

PARELLI: Guh . . . guh. . . .

GIMBLE: He said something. I heard him say something.

LEFFERTS: It didn't make sense. Sanders, move the mike closer to his mouth.

PARELLI: Ah . . . ah. . . .

BROWN: His eyes are open.

GIMBLE: Parelli. Parelli, who shot you? Who was it, Parelli? Why did they shoot you?

PARELLI: Guh . . . guh. . . .

BRISLING: This is obscene.

LEFFERTS: Who planned it, Parelli? Who put up the money? Who was behind it, Parelli? Can you hear me?

PARELLI: Climb planging. No man can ever the building. I said to bicycle of no lad can be to mother.

GIMBLE: What? What?

PARELLI: Or sake to make a lake. We see today not by gun if she does.

LEFFERTS: Can you give him another shot, Doc?

NATHAN: No.

PARELLI: Guh . . . guh. . . .

BRISLING: Fibrillations.

PAGENT: Pulse weakening and intermittent.

NATHAN: He's going.

BROWN: Parelli, listen to me. Parelli, can you hear me? Who shot you, Parelli? Who put up the money? Who brought you here from Detroit? Parelli?

PARELLI: I never thought to. And then I was on the street where. Louise? We saw the car sky and what. Momma. In the sky. It was in. Never a clutch could. Some day she. Fucking bastard. I think that I should.

GIMBLE: Who, Parelli? Who did it?

PARELLI: A bird at song if even wing, the girl herself shall never sing.

NATHAN: Nurse?

PAGENT: No pulse.

NATHAN: Brisling?

BRISLING: No heartbeat.

[Lapse of nine seconds.]

NATHAN: He's gone.

LEFFERTS: Shit.

[92]

Memorandum (Confidential) EXD-794, dated 14 December, 1968, from Edward X. Delaney, Captain, NYPD, to Police Commissioner, NYPD, with confidential copies to Deputy Arthur C. Beatem and Chief Inspector L. David Whichcote.

"This document should be considered Addendum 19-B to my final report NYPD-EXD-1SEP-1968.

"It has been brought to my attention that the attempted armed robbery of the premises at 535 East Seventy-third Street, New York City, on 31 August-1 September, 1968, might have been prevented if there had been closer cooperation between agencies of the city, state, and federal governments, and private investigative agencies. A list of agencies involved is attached (see EXD-794-A).

"While I cannot reveal the identity of my informant *at this time,* I can state without fear of serious contradiction that for several months prior to the commission of the crime, the aforesaid agencies were in possession of certain facts (on tape recordings and in transcriptions) relating to the planned crime, obtained via bugging and other electronic surveillance devices.

"Admittedly, no *one* agency was in possession of *all* the facts or all the details regarding the proposed crime—such as address, time, personnel involved, etc. And yet, if a central pool or clearing house (computerized, perhaps?) for electronic surveillance had been in existence, I have little doubt but that the crime in question could have been forestalled.

"I strongly urge that a meeting of representatives of law-enforcement agencies of city, state, and federal governments be convened immediately to consider how such a clearing house for the results of electronic surveillance can be established. I shall hold myself ready to assist in any way I can to help organize such a project, as I have a number of very definite ideas on how it should be structured."

[93]

Approximately 5:45 A.M. The apartment of Ingrid Macht, 627 West Twenty-fourth Street, New York, New York. This is tape recording SEC-1SEP68-IM-5:45AM-196L.

[Sound of doorbell.]
[Lapse of eleven seconds.]
[Sound of doorbell.]
[Lapse of eight seconds.]

INGRID: Yes?

ANDERSON: Duke.

INGRID: Duke, I am sleeping. I am very tired. Please call me later in the day.

ANDERSON: You want me to shoot the lock off?

INGRID: What? What are you saying, Duke?

[Lapse of six seconds.]

INGRID: Oh, my God.

ANDERSON: Yes. Close and lock the door. Put the chain on. Are the shades down?

INGRID: Yes.

ANDERSON: Get me something—some towels. I don't want to drip on your white rug.

INGRID: Oh, *Schatzie, Schatzie*. . . .

[Lapse of nine seconds.]

INGRID: My God, you're soaked. Here . . . let me. . . .

ANDERSON: Not so bad now. It's inside now. . . .

INGRID: Gun or knife?

ANDERSON: Gun.

INGRID: How many?

ANDERSON: Two. One high up, just below my wishbone. The other is down and on the side.

INGRID: Did they come out?

ANDERSON: What? I don't think so. Brandy. Get me some brandy.

INGRID: Yes . . . let me help you to the chair. All right. Don't move.

[Lapse of fourteen seconds.]

INGRID: Here. Shall I hold it?

ANDERSON: I can manage. Ah Jesus . . . that helps.

INGRID: Is it bad?

ANDERSON: At first. I wanted to scream. Now it's just dull. A big blackness in there. I'm bleeding in there. I can feel it all going out . . . spreading. . . .

INGRID: I know a doctor. . . .

ANDERSON: Forget it. No use. I'm getting out. . . .

INGRID: And you had to come here. . . .

ANDERSON: Yes. Ah . . . God! Yes, like a hound dragging hisself so he can die at home.

INGRID: You had to come here. Why? To pay me back for what I did?

ANDERSON: For what you did? Oh. No, I forgot that a long time ago. It was nothing.

INGRID: But you had to come here. . . .

ANDERSON: Yes. I came to kill you. See? Here . . . look. . . . Two left. I told you I'd get you out some day. I promised you. . . .

INGRID: Duke, you are not making sense.

ANDERSON: Oh, yes. Oh, yes. If I say. . . . Ah, Jesus . . . the blackness. . . . I can hear the wind. Do you want to yell? Do you want to run into the other room, maybe jump out the window?

INGRID: Ah, *Schatzie, Schatzie* . . . you know me better than that. . . .

ANDERSON: I know you better . . . better than that. . . .

INGRID: It's worse now?

ANDERSON: It's coming in waves, like black waves. It's like the sea. I'm really getting out, I'm getting out. Ah, Jesus. . . .

INGRID: It all went bad?

ANDERSON: Yes. We were so close . . . so close. . . . But it went sour. I don't know why. . . . But for a minute there I had it. I had it all.

INGRID: Yes. You had it all. . . . Duke, I have some drugs. Some shmeck. Do you want a shot? It will make it easier.

ANDERSON: No. No, I can handle this. This isn't so bad.

INGRID: Give me the gun, *Schatzie*.

ANDERSON: I meant what I said.

INGRID: What will that do? How will that help?

ANDERSON: I promised. I gave my word. I promised you. . . .

[Lapse of seven seconds.]

INGRID: All right. If that is what you must do. It is all over for me, anyway. Even if you died here this instant, it is all over for me.

ANDERSON: Died? Is this the end of me then? Nothing any more?

INGRID: Yes. The end of John Anderson. Nothing any more. And the end of Ingrid Macht. And Gertrude Heller. And Bertha Knobel. And all the other women I have been in my life. The end of all of us. Nothing any more.

ANDERSON: Are you scared?

INGRID: No. This is best. You are right. This is best. I am tired, and I haven't been sleeping lately. This will be a good sleep. You won't hurt me, *Schatzie?*

ANDERSON: I'll make it quick.

INGRID: Yes. Quick. In the head, I think. Here . . . see . . . I will kneel before you. You will be steady?

ANDERSON: I will be steady. You can depend on me.

INGRID: I could always depend on you. Duke, do you remember that day in the park? The picnic we had?

ANDERSON: I remember.

INGRID: For a moment there . . . for a moment. . . .

ANDERSON: I know . . . I know. . . .

INGRID: I think I will turn around now, *Schatzie.* I will turn my back to you. I find I am not as brave as I thought. I will kneel here, my back to you, and I will talk. I will just say anything that comes into my mind. And I will keep talking, and then you will. . . . You understand?

ANDERSON: I understand.

INGRID: What was it all about, Duke? Once I thought I knew. But now I am not sure. You know, the Hungarians have a saying—"Before you have a chance to look around, the picnic is over." It has all gone so fast, Duke. Like a dream. How is it the days crawl by and yet the years fly? Life for me has been a bone caught in my throat. There were little moments, like that afternoon in the park. But mostly it was hurt . . . it was hurt. . . . Duke, please . . . now . . . don't wait any longer. Please. Duke? *Schatzie?* Duke, I. . . .

[Lapse of five seconds.]

INGRID: Ah. Ah. You are gone, Duke? You are finally out? But I am here. I am here. . . .

[Lapse of one minute fourteen seconds.]

[Sound of phone being dialed.]

VOICE: New York Police Department. May I help you?

[94]

The body of John "Duke" Anderson was removed to the New York City Morgue at about 7:00 A.M., 1 September, 1968. Ingrid Macht was taken to the House of Detention for Women, 10 Greenwich Avenue. The premises at 627 West Twenty-fourth Street were then sealed and a police guard placed at the door.

On the morning of 2 September, 1968, at Police Headquarters, 240 Centre Street, at approximately 10:00 A.M., a meeting was held of representatives of interested authorities, including the New York Police Department; the District Attorney's Office, County of New York; the Federal Bureau of Investigation; the Internal Revenue Service; the Federal Narcotics Bureau; and the Securities and Exchange Commission. Representatives of the New York Police Department included men from the 251st Precinct, Narcotics Squad, Homicide East, Homicide West, the Police Laboratory, and the Communications Center. There was also a representative from Interpol. The author was allowed to be present at this meeting as an observer.

At this time a squad of ten men was organized and directed to search the apartment of Ingrid Macht at 627 West Twenty-fourth Street, the toss to commence at 3:00 P.M., 2 September, 1968, and to be terminated upon agreement of all representatives present. The author was allowed to attend as an observer but not active participant in the search.

The toss of the aforesaid premises commenced at approximately 3:20 P.M., and was, to my satisfaction, conducted with professional skill, speed, and thoroughness. Evidence was uncovered definitely linking Ingrid Macht with the smuggling of illicit narcotics into this country. There was also some evidence (supposition) that she had been involved in prostitution in the City of New York. In addition, there was evidence (not conclusive) that Ingrid Macht had also been involved in the theft and sale of securities, including stock shares, corporate bonds, and U.S. government bonds.

Also, there was some evidence that Ingrid Macht was operating a loan-shark operation, lending sums to persons she met on her job at the dance hall, to pushers of narcotics, and other individuals known to law enforcement officials. In addition to all this, evidence was uncovered (not sufficient for prosecution) that she was a steerer for an abortion ring, with headquarters in a small New Jersey motel.

During the extremely painstaking search of the premises, a detective from the 251st Precinct discovered a small book concealed beneath the lowest drawer of a five-drawer chest in the bedroom. On first examination, it appeared to be merely a diary. In fact, it was a volume bound in imitation leather (in red; imprinted on the front cover: FIVE-YEAR DIARY). Closer examination proved it to be more in the nature of a commercial ledger, detailing Ingrid Macht's personal dealings in stocks and other securities.

Cursory examination of the entries, which included investments (amounts and dates) and sales (amounts, dates, and profits), showed immediately that Ingrid Macht had been successful in her financial dealings. (In a statement to the press, one of her defense attorneys has estimated her personal wealth as being "in excess of $100,000.")

The author was present when the "diary" was discovered and had an opportunity to leaf through it briefly.

On the inside back cover, in the same handwriting as the other entries in the journal, was this inscription: "Crime is the truth. Law is the hypocrisy."